ROCK
THE
WORLD

The spotlight is fading. Darkness is closing in. It's time to ...

ROCK
THE
WORLD

Keith Campion

The manufacturer's authorised representative in the EU
for product safety is Authorised Rep Compliance Ltd,
71 Lower Baggot Street, Dublin D02 P593 Ireland (www.arccompliance.com)

This is a work of fiction. Names, characters, businesses, places, events
and incidents are either the products of the author's imagination
or used in a fictitious manner. Any resemblance to actual persons,
living or dead, or actual events is purely coincidental.

Troubador Publishing Ltd
Unit E2 Airfield Business Park,
Harrison Road, Market Harborough,
Leicestershire. LE16 7UL
Tel: 0116 2792299
Email: books@troubador.co.uk
Web: www.troubador.co.uk

ISBN 978 1836 284 109

British Library Cataloguing in Publication Data.
A catalogue record for this book is available from the British Library.

Printed and bound in Great Britain by 4edge Limited
Typeset in 11pt Adobe Garamond Pro by Troubador Publishing Ltd, Leicester, UK

An Empty Chair at the Table

The table's full, the candles glow,
Laughter veils what we all know.
We pass the bread, we say the grace,
Eyes linger on that empty space.
The fire is lit, the lights are low,
We sit together, voices flow.
It's more than a seat, more than space –
It holds our memories, holds their place.

There's an empty chair at the table,
An empty space, irreplaceable.
No words are said, heartbreak we share,
The ache that lives in the empty chair.

Plates are cleared, the night goes on.
But something lingers, though they've gone –
A quiet love remains, held there,
In the stillness of the empty chair.
Our promise to them, fierce and bright,
Cast in the shadow of stolen light.
A child sits near, so brave, so small –
A piece of them that binds us all.

There's an empty chair at the table,
All our memories, unshakeable.
We see you there with stories to tell,
Your voice a song we knew so well.
Listen – it echoes through the air.
Forever held by that empty chair.

(McCall/Townley)

1

McKenzie McCall was sprawled across a settee, backstage at an old theatre in the middle of the British leg of his '86 tour – Bristol, or was it Bath? He made a hazy note in his mind to check with his manager, Atkinson, before he went on stage. It never went down well when you name-checked the wrong city to a local audience and the press had hammered him last time he did it. Atkinson was absolutely fuming that night. *'Hello, Manchester!'* Except he was in Middlesbrough. *Mack's Manchester Muddle* was one of the kinder headlines the next day.

Lying down, one foot on the settee, the other on the floor, McKenzie had a bottle of beer in one hand and his trademark cowboy hat was pulled down over his face, a message to the room that talking to him was not an option. Around him, people were chatting in huddled groups – laughing, smoking and drinking. A few of them were 'the suits' – the record company executives. They'd just about managed to find time in their jam-packed schedule of sucking up to far fresher, edgier acts to check in on his tour tonight – not that this had inspired McKenzie to make any particular effort. He'd clocked their disinterest before their first half-hearted handshakes. The only bonus of having them around was that Atkinson was slightly less obnoxious and on his best behaviour.

McKenzie's band were sitting on a large settee opposite him. Also milling about was the usual collection of hangers-on who had managed to wing their way backstage – a cousin of a cousin of someone related to the band, or some other tenuous link that allowed them to blag their way in. They would dine out on the story of being backstage with McKenzie McCall for years to come. The man himself hadn't moved an inch from the settee in forty-five minutes so there wasn't going to be much of a tale to tell. McKenzie knew even the slightest acknowledgement from him in their direction would make their day … their year, possibly their life – but he just couldn't bring himself to do it.

It hadn't always been like this, in the early days – '73 and '74 – when he first tasted success, in his mid-twenties, he used to warmly work the room, shaking hands. He was the epitome of charm – patting strangers on the back as if he'd known them forever and asking them something to show willing; he was well-known for being the 'Mr Nice Guy' of rock. Thirteen years later, the days of mustering up that kind of vibe were long gone.

Standing nervously in the corner, whispering and glancing at McKenzie and failing miserably to appear relaxed, were the local radio station competition winners – all McKenzie's worst nightmares. It was almost embarrassing how out of place they looked. Yes, the dreaded 'meet and greet' which McKenzie had rechristened the 'meet and get done'. McKenzie hated the awkwardness of it – the small talk, the posing for photos, knowing he looked rough in each one and that the photo would end up in a local newspaper (*The Day I Met McKenzie!*) and he had no control over it whatsoever. He'd have to smile while answering the same old questions – was there some deep meaning to the third verse of 'Beyond the Line', his breakout hit thirteen years previously? McKenzie didn't have the heart to tell them that the whole verse was built around words that rhymed with 'end'. What's more, it was written with a hangover after receiving a telegram from the record company stating that he had two days to finish recording his first album or he'd have his contract ripped to shreds.

> *In the distance, there's a bend,*
> *Where weary travellers seek to mend.*
> *Whispers of the roads that blend,*
> *Guide us to that journey's end.*
> *Beyond the line, where dreams ascend,*
> *A brighter path, a hand to lend.*
> *Through every trial we transcend,*
> *Together we will not pretend.*

As far as McKenzie was concerned, he'd written stuff that made more sense when he was at primary school. I mean, *how* many times could you fit 'end' into a lyric? But with a pretty catchy melody to go with it, he'd had a surprise hit on his hands and was thrust blinking into the limelight. 'Beyond the Line' eventually climbed to the number two spot, narrowly edged out by Slade and one of their notoriously misspelt songs.

McKenzie listened to the voices around him as he pretended to doze; not for the first time, he realised almost everyone around him was making money from him – everyone dependent on his talent. McKenzie could hear Atkinson in the centre of the room, how could he not? Atkinson's voice didn't so much speak as bark – loud, coarse and with no volume control; he was devoid of any need for discretion. Atkinson Stark was McKenzie's manager, a man entirely lacking in decorum – rude, insensitive and utterly unapologetic about it. Whereas McKenzie was tall with long hair that hung over his face like curtains and lazy beard growth, Atkinson was short and rounded; he had a gleaming bald head and was clean-shaven – his face that of an angry bulldog. Atkinson dressed perpetually in impeccably tailored black suits from Saville Row and matching black silk shirts. Despite his diminutive stature, he cut a sharp and intimidating figure. Gold rings adorned his fingers and a thick gold chain rested on his chest, peeking out from the open collar of his shirt. He wore dark sunglasses even indoors, once declaring to McKenzie that hiding his eyes made him all the more unnerving during negotiations.

Atkinson's carefully crafted attire shouted power, wealth, and untouchability – an image he carefully cultivated. McKenzie once mustered the courage to ask Atkinson why he always wore the same clothes.

'This is the 1980s, Mack. You've got to dress to impress – it's power dressing! If it's good enough for Maggie, it's good enough for me. I've got seven of these suits hanging up in my wardrobe – it saves wasting any time each morning having to decide what to wear, leaving me free to make all those important decisions for you and that's quite a job, Mack. Besides, I've earned these suits, Mack, earned them.'

McKenzie was never quite sure why he hesitated to point out that it was *his* songwriting and performances that paid for Atkinson's flashy suits. Without the songs, there would be nothing to manage. Yet, Atkinson clung to an unwavering belief that their talents were equal and he harboured genuine resentment that the profits weren't split evenly. To Atkinson's credit, though, in an industry notorious for chaos, uncertainty and fickle trends, he had skilfully steered McKenzie through shifting eras – Glam Rock, Punk, New Romance, synthesizers and power ballads – without demanding he reinvent himself too much. McKenzie just did his thing, country-ish rock driven by guitar, bass and drums. Atkinson was shrewd and ruthless and had cemented his status as a legend of the music business. Becoming something of a celebrity himself, his name often appeared in tabloid gossip columns as he tumbled out of fashionable London nightclubs with a stunning woman on his arm night after night. Though only a decade older than McKenzie, Atkinson had nonetheless mastered the role of a bossy, domineering father figure, dispensing tough love with well-practised ease. There were moments when McKenzie genuinely loathed Atkinson, but even in those times, one thing was certain: Atkinson always had his back. If you wanted anyone to have your back, it was probably Atkinson. He looked after McKenzie, protected him and made decisions on everything – from the wrong type of cheese on the rider to huge music contracts – without blinking an eye. All for a twenty per cent cut.

Atkinson's right hand always gripped a large Filofax which was bursting at the seams. His left hand alternated between a Cuban cigar and a flute of Cristal Champagne.

He had two pockets on the inside of his suit jackets – in one lived a large wad of crisp bank notes, ready to whip out to impress anyone who needed impressing when he settled a bill. In the other pocket was his pride and joy, a cutting-edge mobile phone – his Roamer. It was the size and weight of a brick and hardly anyone else had one, but it meant Atkinson was always able to be in touch with people at any time, with the press of a few big buttons. Carrying it around with him wherever he went – well, it *looked* impressive.

Atkinson had been McKenzie's manager since the beginning, when McKenzie had played the local Manchester pub scene with his trusty old guitar in the early '70s. Atkinson was the landlord of one of the pubs and always had a word of advice for McKenzie.

'You're pretty good – why are you wasting your time playing this namby-pamby 1960s folk music? Rock music is where the big time is going to be. You need to toughen up your image – start acting like a star. Until then you'll *never* be one.'

Over time, Atkinson took on the role of manager without McKenzie ever really asking him to, it just seemed to happen, but within two years McKenzie McCall was a household name and had been ever since.

McKenzie lifted his head off the arm of the settee to steal a look around the room. All eyes turned towards him expectantly. With a heavy sigh, he dropped his head back down again.

2

The summer of 1986 – an iconic moment at the height of the 1980s. Madonna reigned as the Queen of Pop; Michael Jackson was the undisputed King. The Pet Shop Boys, A-ha, Billy Ocean and George Michael had all topped the charts by the time the long, hazy summer arrived – a music soundtrack to a memorable year brimming with unforgettable energy. The top forty was full of classic song after classic song playing on radios in kitchens, in cars and in parks across the country. Queen were in the midst of a huge tour, performing to hundreds of thousands of adoring fans, riding high after their triumph at Live Aid the previous year. At Wembley Stadium, Wham! took their final bow with a farewell concert that defined an era. Roland Rat and *Wacaday* with Timmy Mallett were must-watch staples of summer holiday TV for children, filling the early mornings before they were ordered outside to play. Televisions flickered with the drama of England's and Scotland's World Cup campaigns in Mexico, while children swapped football cards in playgrounds and parks – the shiny silver ones being the true currency of the moment. England's hopes soared as they reached the quarter-finals, only for Maradona's infamous 'Hand of God' to shatter hearts. Meanwhile, a buzz of anticipation built for a summer royal wedding, as households eagerly added to their collections of commemorative mugs and decorative dishes featuring Andrew and Sarah. Fashion in 1986 was bold and unapologetic – neon colours, power-dressing shoulder pads, striking prints and voluminous hair dominated the scene. At the political helm, Margaret Thatcher stood at the height of her power, both revered and reviled. Yet, beneath the surface of this seemingly idyllic summer, the nation wrestled with lingering tensions. The scars of the miners' strike were still raw, a stark reminder of divisions deepened by economic disparity – the rich grew richer, while poverty spread. On the horizon, more dark clouds loomed, poised to shatter the carefree façade and send shockwaves through the fabric of British society.

Liverpool was the best football team in the country, the club everyone wanted to support. Despite living in a Manchester suburb, Andy Townley had no qualms about betraying his hometown to cheer for Kenny Dalglish's legendary Liverpool squad. He wasn't alone – most of his classmates at the comprehensive school followed suit. Manchester United weren't awful by any means, with Norman Whiteside and Bryan Robson orchestrating the play, but Liverpool had the glamour: Grobbelaar, Barnes, Hansen, McMahon and Rush. For a twelve-year-old, supporting a winning team was everything and the magic at Anfield was impossible to resist. United? They weren't going to win the league in a million years. And Manchester City? Well, supporting them was something you did only if fate had cursed you with a City-supporting family.

Andy lived in a terraced house with his mum, Debbie, in Massleforth, a small suburban town a bus ride away from Manchester. His road was lined with long rows of houses on both sides, where residents stepped directly off the street into their homes. Cars were parked tightly along the kerbsides. Andy's dad, Tony, had moved out a couple of years ago and Andy hadn't seen him since. The details were hazy. His mum was clearly hurting but whenever Andy tried to talk about it, she shut down, leaving him confused and unsure of what to do. Andy's feelings were conflicted. His memories of Tony were happy but he was angry at the way his mum had been let down. At his school, coming from a single-parent family wasn't unusual, yet Andy couldn't shake off his self-consciousness about it.

But through shared adversity, Debbie and Andy had developed an inseparable bond. Debbie was a fun-loving and extroverted lady in her mid-thirties, which accounted for Andy's more reserved character – Debbie's personality was big enough for both of them. She was a whirlwind of coordinated chaos, with a perpetual sparkle in her eye and some choice sarcasm for anyone who dared to intrude on her positivity. Debbie had an unwavering determination and Andy felt her support and encouragement like an arm round his shoulder, guiding him forwards. They shared an unspoken understanding: each day was an adventure or a challenge to face together. Evenings were their favourite time, the moment they could close the door of their tiny terraced home and leave the world outside. After dinner, they would settle in the cosy living room, books spread across the coffee table. Debbie patiently helped Andy with his homework, while Andy, eager to entertain, would launch into animated tales from his school day. He loved making her laugh, often exaggerating just to see her burst into hysterics. Debbie was not going to let Tony's leaving define them, but the grief was evident in her face. Andy felt a deep sadness too, a lingering heartache that hung between them, suspended and unspoken. Pictures of Tony still stood on the mantelpiece and on top of the TV – like a ghost of the past smiling down on them. There was a Tony-shaped hole in their lives.

Despite Debbie's vibrant spirit, it was becoming impossible to ignore the reality that she was ill. Her body seemed to be quietly betraying her. At first, the signs were easy to dismiss – she hid them well – but the cracks began to show when she left her job as a legal secretary to focus on her health. Money became tight and Andy sensed the shift, even if Debbie tried to shield him from it. Beginning not long after Tony left, there was a relentless fever she couldn't shake off, like an unending flu. Then came the night sweats – drenched sheets and vivid nightmares that left her pale and trembling by morning. Andy's grandparents brushed their daughter's illness off as stress, blaming the upheaval of Tony's departure. Debbie tried to laugh it away, insisting she was *never* ill, but even her humour couldn't mask the unease growing in her eyes.

This went on for a few weeks until slowly, to everyone's relief, she recovered. But then she lost weight and the skin on her face looked lumpy and ashen. Debbie had promised all kinds of activities over the school summer holiday, cheap and cheerful days out, but she was getting tired easily and had coughing fits and they hadn't really done much at all. She apologised profusely and promised that – as soon as the doctors got her on the right medication – she'd have more energy. Andy was worried, but a conversation about it was off limits. Debbie was still loud and funny, but it was becoming harder to ignore the fact that she wasn't returning to her old self.

Sometimes, when Debbie let her guard slip – sipping a bottle of Heineken and allowing Andy to have a weak shandy over a quiet game of cards – he'd find the moment to bring it up. Debbie would stumble through a blustery explanation … problems with her blood, a bad chest, maybe her liver, they thought it might be cancer but it was all fine … doctors have got it all under control, she said. They were searching for the right treatment and it wasn't a huge concern. It was during these times she was more inclined to talk about Tony. With moist eyes and bottle in hand, there was a chink in her armour and confusion and dejection were plain to see.

'Tony was a good man, a great father – it was like he had a breakdown and just couldn't cope with family responsibility any more, so he turned his back on it all. He packed his bag and closed the door on us without looking back.'

Debbie didn't drink often but sometimes she'd lose herself and reveal a bit more than she meant to.

'There was that new crowd of pals from work, he'd not come back until the morning sometimes. I was pleased for him, at first. I thought he just needed a bit of space, maybe marrying meant he missed out on a bit of socialising. I know I should be angry, but … I don't know …'

Andy remembered Tony as a kind and gentle man, who used to take him to the local park on Saturday mornings so Debbie could catch up on her sleep after a busy week. He'd stand patiently in the cold while Andy played on the monkey bars, encouraging him when Andy got frustrated because his small arms couldn't reach all the way across. The day Andy finally made it, Tony carried him all the way home on his shoulders, beaming with pride, to an equally proud Debbie. He took Andy back the next day with the camera so he could photograph this achievement as if it had just happened. They'd go to the local woods, where Andy would climb trees and they'd chat happily about school, football, music – anything that came into their heads. It was difficult to understand any of it. Andy remembered Tony as the one who used to hold him up, steadying him when he felt like he was falling. Now, he wished Tony was still there to do the same for Debbie.

3

'You nearly ready, Mum?' Andy called towards the locked bathroom door upstairs. He stood by the front door, the late-September sun streaming through the semicircular stained glass, scattering warm, colourful light onto the hallway. It had only been a couple of weeks since school started, but Andy had already been late twice, waiting for Debbie to get ready in the mornings. Lately, she'd been spending long, uneasy stretches of time in the bathroom and Andy didn't want to rush her. Finally, he heard a cough from upstairs, followed by the flush of the toilet. The landing creaked as Debbie appeared at the top of the stairs. Gosh, she looked thin, Andy thought, a familiar knot tightening inside him.

'Sorry, love. Bad stomach again,' she said, wincing as she made her way gingerly downstairs, gripping the banister. Debbie joined Andy on the walk to school some mornings. Passing streets of terraced houses, they would turn left towards the main road where Debbie caught a bus to Manchester for medical appointments, while Andy continued on to school. Debbie limped alongside him, the pain in her foot slowing their pace. A wound had lingered there for weeks, stubbornly refusing to heal.

'Is there nothing they can give you, Mum? For your tummy, I mean. And have you shown the doctor your foot? What did he say?'

'They're trying different things, Andy. We just have to be patient and hope the right medicine comes along. Well, you know, the right medicine to start improving things. The doctors are considering different approaches. I just have to wait for more tests, that's all.'

Andy and Debbie's life had become increasingly solitary – just the two of them against the world, Debbie liked to say. It used to be her battle cry, a defiant rallying call, but it didn't sound quite so steely these days. Andy used to have friends over, but Debbie had become non-committal and cagey about when they could come and Andy sensed her unease at having people around her, so he didn't push it.

As they closed the front door behind them, the door of the house to the right swung open.

'Debbie! How are you? Oh Debbie, you are skin and bone – nothing more. Have you been eating my meals? I worry, Debbie!'

'Morning, Mrs Silva. Of course we have and they're just as delicious as ever,' Debbie said with an affectionate smile. Mrs Silva had lived on the street with her husband for nearly thirty years since arriving from Portugal seeking employment opportunities. Both were recently retired – Mr Silva was a postman and Mrs Silva had worked in the local bakery. Despite her diminutive stature, Mrs Silva was a formidable and proud lady. Her voice, though soft and melodic, carried authority and wisdom. She almost always wore a dark skirt that swayed just above her sturdy leather shoes, paired with a faded floral blouse neatly tucked at the waist and a thick knitted shawl draped over her shoulders. A patterned headscarf, tied under her chin, framed her weathered face, while a gold cross on a delicate chain glinted faintly at her neck. They had always kept themselves to themselves, Mr and Mrs Silva, but when they started to notice that Tony was no longer there, they'd taken it upon themselves to become protective of Andy and Debbie with a lion-like ferocity.

'I worry, Debbie,' Mrs Silva repeated. 'Look at you!' She stepped off her doorstep and reached up to cup Debbie's face. Debbie flinched, jolting her head back and stepping away from the raised hands.

'No! No … thank you … Mrs Silva. I'm OK,' Debbie replied sharply. Hurt was written all over Mrs Silva's startled face and Debbie softened her tone. 'I'm OK, honestly, you don't need to worry. But thank you … for your kindness.'

Debbie's reaction played on Andy's mind as they made their way up the street. Mrs Silva had never been one to worry about personal space, it was just her way. Still, it wasn't like Debbie to snap at someone, even when she wasn't feeling her best.

At school, Andy was in Mr Harris's form group. Mr Harris was a tall, burly man who wore a crumpled white shirt with rolled-up sleeves. The top button was always undone with a tie loosely knotted around his neck. This always gave him the look of someone who had already undertaken a hard day's graft, even at 9 a.m. Mr Harris was balding on top and spoke with a Welsh accent. He played rugby at the weekend which accounted for a cauliflower ear. On both forearms he had large tattoos of anchors. Mr Harris had a flat nose and an urban myth circulated the school that, as a young man, he'd been a skilled amateur boxer, which earned him instant respect. Mr Harris frequently faced arm-wrestling challenges from some of the cockier pupils, who he sometimes humorously indulged, conducting the contests across his desk at the front of the classroom. With an air of idle bemusement, he would watch as the students struggled to budge his arm even an inch, their faces growing redder with each futile attempt. Despite his fearsome reputation, Andy adored Mr Harris. He carried an air of firm authority that conveyed a clear you-don't-mess-around-in-my-classroom message without ever needing to say it. Yet beneath the stern exterior, he was kind and warm, with a genuine interest in his pupils. As one of the school's deputy heads and Andy's science teacher, Mr Harris brought a seasoned approach to his lessons. His dry humour, honed over twenty years of teaching the same material, engaged the pupils and made the subject enjoyable.

Andy arrived late into class. It was form time and the class were chatting. Mr Harris sat with his feet up on the desk, hands clasped behind his head. Form time was meant to include structured activities focused on personal and social development, but Mr Harris held a rather loose interpretation of this. Mr Harris spotted Andy trying to sneak in.

'Here he is, another Manchester traitor. Easy win for Liverpool at home – Charlton didn't even put up a fight. But the big story? Man United! Your *own* city team pasting Southampton five-one. This is our year and you lot will be crawling back to support us. Ron Atkinson's got the squad this year, you mark my words!'

The class had gone quiet, enjoying the moment, before bursting into laughter. Andy smiled shyly – he loved Mr Harris's banter, though he didn't quite have the confidence to give it back. Someone called out asking why Mr Harris didn't support a Welsh football team. Andy missed the reply as he sat down and settled himself, but the class burst into fits of laughter again at whatever Mr Harris replied.

When everyone returned to discussing the previous night's *Top of the Pops* and *EastEnders* episode, Mr Harris considered Andy for a moment before rising from his desk. As he wandered over, he mock-clipped a boy around the ear and pointed at the floor, a wordless command to stop swinging on his chair. With his back to the class, Mr Harris perched on the table beside Andy and spoke softly.

'Everything OK, Andy? Genuinely, you're not in trouble but I have to put you down as late in the register and they're going to start noticing – my leadership colleagues. I'll stick up for you but I don't want them on your case with detentions and whatnot. Is there anything I can help with?'

The rest of the class were immersed in their conversations. Andy bit his lip and moved his chair forward.

'Things are just a bit difficult at the moment, sir. My mum's not very well, it might be cancer or something. She doesn't like talking about it, but it takes her a bit of time to get ready and her tummy is bad in the mornings too. She's got an appointment today so she left the house with me, that's why we were late. I'm really hoping they try her on some new treatment.'

Mr Harris nodded and offered a sympathetic smile. 'That sounds tough. I could tell something was going on – teacher radar. Listen, I know I'm only an old fuddy-duddy teacher but if there is anything I can do, let me know, OK? I'll have a little word with the head of year so they can back off too. My mum, God bless her, went through some ill health over the years so I understand, Andy.'

'Thanks, sir,' Andy replied, a warm rush of appreciation swept over him. He was being noticed and cared for. The bell shrilled from outside the door and teenagers started pouring from all directions in the corridor.

'Right you horrible lot,' Mr Harris barked, making his way back down the classroom between the desks. 'Get yourselves out of my classroom. And remember – be kind. You never know how someone is feeling inside. Don't take any chances, just be kind.'

4

cKenzie lifted his hat then hauled himself up into a sitting position and blinked a few times, scratching the rough stubble on the side of his face. Another city, another lively dressing room buzzing with pre-show energy but McKenzie was struggling to find the enthusiasm to match. He had that mid-tour feeling when travelling around the country performing at different venues each night and it unsettled him. Moving from city to city – tour bus by night, hanging around by day and waiting for the next performance – he quickly lost track of real life. This monotony had gone on since early August and it was only the UK leg of the tour – gigs in Germany, Austria and France were to come later that autumn. If he was lucky, he might manage to sneak out for lunch or dinner, but exploring the latest town or city, taking in the sights and seeking out some culture? Not a chance.

McKenzie hated being recognised. He struggled to relax if he was in a shop or a museum, knowing fans were waiting outside for him. Some in the industry loved it, despite pretending they didn't. McKenzie knew one fellow rock star who, during an infamous appearance on Terry Wogan's chat show, complained bitterly about his privacy, while simultaneously tipping off the paparazzi about his comings and goings. Wherever the paps went, crowds usually gathered. McKenzie would love nothing more than to wander around a city, but he knew from bitter experience what always followed. It went through the same stages: first, the glances and whispers, then the shout '*It's McKenzie McCall! Hey, Mack!*' and finally, screams and jostling as he was engulfed by a throng of excited fans. McKenzie didn't understand the fuss. He was just him, flaws and all – someone who had written a few songs that some people enjoyed humming along to.

McKenzie had played bigger venues than Newcastle City Hall – much bigger – but his latest album had … well, in industry terms, it had tanked. Bombed. Sunk. However you wanted to say it, the reality was the same. It was an unusual feeling, suddenly not being *the man with the golden touch*. McKenzie felt the pressure that his career was on the slide, his star waning. He was realistic enough to know this moment would come eventually, when his time in the spotlight would fade. Atkinson was tenser and louder than usual. He proposed a tour with 'more intimate' venues (code for *small*) to create the illusion of sold-out shows and prove that McKenzie was still popular and relevant. Atkinson called it the 'Mack's Crazy Tour' – branded as a chance for McKenzie to reconnect with fans in cosier settings. There would be nothing worse than the tabloids crowing that McKenzie McCall had failed to fill arenas – something they would relish.

The demoralising thing for McKenzie was that the album was pretty damn good – ten great songs. The recording sessions had gone perfectly, coming together like a dream and McKenzie had felt rejuvenated. So much so, he called the album *Rejuvenation!* Atkinson later claimed to regret the inclusion of the exclamation mark. In hindsight, it made a bold statement that set the album up to fail. Atkinson argued there was no killer single to grab attention – just nicely crafted songs. *Nicely crafted?* McKenzie had poured his heart and soul into them and they hadn't come easily. The tabloids had initially gushed over the album, giving it five-star reviews. But days later, when sales were mediocre, they turned on it like a pack of hyenas – *McKenzie Misfires!* was one of the predictable headlines.

McKenzie began preparing for the show, slipping a shirt over his white vest and fastening a couple of buttons before adjusting his dog tags so they hung prominently over the vest – this had been his signature look for years. A couple of hours earlier, Atkinson had read him the riot act about his lifestyle and was now giving McKenzie the tactical silent treatment. There was no escaping that McKenzie *had* been drinking recently, more than ever before – his face was a flushed, blotchy red and his eyes were bloodshot. He'd developed a slight paunch around his middle and Atkinson wasn't shy in pointing it out.

At 7.27 p.m. – just over half an hour until showtime, Atkinson appeared at the door and glared at McKenzie then barked to the room, 'Right everyone, out! Out you go. Just the band to stay – out!'

McKenzie always spent the final half hour before a performance alone with his band, focusing on switching to performance mode and shutting out distractions. His onstage persona was very different from who he was offstage and it took work to summon the confidence needed to step into that role. Those moments were dedicated to putting the finishing touches to his stage gear and having a quick chat with the band to review the setlist, including any last-minute changes. They warmed up with a few harmonies, their voices blending effortlessly as they sipped drinks to keep their throats hydrated.

Not long ago, McKenzie would have frowned upon drinking alcohol before a show, deeming it unprofessional. But now, he found himself reliant on it to settle his nerves. He knocked back a shot of vodka, feeling its warmth spread as he steadied himself for the stage. With ten minutes to go, his head roadie, Snakes, knocked lightly on the door and poked his head inside.

'Ten minutes, Mack.'

Snakes had been with McKenzie since the earliest days – a true 'Road Dog', one of the crew members who thrived on the nomadic touring life. Road Dogs were untethered, free from responsibilities at home and always ready to go out on tour. Snakes earned his nickname for his uncanny ability to slip into the tightest spaces on lorry trailers to retrieve equipment. While McKenzie usually commanded the stage with his famous old guitar, for one of his slower songs, 'The Moon and Stars' from his debut album, he began at the piano. After a few verses, Snakes would crouch behind him, waiting silently in position, before handing McKenzie a microphone. McKenzie would then stroll to the front of the stage to finish the song, standing before an audience who would inevitably sing along. It was a well-rehearsed routine – Snakes had performed this duty four hundred and thirty-four times and counting.

Snakes had always worn the same outfit for as long as McKenzie had known him, regardless of the weather: denim shorts, a white T-shirt and a short-sleeve Hawaiian-style shirt thrown over the top. McKenzie appreciated the loyalty of people like Snakes, who would literally do anything for him, but he rarely engaged in long conversations. Aside from McKenzie's dread of small talk, Snakes' tales often bordered on the absurd, most of them starting with, 'When I …': *When I was at Princess Diana's wedding … When I was in the marines … When I was chatting with Margaret Thatcher … When I sold my guitar to Prince.* McKenzie never knew which were true, which were distorted versions of the truth or which Snakes had concocted entirely on the spot. After delivering the ten-minute call, Snakes would offer his assessment of the crowd: 'They're on fire tonight, Mack; they're absolutely buzzing!' or, more ominously, 'Bit quiet out there, Mack; it's like a graveyard. Think you're going to have to bust a gut to get them going.'

Either way, the challenge at that point was to muster the enthusiasm to deliver the same old songs.

5

Debbie was sitting in her bedroom at her dressing table in front of the window, removing her makeup with cotton pads. The flowery curtains were closed in front of her and the matching lamp on the bedside table lit the room with a soft glow. The clock radio was tuned into an early evening love songs programme and 'Different Corner' by George Michael played in the background. Her skin used to glow, Andy thought. Her eyes used to sparkle. She was still the same person but she looked different – it was hard to put his finger on it, but he still thought she was beautiful.

Andy respected Debbie's reluctance to discuss her illness but no matter how hard he tried, he just couldn't wrap his head around it.

'Why don't they know what's wrong with you? They're doctors, aren't they? I thought you said it might be cancer. I don't want it to be cancer, obviously, but at least we'd know what you're dealing with. We'd have something to fight then and they'd know what medicine to give you. You need to tell them to … to … get their act together. I'm coming with you next time!'

His voice was rising, frustration and fear getting the better of him.

'OK, Napoleon, stand down. We're not going into battle,' Debbie replied, smiling weakly under the onslaught. "Bringing you up with the same feisty, questioning attitude I had when I was young is starting to backfire on me!"

'What did they say about your foot? They must have looked at it?' Debbie's foot was wrapped in a neat, fresh bandage. There was a sharp edge in his voice now but enough was enough.

'It's definitely healing and getting a bit better now, love. I'll be dancing around the kitchen with you in no time,' Debbie replied, rubbing some Nivea cream into her face.

It wasn't Debbie's fault she was ill and Andy hated seeing her struggle. She was his mum and he loved her more than words could express but in that moment it felt good to unleash some buried anger. Andy wanted to hug her and stomp out of the room, slamming the door behind him all at once. Unsure of which he would choose, there was something in her expression he had never seen before – weakness, maybe. But then his attention was drawn to something even more startling: a mauve mark on the side of her face, close to her ear, about the size of a squashed pea. It stopped him in his tracks. This was new. Andy rarely saw his mum without makeup, but surely he would have seen a birthmark at some point. It wasn't large, but its presence made Andy uneasy.

'Listen,' said Debbie, rubbing cream into her hands. 'I'll walk with you tomorrow morning. I need to get the giro and do a few bits and bobs in town and I'll pick up something nice for tea, OK? A proper Friday night meal a la Mum, the hottest chef in … well, just this house, really.'

Andy smiled, trying to let go of some of the tension. 'Love you, Mum. I'm sorry. It's just … I don't know … I'm sorry.'

The next morning, as they closed the door behind them, Mrs Silva opened her own door gingerly a few inches and peered out.

'Hello, Debbie.' She sniffed through the gap, pointedly showing she was still offended by the incident a few days previously.

'Morning, Mrs Silva. How are you?' Debbie said brightly, although her voice was croaky, having developed an overnight rasp that didn't quite convey the effect she was probably hoping for.

Mrs Silva swung the door wide open and stood up to her full height of five feet, looking Debbie over, scrutinising her coat, hat, scarf, and gloves despite it being a mild November day.

'Never mind how I am,' Mrs Silva continued, 'how are *you*, Debbie?'

Mr Silva joined her at the door. Just slightly taller than Mrs Silva, he had silvery hair and was wearing a grey cardigan and burgundy slippers.

'Are you going somewhere, Debbie?' Mr Silva asked quietly. Mrs Silva glared at her husband before raising an eyebrow at Debbie as if to say, *Are you?*

'Oh, just popping into town to get a few bits,' Debbie replied, her voice uncertain. 'I'm cooking tea, aren't I, Andy?' Andy sensed her discomfort at being thrust into this casual gathering. Debbie used to fill a room with her personality but since she became ill, she seemed to have shrunk – less sure of herself, less comfortable around people.

'You shall not!' barked Mrs Silva, taking everyone by

surprise and making her husband jump. 'I shall make you tea. Bife à Portuguesa?'

Andy adored Mrs Silva's cooking and nodded his head vigorously. His mum couldn't compete with an offer like that.

Debbie smiled. 'There was me, going to the trouble of Birds Eye fish fingers and chips in the chip pan. Thank you, Mrs Silva, that would be lovely.'

'I shall cook,' confirmed Mrs Silva, without acknowledging Debbie. She nodded haughtily and Andy couldn't help but wonder how anyone could be so unfailingly kind without a hint of a smile. Mrs Silva went to close the front door, wafting at Mr Silva to step backwards. She paused and narrowed her eyes at Debbie. 'I see your cheek bones, Debbie. We need to feed you up.'

'Well, all the top models have them, Mrs Silva. I've been trying my best to look like Jerry Hall or Grace Jones for a while now. I'm not even forty yet; there's still time for me to strut the catwalks of Paris.' Debbie giggled, which made Andy laugh. With one last withering look, Mrs Silva closed the door.

Reggie, Andy's closest friend from his form group, came puffing up behind them as Andy and Debbie walked up the street. He had a rucksack slung over his back and carried a football boot bag – red, with the Liverpool emblem proudly emblazoned on the side. Previously, Reggie had worn his Manchester United top with pride, stubbornly ignoring Liverpool's dominance and clinging to a crumbling loyalty. He'd even dish out half-hearted banter about Liverpool fans being nothing but glory-hunters. But then, one fateful Monday morning, he turned up at school in a brand new, gleaming Liverpool shirt — tags freshly snipped, sleeves just slightly too long — looking both sheepish and defiant. He'd clearly braced himself for the inevitable ridicule. He didn't fight back. He just shrugged and muttered, "Liverpool's just better, alright?" From that moment on, Reggie went full Scouser. He rewrote his footballing history with complete conviction, now claiming he'd always been a Liverpool fan — "since I was, like, four" — as if no one remembered that buried beneath the new Ian Rush poster on his bedroom wall was a slightly curled one of Bryan Robson.

Reggie was the same height as Andy but stockier, with a shaved head and a perpetually dishevelled uniform. At least one side of his shirt was always untucked and despite being in high school for over a year, he still hadn't mastered tying a proper knot in his tie. Today, it was hastily fastened in a crude, uneven loop. His blazer pocket sported a tear and a smear of toothpaste adorned the front for good measure.

'Hi, Andy. Hi, Mrs Townley,' Reggie said brightly.

'Hi, Reggie. Look at your tie! Give it here.'

Reggie grinned, slipped off his tie and handed it to Debbie, who draped it around her own neck. Andy caught Reggie's double-take as his gaze lingered on Debbie's face. Andy was getting used to these reactions – the surprised second glances, the barely concealed shock at how her appearance had changed. Debbie tied the tie loosely, then pulled it back over her head and placed it around Reggie's neck with a satisfied nod.

'Just adjust it up now. You look smarter already, Reggie. We'll make a gentleman of you yet.'

'Thanks, Mrs Townley,' Reggie replied uncertainly. He turned to Andy. 'Aston Villa at home tomorrow. We need to bounce back from that Southampton match. Mr Harris will love it if Liverpool lose again. Not that he can talk – United are practically at the bottom of Division One.'

Debbie hobbled alongside them, slowing them down noticeably. Reggie checked his watch and let out a low whistle.

'I'll jog on ahead, Andy. I'll, erm, let Mr Harris know you might be a bit late. Bye, Andy. Bye … erm … Mrs Townley.'

'You run on ahead, Andy. Go on, go with Reggie. I don't want you to be late, I'll…' Debbie wheezed, struggling to catch her breath – 'I'll be fine.' She stopped abruptly and lowered herself onto a garden wall.

Debbie closed her eyes tightly, drawing in a few deep breaths. When she opened them again, there was the slightest look of fear in her eyes.

'Forget town, Mum. Let's get you home – have a quiet day. It doesn't matter if I'm a little bit late, I'll explain to Mr Harris. He's always great about it.' Andy perched next to her. 'It's half term in a few weeks, Mum. Whatever you say, I'm coming to the doctors with you. We need to get this sorted.'

Debbie pulled herself up and, with a slight wobble, steadied herself on the gate post.

'See, all fine, just needed a little breather.' She attempted a smile. 'Come on, love, I feel OK and I fancy a mooch around Woolworths. It'll do me good, I was looking forward to getting out – I'll get you some pick 'n' mix. Besides, I can't face Mrs Silva's interrogation if I go back now.'

Andy just arrived for the end of form time, plonking himself down next to Reggie before the bell rang and the class bustled out of the door in high spirits.

'Andy, you got a sec?' Mr Harris called. He pulled down the roller chalkboard, considered what was written on it, then rubbed it off with the board rubber. He wafted his hand and coughed over-dramatically at the chalk dust and smiled. 'Everything OK? Bad morning today?'

Andy shrugged. 'Mum was a bit shaky, that's all,' he replied. 'I don't really understand it, sir. She doesn't seem to be getting any better. She takes lots of these pills but they don't seem to be doing anything. I can tell it's worrying her but she doesn't want to speak about it – it annoys me sometimes … but it feels scary too.'

'I understand, Andy, but she won't want to bother you with it, that's all. She'll feel she's protecting you and, in a way, that will comfort her. If there was something important for you to know, she would tell you. She'll want you focused on school. It sounds to me like she's doing her very best for you. Your dad, he's not around, is he?'

Thinking about his dad was acutely painful for Andy. Just the mention of Tony sent a jolt through him.

'No, sir. We … we don't know where he is.'

'I'm sorry about that, Andy. You're doing amazingly – respect to you. You come in each day and get on with it – and to top it all off, you have to put up with supporting Liverpool too!'

Andy smiled.

'I know I've said it before,' Mr Harris continued, 'but if there's anything I can do to make this easier, just say. Even if it's someone to talk to, my door is open. Got that?' Mr Harris performed a mock punch to Andy's chin and Andy nodded. 'You're tougher than most of the guys I used to fight. Now off you go.'

'Thanks, sir,' Andy said, picking his bag up from the floor. 'Sir? *Did* you used to fight?'

'Welsh Youth Champion no less,' Mr Harris said proudly. 'Thirty-five bouts, thirty-four wins. I only lost one because I reckon they'd slipped the judges a bung and I lost on points – I was robbed that night. Still bugs me that does. Hurricane Harris is what they called me – I've still got the newspaper clippings.'

Andy nodded, impressed, and headed towards the door.

'Hey,' Mr Harris called after him. 'You're the only person I've told that to, mind. That's between us, OK? Let's leave it to the rumour mill, shall we?'

Andy put his thumb up and joined the crowded corridor.

6

cKenzie was standing on a stage in a freezing, disused theatre tucked away down a litter-strewn side street in London. The November chill seemed infused into every brick of the building. The filming of the video for his second single off the *Rejuvenation!* album was in full swing. The song was titled 'Waking the Ghosts' and the storyboard followed a fairly obvious concept: McKenzie would stroll onto the stage of a run-down theatre to perform, his song somehow awakening the ghosts of past audiences from the theatre's heyday – or something along those lines. Atkinson had explained it in detail but McKenzie had questions. Why would he be wandering onto the stage of a disused theatre? Why would he even be *near* a disused theatre? And why on earth would the ghosts of an old audience be interested in watching him? Even his own fans were losing interest, let alone ghostly ones. If McKenzie found himself with time to kill in the middle of London, there was no chance he'd be standing alone on a draughty stage in a derelict theatre. No, he'd be seeking out one of his members-only clubs for a drink. Atkinson was furious at McKenzie for looking the worse for wear again after a heavy night. Watching McKenzie gingerly plink two Alka-Seltzers into a glass of water, Atkinson's face was thunderous *without* him questioning the video concept.

McKenzie had once relished video shoots, so much so that his perfectionism often compelled him to take over the directing, insisting on nothing short of his exact vision. This was a few years ago, when his singles sold by the truckload and no expense was spared on lavish productions filmed in aircraft hangar-sized studios. 'Waking the Ghosts' had a shoestring budget and was scheduled to be filmed in under a day, entirely in black-and-white. Atkinson claimed this choice lent the production an artistic edge, but McKenzie knew it was all about cutting costs. To save even more, the ghostly audience extras were recruited from his fan club, sparing the need for paid actors. Atkinson was well aware the song wasn't going to trouble the upper reaches of the chart. Duran Duran, Kim Wilde, The Bangles, Mel and Kim and The Pretenders were all releasing songs that autumn, so why spend more than was absolutely necessary?

McKenzie could hear Atkinson berating someone somewhere in the theatre. At least, it *sounded* like berating – with Atkinson, it was hard to tell; even in his most ecstatic moments, he sounded irritable. McKenzie had already fallen out with Atkinson a number of times that morning and the mood was edgy. Not only had Atkinson spent an hour making snide remarks about McKenzie being hungover *again* but he'd also managed to coax him, begrudgingly, into a white suit jacket with rolled-up sleeves coupled with a pink T-shirt. McKenzie's straggly hair had been trimmed, slicked with 'wet-look' gel and styled forward into curly tassels that hung over his face.

'Jesus, Atkinson, I look absolutely bloody ridiculous. You've bought me a seat on the 1980s bandwagon,' McKenzie said, looking in horror in a full-length mirror after the make-up and wardrobe people had finished with him. 'What did you do, raid the *Miami Vice* costume department?'

'We need to get you up to date, Mack. You can't dress like a rhinestone cowboy forever.'

Atkinson exhaled cigar smoke and laughed wheezily at his own joke.

'One – I look like Simon Le Bon's dad. Two – this video is being shot in black-and-white, why the hell do I need the pink T-shirt?'

'It's called fashion, Mack, fashion! Get those sleeves rolled up, they keep slipping.'

'Yes, Atkinson,' McKenzie replied, shaking his head at the mirror, 'because having a bit of forearm on display will suddenly make this a good song that people will want to buy.'

'It's a … solid song, Mack. It's a grower – you have to listen a few times to appreciate it. Good God, man, if you don't believe in your songs how can we expect the public to!' Atkinson paused, looking McKenzie up and down critically. 'Maybe do a button of that blazer up, Mack, we can see your paunch. *Growing* paunch, I might add.'

You'd think making music videos would be exhilarating, but most of the time was spent sitting around doing nothing. The endless waiting left McKenzie restless, craving a drink and increasingly irritable. MTV had launched in the United States a few years earlier to great fanfare and was set to air in the United Kingdom soon, making music videos a necessary evil for every song. McKenzie had been standing in the same spot on the stage for twenty minutes while the crew set up the lighting, and his head was pounding. Despite his ease performing in front of 15,000 people while strumming a guitar and singing, McKenzie felt oddly self-conscious and awkward when being filmed.

'I'm a musician, *not* an actor,' he moaned to Atkinson.

McKenzie had been in make-up an hour earlier and he could sense the make-up artist's disappointment upon seeing him in the flesh, which did nothing to bolster his wafer-thin confidence. He had let himself go – there was no denying it – and he was dreading the video shoot because he knew it would draw attention to it. The previous week, *McKenzie's Multiplying Midriff* was a headline on page four of the *News of the World*, accompanied by a rather unflattering picture of McKenzie lifting his guitar over his head, his T-shirt riding up to reveal his belly in all its hairy glory. The worst part was that Atkinson suspected the picture had been taken by a member of McKenzie's own road crew and leaked to the press. Furious at the betrayal, he lined up the entire crew and fired them all on the spot. Moments later, realising this was hardly the wisest of moves in the middle of a tour, he grudgingly reinstated them – though not without continuing to berate them.

'OK, you can step down, McKenzie. We think we've got the lights. We'll call you again when we've talked it through with the camera operators,' a voice from a loudspeaker told him. Stepping out of the glare, McKenzie was immediately met by a personal assistant who helped him into a dressing gown. McKenzie always found this faintly ludicrous. Why would he need a dressing gown after twenty minutes of standing doing nothing? At the bottom of the steps leading from the old theatre's stage, he was met by some of the fan club members who were holding out albums, posters and T-shirts for him to sign. McKenzie understood why this was a big deal for them and signed away – a squiggle that took a millisecond, one he had perfected over the years. He even managed to ask a few 'Where have you come from?' type questions to show an interest. What truly annoyed McKenzie was when people continued to pester him even after he had signed something and they had taken a few photos – those who invaded his personal space or lingered a bit too long. McKenzie hated it when he was eating out and someone approached him. He deserved to enjoy a meal in peace, especially given the steep prices at those trendy London restaurants. It was bad enough knowing fellow diners were watching him. He could sense their attempts to act nonchalant about sharing a dining space with a celebrity, but he caught them stealing glances from the corners of their eyes, fully aware they were scrutinising his every move. For this reason, he never ordered soup or spaghetti – *'Oh, we saw McKenzie McCall in Le Caprice the other night; he spilt the vichyssoise all down himself.'* No thanks.

The problem with video shoots, McKenzie decided, was *people*. There were people everywhere. Proving his point, as McKenzie finally managed to extract himself from the overenthusiastic fan club members, he was intercepted by a young production assistant. The assistant was wearing black headphones, clutching a clipboard and sporting the slightly bewildered look of someone unsure of their actual role on set.

'Excuse me, McKenzie...' the young man said, raising an apologetic hand. *Oh, God.* '... can I just say, all that 1970s stuff you did – it's so good. You really should be held in such high-esteem. Like, up here.' He raised his hand above his head to emphasise the sentiment.

'Well, erm, I *am* kind of held in some esteem, I think...' McKenzie replied, already bristling at the exchange.

'No, no,' the assistant insisted, pressing home his point, 'I think you should be *really* respected for what you've done...'

'Well, again... I would hope I am *slightly* respected,' McKenzie said, his voice laced with faint irritation. 'I've still got a *few* fans left around the world ... but thank you.'

'No, I mean... *revered*,' the assistant blurted out desperately, not giving up, but his confidence evaporating.

McKenzie sighed inwardly. He'd always thought those stories about music stars who demanded no one approach or engage with them on set were ridiculous. Now, he wasn't so sure. He made a mental note to ask Atkinson to implement a you-don't-speak-to-McKenzie policy next time.

In a foul mood, McKenzie returned to a small dressing room at the end of a gloomy corridor in the depths of the theatre. Although they'd tried to spruce it up a bit for their special guest, with the addition of a nice velvet settee and a chair, it still looked as run down as the rest of the dilapidated building. Atkinson was sitting reading *The Sun* and shaking his head.

'They're going after Elton again, dear oh dear. This article is brutal. I'm glad I'm not his manager this morning.' He chuckled.

McKenzie looked at him incredulously.

'You're saying you're glad you're not Elton John's manager – one of the most talented musicians in the world? What a ridiculous thing to say, Atkinson.'

Atkinson lowered the paper and locked eyes with Mack.

'Well, someone's a bit of a grouchy pants this morning. We're all here for you, trying to make you a decent video, but do you appreciate it …?'

McKenzie opened his mouth to express exactly what he thought of the theatre, the video, the director and how he felt like the Phantom of the bloody Opera lurking in the bowels of the building. Instead, he slumped back on the dusty settee. Atkinson shook his head at him, straightened the paper with a dramatic flick and went back to tutting and smirking at whatever gossip he could find. Radio 1 blared from the ghetto blaster on the shabby table beside Atkinson, with Simon Bates introducing 'A Kind of Magic'. McKenzie loved Queen; he admired Freddie Mercury's soaring vocals and live performances and longed for even a fraction of Brian May's guitar genius. He envied them being in a group, bouncing ideas off each other and supporting each other. McKenzie had his backing band, but he still felt the burden of being a solo artist; all the pressure was on him to perform and write the songs and when times were tough, he alone bore the weight of it all.

'Turn it up, Atkinson,' McKenzie said. Atkinson tutted at McKenzie's foot, which began tapping as John Deacon's lively bass line kicked in. Atkinson ignored the request.

'One of *them*, Mercury is. You know' – Atkinson lowered his voice and glanced around – '*gay*.'

Atkinson studied McKenzie, waiting for his reaction but none was forthcoming. '*And* Elton John. Don't even get me started on Boy George, they're all at it – they're taking over the music industry. Everyone knows it. It's an open secret with Mercury. They all need to be careful with their…

lifestyle… says so 'ere.' Atkinson prodded the front of *The Sun* with his stubby finger. 'Look!'

McKenzie scanned the front page. *Gay Plague! Killer AIDS Virus!* The headline was a little too pleased with itself.

'AIDS,' confirmed McKenzie. 'Seems pretty awful from what I've read.'

'Apparently it's spreading like wildfire through these … communities.' Atkinson pulled a face. 'Tory MPs are saying if they choose to live that way, what do they expect? Once you've got AIDS, that's pretty much it – two years, tops.'

'Are we really taking behavioural advice from Tory MPs now, Atkinson? Don't you think if it were straight people affected, I bet those same MPs would impose some kind of nationwide lockdown until a cure was found? But since it's mostly gay people, we'll just stick the boot in.'

McKenzie was in a combative mood and the endless hanging around for the world's most absurd video shoot to begin only fuelled his irritation.

Atkinson sat up and slammed the paper down. 'Mack, will you *keep it down*,' he hissed. 'How many times? You've got a mole in your camp and you're here supporting the gays. *The Sun* will have a field day with that.'

Atkinson sat back into the chair, a smirk spreading across his face. 'I remember when you did that song, "Dance Time", and you became a bit of a gay icon didn't you, Mack? Deary me, I had to spend the next six months toughening up your image and planting pictures of you chatting to women in the press. Nearly ruined you that did.' Atkinson laughed so hard that he descended into a wheezing cough, his face turning beetroot as tears streamed down his cheeks. McKenzie regarded the big, round tomato in a suit before him. Atkinson really did disgust him sometimes. Yet he wasn't done; he had more to say. 'You have to be careful with these things. I keep saying, we could do with getting you settled down. You know, for your career. What are you now, thirty-seven or thirty-eight? People will start to question it. We need to get you photographed with a bit of arm candy to keep the gossip columns happy.' Atkinson gave McKenzie a knowing look.

McKenzie rolled his eyes – Atkinson spent most of the time in the gossip columns himself, with a different woman on his arm each night. McKenzie had no idea how he attracted them; it must have been the size of his wad … of cash.

'Ah yes, what better reason could there be to find a lady to spend the rest of my days with than for my image? That's the foundation of a healthy relationship, for sure,' McKenzie said.

Atkinson nodded an *exactly*.

It *was* true; McKenzie hadn't met anyone in a long time now, but who would want to date a washed-up seventies rock star who was past their sell-by date and trying to cling on to a career in the eighties? Besides, McKenzie hated going on dates, not really knowing whether he was expected to be real McKenzie or rock star McKenzie.

'Let's all take a moment to consider *your* love life, shall we, Atkinson? In thirteen years of knowing you, I've not actually *met* one of these girlfriends. What happens – they quickly realise what you're actually like and jump ship? A nice relationship might actually bring out a more endearing side in you … and maybe you'd leave me alone and stop coercing me into things.' McKenzie was losing his temper, exacerbated by a hangover of epic proportions that showed no sign of abating.

'Hey!' barked Atkinson. 'I dedicate myself to you and your career, there's no bloody room for anyone else in my life. Married to my job, I am. And do you appreciate everything I do? No you bloody do not! And I am shocked, Mack, shocked! I have never once tried to coerce you into anything. Look after you and your career out of the goodness of my heart? Yes! *Coercion?* No!'

'My name is Michael, Mike McCall! You told me no successful musician can get anywhere being called Mike and you changed my name on all the promotional material *without* telling me first. Well, Michael Jackson must be kicking himself, Atkinson. Being a Mike has really damaged *his* career. Oh, and you get twenty per cent, Atkinson, that's more than enough appreciation. Let's get this godforsaken video over and done with. I want to get to the club for a dri— I mean home.'

7

'**N**ow, wait for the *fireworks!*'

Mr Harris stood at the front of the room, savouring the rapt attention of twenty-eight wide-eyed pupils. Eye-protection goggles firmly in place and a white lab coat adding an air of importance, he grinned like a showman about to dazzle his crowd. This was the highlight of the lesson – a magnesium strip about to burst into brilliant light. He raised the burning splint with dramatic flair, ready to ignite the strip and bask in the inevitable gasps of awe. But before he could strike, the attention in the room shifted away from him, much to his dismay. There was a timid knock at the door. Mrs Taylor from the office hovered there, her hands clasped nervously. A mousy figure in a knitted cardigan and thick glasses, she looked distinctly uneasy about interrupting. Mr Harris sighed, the splint suspended in mid-air. He turned to her and raised his eyebrows, his smile now thin and strained. '*Yes*, Mrs Taylor?'

'I'm *so* sorry, Mr Harris, erm Andrew? I could do with Andrew Townley – is he in your class? It … it is quite important. He will need his bag and coat.'

'OK, Andy.' Mr Harris extinguished the splint. 'Get your stuff and off you go.'

***

Andy's stomach lurched as he scrambled to grab his bag from the floor and his coat from the chair. Reggie shrugged. 'Looks like you're going home, Towns.'

Mr Harris followed Andy out of the door and pulled it shut behind them, holding on to the handle with one hand. Andy could hear the class erupt into chatter behind him.

'Everything OK, Mrs Taylor? With Andy, I mean?'

Mrs Taylor turned to Andy, her face warm and full of concern.

'Andy, your mum had a bit of a funny turn in town … while shopping. She went to hospital and it's OK, they quickly released her and she's home, but she's obviously feeling a bit under the weather and shaken up. Your gran rang and thought you'd want to know, she says it's OK for you to walk home.'

Tears pricked Andy's eyes and he gulped – he *told* her not to go. He *knew* it wasn't a good idea.

Mr Harris put a hand on his shoulder. 'Listen, Andy, don't worry. It sounds OK – the hospital wouldn't have released her if it was serious. People faint and whatnot all the time. Go home, look after her and it'll be OK. We'll have a chat in the morning and don't forget we're here for you if needed. Tell your mum not to worry about parents' evening tonight – we can rearrange, it's not a problem.'

Andy hurried home, a stitch pinching his side. As he rounded the corner onto his street, he couldn't help but notice how shabby his house appeared amidst the row of terraces, especially in comparison to the well-kept homes on either side. The window frames were splintering and the paint was cracking – the front door, which used to be white, was a grimy grey colour. His dad was always the one for getting DIY jobs done around the house. Andy tried to push thoughts of Tony from his mind; it was his coping mechanism. Yet, a deep bitterness coursed through him as he grappled with the betrayal of watching his mum face her illness alone while Tony was enjoying the freedom and social life he must have longed for.

As Andy pulled his key from his pocket, Mrs Silva's door swung open and her head shot out. She wore a faded floral housecoat and plastic rollers peeked out from beneath her well-worn headscarf.

'Andy! This is no good. We are all telling Debbie she is not well and needs to slow right down but she will not listen – now look!'

'I'm going in to her now, Mrs Silva. She's just fainted, I think – it's not her fault. Mr Harris said people faint all the time,' Andy replied, fiercely loyal to his mum. Mrs Silva looked unconvinced.

'I still bring your food in two moments and you can heat it later. Tell Debbie she needs to eat too. Your grandmother is in there and thank goodness for that.'

Andy opened the front door and paused in the narrow hallway, finding immediate comfort in the muffled voices drifting from behind the sitting-room door. After kicking off his shoes, he stepped inside. On the settee against the far wall, Debbie sat upright. Andy's gran, Pam, fussed behind her, adjusting the pillow that supported her. Both women turned and smiled at him. Despite the lack of colour in Debbie's face and the shadows under her eyes, she looked better than he had anticipated.

'Here,' said Pam, handing Debbie a glass of water and a couple of pills. 'What are these, anyway?'

Pam was a sprightly lady, in her mid-sixties. She was still playing tennis every day with Brian, Andy's grandad, who was sitting in the armchair by the window. They were both dressed in white sports gear.

'They're … just some medication the consultant is trying me on,' Debbie replied.

'Well I didn't think much of those doctors,' said Pam. 'Did you, Brian?'

Brian was wearing a headband and matching wristbands like an ageing John McEnroe. He looked up from his newspaper.

'Very abrupt, they just wanted us gone as fast as possible. Wouldn't even let Debbie have a bed, Andy. They took her off to some side room then discharged her straight away. Disgraceful really. What's happened to the NHS? Maggie Thatcher needs to sort them all out.'

'They could see I was fine,' Debbie argued, a hint of exasperation creeping in. She had clearly endured this conversation for the better part of an hour.

'Fine? You collapsed in Debenhams and were convulsing!' Pam glanced at Andy, noting his concern and softened her tone. 'Sorry, Andy, but we're worried. It nearly gave me a heart attack when we got the call. Just leaving for tennis, we were. Poor Marge and Harold will be wondering where on earth we are, they were expecting a game of mixed doubles.'

'Probably still standing there waiting for you to serve,' muttered Brian from behind a newspaper. 'Can't stand Harold anyway. Ever since he got that metallic silver Ford Sierra he's been insufferable, the flashy sod. I hope it rusts.'

'Brian!' Pam admonished as she ran a finger across the top of the TV. 'Good heavens, Debbie, when was the last time your surfaces saw some Pledge and a duster?'

'I hadn't eaten breakfast and got light-headed. I feel fine now,' Debbie said to Andy, ignoring her parents. 'We've got Mrs Silva's world-famous cuisine on the way, then I've got parents' evening to get to.'

There was a knock at the door.

'Debbie, you are *not* going to parents' evening, I *won't* allow it …' said Pam, heading for the front door. Pam pulled the sitting-room door to and they could all hear her thanking Mrs Silva profusely and discussing Debbie's current health status, without any concern as to who might hear.

'… I know, Mrs Silva,' they could hear Pam say, 'and she thinks she's going to Andy's school tonight, not a chance of it. She needs rest! I think she's taken a shine to that Mr Harris, Andy's form tutor – but you rest assured, Mrs Silva, I will not let her past this door!'

Andy glanced from Brian to Debbie; they were all thinking the same thing.

'I know you're going, Debbie, no matter what Pam says.' Brian sighed. 'But I'm driving you, staying with you *and* dropping you back here. Pam's not going to let me hear the end of it when I get back, though – just so you know, Debbie.'

***

Debbie had met with most of Andy's teachers, guided around the building by Brian. It was the same school she had attended as a teenager. Each teacher had said more or less the same thing and her heart swelled with pride – Andy was a delightful, well-mannered boy who, though he sometimes drifted off a little, was otherwise dedicated and hardworking. Debbie found herself needing to justify his wavering focus, explaining they had been through a period of adjustment after his dad left the home. The teachers were kind and understanding. The corridor was quiet as Brian and Debbie sat in a row of small chairs outside Mr Harris's room, waiting for their last appointment. Brian idly studied the noticeboard in front of them.

'He's nothing like you. Andy, I mean,' he said, chuckling. 'I remember sitting outside these rooms dreading going in to see your teachers. They would say you were headstrong and always ready to give an opinion, even if it wasn't asked for. That's why we only ended up having you – you took up enough of our attention. Andy must take after Tony …' Brian's words tailed off, leaving a silence hanging in the air between them. He turned to Debbie. 'Where *is* Tony, Debbie? This isn't good enough – you are struggling with your health. Even if things didn't work out for whatever reason, he should still support you. How can a man *change* like that? I liked Tony. I thought he was a sound bloke. Pam did too – we all did. It's Andy's parents' evening … where in God's name is he?'

'Don't, Dad.' Debbie paused. 'Tony was … Tony was always a bit different, but he was interesting … that's why we got together. He was a bit of a loner, outwardly happy-go-lucky but there was something always there. He was always searching for *something* – a new house, different furniture, a new carpet, a new bathroom. He just couldn't quite settle. I'm not sure anything could make him truly happy.' She sighed. 'It was like he had to build a cold barrier to help himself leave, to protect himself from guilt or his conscience. When he found that new group of workmates, maybe he felt he'd missed out on life. Who knows? Maybe he met a new woman.'

Brian shook his head. 'I just don't know how you're not angry.'

Debbie considered this for a second. 'Because I *loved* him, Dad ...'

'Mrs Townley?' The door swung open and the bulky figure of Mr Harris filled the doorway, smiling at them both. 'Please, come in.' He gestured with a sweeping arm towards the room. 'Are you coming in as well, sir?'

'Oh ... no, I'm just the chauffeur, well dad, Debbie's dad ... Andy's grandad. This is the last appointment, then we'll get Debbie home – she's a bit under the weather but she was determined to come. I'll wait here.' Mr Harris's imposing presence often had this nervy effect on people.

'Yes, it's good to see Mrs Townley here and it's a wise decision, sir. I wouldn't want you to have to hear the truly terrible things I've got to say about Andy.' Mr Harris laughed loudly and gestured again for Debbie to enter.

Mr Harris spoke warmly of his huge respect for Andy and it was clear to Debbie they had a strong relationship. He said he appreciated that there were challenges in their life, but that Andy was coping brilliantly and was such a mature and grown-up boy. Mr Harris reaffirmed that if Andy needed someone to chat to, he was there for him. Debbie could see why Andy liked him so much. Mr Harris had a big heart and a way of making someone feel important and valued. Debbie couldn't help smiling. She was so pleased that Andy was doing well, despite everything. This was *her* boy and he had been through so much but he was still trying his best. Her heart felt close to bursting. The strange and sudden dizziness and flashing lights she'd experienced earlier were a distant memory. She felt re-energised. In a strange way, it was refreshing, chatting to another adult who wasn't one of her parents, Mrs Silva or a medical practitioner. She didn't have nearly enough normal moments any more. Relaxing, Debbie moved a hand upwards to casually brush her fringe aside as she listened to Mr Harris, causing her sleeve to ride up her arm slightly. A dark, mauve blemish became visible on Debbie's wrist. Almost in slow motion, Mr Harris's gaze shifted from Debbie's face to the mark on her arm. She was still laughing at his recounting of how Mrs Taylor's interruption earlier that day had almost caused him to burn his eyebrows off. His smile froze. Debbie was now responding and smiling as she spoke, but he didn't hear what she said.

'Right well, I'm sure you need to be going,' he blurted, interrupting her mid-sentence – with a rigid, expressionless face. 'I mean, I'm sure you want to get back to Andy and it sounds like you've had quite a day.'

He rose and opened the door.

'Oh … oh yes, of course. Sorry, I'm keeping you,' Debbie replied, surprised, her smile fading. She pushed herself up using the table. 'Thank you for everything you've been doing for Andy, he really appreciates your support.'

Mr Harris nodded, his smile still strained as he glanced at the table where Debbie's hands had just been resting.

'Bye, then. Thank you.' Debbie said as she exited. Mr Harris leaned back, turned his head away and held his breath as she passed by.

8

'Number thirty-one?' McKenzie repeated back to Atkinson. 'It could have been worse, I guess. At least it hit the top forty.'

The atmosphere in the back of Atkinson's Rolls Royce Silver Spirit was tense. They were en route to The Roundhouse for the final gig of the UK tour before heading to Europe. Outside, the late November afternoon was already fading into dusk and the car lights of the busy London traffic sparkled and dazzled against the wet streets. Normally, the last show of a tour would reinvigorate the crew and band, creating a celebratory atmosphere. However, Atkinson had been in a foul mood all day, leaving everyone walking on eggshells.

No one was surprised by the swift stay of 'Waking with Ghosts' in the top forty. The only press attention it received was a small article in *The Mirror*, which barely even mentioned the song. Focusing on McKenzie's rash change of fashion – *Mack's Makeover Misery* – the article ridiculed McKenzie's evident discomfort at the pink T-shirt and blazer combo. It claimed Atkinson had pressured McKenzie into wearing the outfit as a desperate attempt to appear 'with it'. Ironically, it was one of the few articles written about him which was actually true. As the car edged down Camden High Street, Atkinson jabbed his cigar in McKenzie's direction.

'You've lost your fight, Mack. You used to want to conquer the world, now you're not even bothered about conquering this drab London suburb we find ourselves in. It's slipping away, Mack. You want to know who is ahead of you in the top forty?' Atkinson glared at McKenzie, demanding a response. McKenzie sank deeper into the deep, plush seat – upholstered in fine cream leather – and stared out of the window. He pulled the sleek brim of his grey cowboy hat down lower, further irritating Atkinson.

'I'll tell you, Mack, I'll tell you!' Atkinson continued, his face turning bright red. 'Cliff Richard with a song from some bloody musical, Shakin' Stevens ... and some bird from *EastEnders*!'

'Hey, I *like* her song!' McKenzie replied wryly from beneath his hat.

Atkinson stubbed out his cigar aggressively and took a sip of expensive champagne from an equally lavish flute resting on a polished wood table between them, which featured convenient glass-shaped depressions. The dashboard and door trims also gleamed in polished wood; the car was Atkinson's pride and joy. To McKenzie, it always seemed faintly ridiculous to see Atkinson drinking champagne; his burly frame suggested he should be nursing a pint of bitter instead. Atkinson had expensive tastes and a carefully curated image of success to uphold. He turned to McKenzie again, lowering his voice into a slow, steely and slightly sinister whisper.

'It's showtime in a few hours, Mack, and you are going to go out there and deliver such a great performance that you are going to send the audience home with their pants on fire. Then, Mack, you'll have one week off. And do you know what we're going to do before the European leg? We are going to book you and the band into the studio and *you* are going to bring the songs you will have been working on during that week off. Creativity, Mack – that's what you used to do. And *I'm* not going to sit on my backside either – *I* am going to find you a new producer, one that understands what's hot right now. It's all synthesisers and drum machines, Mack – guitars are relics of a bygone age. Are we on the same page here? We'll sort this, Mack. We'll sort it.'

McKenzie looked at Atkinson with a face that made it clear there was absolutely no agreement to anything whatsoever. Undeterred, Atkinson thumbed roughly through his hefty Filofax. Turning his back to McKenzie, he pulled his Roamer from his jacket pocket and thumped out a phone number with a heavy finger. As he waited, he took a sip of champagne and a drag from his cigar.

'Charlie? Atkinson Stark!' Atkinson boomed. 'How the devil are you and how is your diary looking next Thursday? I've got a proposition for you. Bear with me on this one …' Atkinson cackled a loud throaty laugh to whatever Charlie replied. McKenzie groaned.

***

It turned out that Charlie was actually *Charley* – Charley Okorie, one of the most in-demand producers in London, known for working with all the New Romantic bands over the past few years. Her presence brought a fresh, fashionable and *female* dynamic to the studio, injecting a sense of style and energy that was hard to ignore. Charley wore shiny pink cotton trousers paired with a loose-fitting pink and white striped top. McKenzie felt old and uncomfortable. Charley sat on a swivel chair in front of what resembled a Star Trek control panel – sliding controls, flashing buttons and oscillating dials. Meanwhile, McKenzie and the band were perched awkwardly on stools in the centre of the studio. Microphones were suspended from the ceiling, poised to capture the magic of the demo they were supposed to be producing. Atkinson was pacing restlessly behind Charley, before stopping abruptly. Leaning into the microphone on the control desk, he pressed a button, his glare fixed on McKenzie through the glass window. Atkinson's voice blared into the band's earphones. With Atkinson, there were only two tones: loud and *louder*.

'Go back to that riff you came up with a few takes ago – it had potential, you were going somewhere with that. It was … catchy – kind of.' His voice was croakier and courser than usual and he was dabbing his forehead with a black silk handkerchief.

'You know, if you twiddle the knobs on the side of your headphones you can turn him right down,' McKenzie said under his breath and the band stifled a smile. They knew Atkinson was not someone to upset, especially if your livelihood depended on it.

Atkinson pressed the button again. 'I heard that, Mack. You've got microphones in front of you, you know. It's only costing me a couple of hundred pounds *an hour* to be here, listening to you guys faff around. I thought the song was ready to go, Mack?'

'*Me*, Atkinson,' Mack said, leaning closer to his mic. 'It's costing *me* – you deduct all costs before taking your cut. Why don't you go get tucked up in bed with a hot lemon or something, leave us to get on with this. You sound a bit run down, Atkinson? We'll be fine, you get yourself off home.'

Atkinson pressed the button again.

'It's stress, Mack. It's the stress of managing you – it's taking its toll!'

McKenzie looked at Charley, who was pretending to adjust some of the sliding controls. She must wonder what she was doing there with an old fart like him who was unable to develop even the simplest of songs.

'We love each other really, Charley,' McKenzie said dryly. 'And when I get my *new* manager, I'm sure me and Atkinson will still be friends, eventually. I bet you don't get this lack of professionalism from the teenyboppers you usually produce?'

McKenzie noticed the flicker of hurt on Charley's face and regretted it instantly. Sometimes, he thought, he really could be an arse.

Recording didn't use to be a chore. McKenzie used to revel in this process: sitting in a room with talented musicians – leading the way, creating the first seedling of a song, playing it for the band, watching it develop and writing the lyrics. This was his dream all those years ago, when he used to busk outside Covent Garden tube station, after Atkinson had persuaded him to take the plunge and move south. Just a few years ago, he carried a Dictaphone with a tiny cassette, capturing ideas as they struck him – walking down the street, sitting in the bath, even shopping for antiques. Quickly pressing record, he'd hum or sing a line or melody into the little machine. Sometimes people would turn in surprise and he'd smile and wink as he sang into it, right there in some random spot, secure in the knowledge that another potential song was safely captured. It was a joy to be part of developing a song from that single hummed line into a fully-fledged hit. Working with musicians at the top of the game, giving them direction but letting their talent interpret where to take the song during the recording process. A studio can be an intimidating place – hired by the hour, with every tick of the clock a reminder of the cost. McKenzie had seen experienced musicians crumble under the pressure of needing to perform in a few takes. McKenzie needed musicians who could understand his vision immediately and run with it on the spot. Playing live and recording in a studio were two different beasts. McKenzie remained loyal to his band – they'd been with him since the early days, both on stage and in the studio. It was a professional relationship that had never strayed into close friendship territory. Maybe there was always an awkward feeling, as if he was the boss and they could never quite get past it.

'That's not quite working, McKenzie,' Charley's strong cockney voice snapped him back into the present. 'Maybe leave it for today, or do you want one more shot at it?'

McKenzie sighed and lifted the guitar strap over his head.

'These things happen,' Charley said when McKenzie joined her in the control room. 'At least you were here. You wouldn't believe how many times I've shown up at the studio only to find a note on the mixing desk saying *gone to Barbados* or something like that. You know what these teenyboppers are like.'

She smiled to lighten the mood after McKenzie's clumsy comment and he returned what he hoped was an apologetic expression, despite his irritation with the session.

'You record your own stuff, I really respect that,' Charley continued. 'Sometimes there's going to be dry spells where the songs take a bit more teasing out. Some of these bands nowadays, they have writing teams that write the songs, mixing teams that mix the songs, fashion teams that dress them and publicity teams to promote them. The actual performer shows up before a night out, sings into the microphone for half an hour and then heads straight out to a club. You're not part of a machine like that, McKenzie. The songs will come.'

McKenzie watched Atkinson shouting into his Roamer in the corner of the room. He turned to McKenzie, waving his arms in a gesture that said, *Don't worry about this; I'm handling it!*

'Actually, Charley, I've got a vacancy for a new manager if you're interested?' McKenzie joked, with a wry smile.

9

ndy felt an unfamiliar but welcome sense of positivity during form time. The class buzzed with chatter around him and as Reggie excitedly described his Kim Wilde poster collection, Andy realised – perhaps for the first time in a while – that he felt part of it all. Debbie had returned from parents' evening brimming with pride and they'd stayed up later than usual, talking about anything and everything. That morning she was up again and chatting happily as Andy got ready for school, cramming his books into his bag. Pam and Brian had spent the night in Andy's room to ensure Debbie was recovering from her fall. Despite a restless night on the settee, it was a relief to Andy that someone was at home to look after her.

As usual with Reggie, the conversation turned to football. Liverpool had found their form again with a 2-0 home win against Coventry over the weekend. But as December approached, it was Everton who were surprising everyone with a commanding 4-0 victory over Norwich, propelling them to the top of the table. A young forward named Gary Lineker was scoring goals for fun. Manchester United had appointed a new Scottish manager, Alex Ferguson. Reggie tried to tease Mr Harris about it – after all, the new boss wasn't doing much to improve United's fortunes and Reggie joked he'd be gone by the end of the season. Mr Harris looked up from the books he was marking, nodded and smiled thinly before returning to his work. After registering the class, he had given them a dressing down about their personal appearance – jewellery and the wrong colour socks. When the bell rang, Mr Harris looked up again.

'Off you go, you horrible lot, and stay out of trouble. I don't want to be spending my lunch hour sorting out your mess with the head of department, just because you can't behave.'

Andy lingered, pulling on his coat and carefully wrapping his Liverpool scarf around his neck. Mr Harris kept his head down, a pen resting against his lip as he reviewed the workbook in front of him, then marking it with a flurry of ticks. Finally, hoisting his Puma rucksack over his shoulder, Andy stepped in front of Mr Harris's desk.

'Erm … sir? Sorry. You … you said we might chat today, you know, about what happened yesterday?'

Mr Harris looked up and leaned back in his chair.

'I've got a full timetable today, Andy. It's a busy day today. Mrs Taylor, in the office, is there for pastoral issues. Any problems and I'm sure she'll help.'

Andy stared at him for a moment, thinking he might be joking – sometimes it wasn't always clear with Mr Harris, but he didn't break into a smile and Andy stood rooted to the spot.

'You're going to be late, Andy – first lesson, English, isn't it? That's on the other side of the building. Mrs Grainger will be waiting for you and I need to get to Mr Dean's office.'

'S-sorry, sir,' Andy mumbled, bewildered.

Halfway down the corridor, Andy turned back to the classroom, double-checking for some sign of a mistake. Mr Harris was gingerly moving a chair with his foot, like it was radioactive and prodding it to the back of the classroom. It was the chair Andy had been sitting on.

When Andy arrived at his English lesson, Mrs Grainger was waiting at the door.

'Come in Andy, come in,' she said. She looked both ways up the corridor, before turning to gesture into the classroom. The class were sitting at tables in pairs.

'Maybe you sit here today, Andy?' She pointed at the table in the front corner, nearest the door. The table behind was empty. Andy slid into his seat, catching Reggie's eye, who responded with a trademark bemused expression. It took the class a while to settle as they pulled out books and pencil cases. There was a buzz of gossip about the previous night's *Grange Hill* episode on TV and Zammo descending into drug use – an event that had caused genuine shock and *needed* discussing. Mrs Grainger stood at her desk, flicking distractedly through a file while glancing towards the door. She wore a striped jacket with large shoulder pads – power dressing – but seemed less poised than usual, exhibiting a flustered and distracted demeanour. Eventually, she began the lesson by gaining the class's attention with a countdown from three.

'Now, erm, let me … yes, Macbeth, page thirty-three. What was Lady Macbeth …' Her expression shifted to one of relief as a knock sounded at the doorway. 'Ah, Mr Harris and Mr Dean, *there* you are.' The class began to stand in the traditional show of respect when an adult entered the room.

Mr Dean, the headteacher, gestured for them to remain seated. He was a tall man, balding, with spectacles, dressed in a brown suit and matching brown shoes.

'Thank you, class. Andy, can you come with us, please?' Mr Dean looked directly at him and Andy briefly wondered how the headteacher had recognised him so easily – they'd never crossed paths before, as far as he could remember. Andy's stomach flipped. His mum – it must be serious this time if the headteacher was involved. Rising to his feet, his thoughts spiralled about what could've happened.

'You'll need your things, Andy. Bring everything with you,' Mr Harris said bluntly from behind Mr Dean.

Andy followed them out into the corridor. Mr Dean offered a small smile.

'We're just going to have a chat in the hall, Andy. It's really nothing to worry about. You walk on ahead.'

When they reached the hall, a table had been set up in front of the stage, where the other deputy head, Mrs Dawes, was already seated. A single chair stood about fifteen feet away, positioned squarely in the middle of the room.

'Take a seat, Andy, there's a good lad,' Mr Dean said, as he and Mr Harris took their places alongside Mrs Dawes at the table.

Andy perched on the edge of the chair, unnerved, his bag and coat resting at his feet. Exposed, he was unsure how to sit or what to do with his hands. Biting his lip, he absentmindedly picked at the skin around his thumbnail – a habit he'd developed without realising. The side of his thumb was red and raw. Mr Harris's impassive stare bored into him, amplifying the suffocating silence. Andy's chest tightened with the weight of it, until at last Mr Dean spoke.

'Now, Andy, this might seem a bit strange and unexpected, but please try not to worry,' Mr Dean began, his tone measured. 'We – the leadership team – had a long discussion with the governors last night about your ... well, your home situation. Particularly concerning your mother, who we understand isn't too well at the moment.' He paused, adjusting his tone as if searching for the right words. 'Well, Andy, we've decided that the best place for you right now – the *kindest* thing we can do – is to suggest that you stay at home with your mum for a few days, to support her while we work out how best to support you too.' He attempted another empathetic smile. 'We've just phoned your home and ...' His voice trailed off as he glanced down the table, looking for support.

'We don't think school is the right place for you at the moment, Andy – not with everything going on at home,' Mr Harris said tersely, his back stiff and his hands clasped in front of him. His deep Welsh accent echoed through the hall.

'Honestly, things are fine,' Andy said, frowning. He couldn't believe Debbie would want him to miss school. 'Mum seemed much better this morning. My gran's with her too, so I really don't need to—'

'Andy, for the time being, we just think it's best—' Mr Dean started, his voice softer, but Mr Harris cut him off.

'You can go home now, Andy – to your mum. She knows you're on the way.'

Mr Harris extended a steady hand, pointing towards the double doors behind Andy.

***

Andy wandered down the main road towards home, his rucksack slung over his back, hands buried deep in his pockets and head bowed. He barely registered his surroundings. It was always strange to realise that life carried on normally outside the school gates during the day. Now, walking among it when he should have been in class, he felt out of place. Cars glided past – Vauxhall Cavaliers, Ford Escorts, Volkswagen Golfs – and Andy watched them with quiet envy. Did their drivers all have normal lives to live and enjoy? A heavy sense of foreboding settled over him. He couldn't make sense of Mr Harris's sudden change in behaviour. Had he decided Andy wasn't worth the effort any more? Maybe he thought Andy was getting too much attention. Perhaps he'd been too needy, too clingy and Mr Harris had finally had enough, deciding Andy was taking up too much of his time.

The thoughts dragged him down. It was hard enough having a mum who was unwell. Now it was like he'd done something wrong and he didn't know what.

When Andy arrived home, he could hear Pam pottering in the kitchen, while Brian read a newspaper in the same armchair he'd been occupying when Andy left. The settee was empty.

'Alright, son?' Brian called out as Pam appeared in the sitting-room doorway, wearing a flowery apron and wiping her hands on a tea towel.

'You OK, Andy? School rang and said you were on your way. They mentioned you wanted a day or two with your mum. What a lovely man Mr Harris is – so considerate,' Pam said with a soft smile. 'We told them you'd probably be fine but he insisted you take a little break to be with Debbie.'

Andy frowned – *he* wanted time at home? Was he imagining the conversation that had just taken place at school?

'You mustn't let it get to you, Andy,' Pam added gently. 'Debbie has another appointment with a consultant next week and she should know more then.'

'Where's Mum now?' Andy asked warily.

'We told her to go back to bed and get some rest, Andy. She looked exhausted – I think parents' evening was a bit much after what happened at Debenhams. I did tell her – she's overdoing it. And I told *you* too, Brian,' Pam said, shooting her husband a disapproving look. 'We'll head home a bit later. We'll just wait until she's up again, but we're always at the end of the telephone if you need us.'

Andy wandered into the kitchen and Pam sank down onto the settee with a dramatic sigh. They had tuned the stacked hi-fi to Radio 2, where the Scottish accent of Ken Bruce, one of the newer DJs, was chatting away cheerfully. Andy poured himself some juice and he overheard Pam telling Brian she wasn't sure about Ken and whether he'd last; she missed Terry Wogan in the mid-morning slot.

As Andy drank, he peered down the length of the glass, his eye settling on the small kitchen table before him. Unusually, Debbie had left one of her little brown medicine bottles out. Andy placed his glass in the sink, listening for any sign of movement from behind the sitting-room door to his right, before heading over to investigate. He knew his mum was taking medication for her illness, but she had never actually revealed what it was or left any evidence lying around. Picking up the bottle, he squinted at the label:

Azidothymidine (AZT)

There was something about those letters that sparked a faint flicker in the depths of his mind. He searched through his muddy memory. Was it something he'd heard on the TV? His mum often had the news on. Instinctively, Andy slipped the medicine bottle into his coat pocket and wandered into the lounge.

'I'm just nipping out… to get some lunch,' he said. 'I'll be back in an hour or so and hopefully Mum will be up and about then and you can get off.'

Pam paused her knitting and reached into the handbag resting at her feet.

'OK, love. Take this 50p and get yourself a pasty. And here's 10p in case you need to call us.'

Taking the bus into town, Andy was determined to regain some control. Mr Harris's behaviour had shaken him, leaving him with a multitude of unanswered questions and a growing sense of losing his grip on reality. For the first time in a long while, he was taking proactive steps and it felt empowering. If there was a way to help Debbie, he would find it – some detective work was in order.

The town library was an old black-and-white timber and brick building, with worn stone steps leading up to a set of huge wooden doors which were open. Through this main entrance was a horseshoe-shaped front desk, where a couple of staff members milled about in the middle. A gentleman with glasses and silvery hair stamped books for customers with a loud clunk, while an older lady in a bright cardigan placed books onto a trolley, her hair scraped back in a tidy bun. When Tony used to bring him to the library on Saturday mornings, Andy loved the experience – the musty smell of books, the thrill of knowing it would feel somehow dangerous to make a noise and the excitement of choosing new titles before taking them to the desk to be stamped out. Weaving around the shelves with his hands in his pockets, Andy felt the hidden medicine bottle in his right hand as he scanned the shelves of books. The library was quiet, save for a couple of students in Bon Jovi T-shirts sitting at desks, surrounded by open books. They were reading and making notes, their pens poised between their teeth. An older gentleman rested in a comfy chair, reading a newspaper, and nodded a greeting to Andy. Finally, Andy spotted what he had been searching for: a sign hanging ominously from the ceiling above the bookcase in the corner of the library – **Science/Medical**.

The librarians stamp echoed across the old building. *Thump. Thump.* Andy dragged a finger across the spines of the books, examining the titles. He didn't actually know what he was looking for: medical literature wasn't exactly his usual reading material. At the end of the row, his finger paused over a huge book spine, maybe ten centimetres wide. Andy struggled to pull the book free from the shelf, its weight heavy and unwieldy in his hands. *Thump.* He turned the cover and read the title. *The Faber Medical Dictionary* in bold letters filled the front cover. A librarian was placing books on a shelf further up the row, casting a brief look at him over the glasses perched on her nose. Andy carried the dictionary to a desk away from the students, facing a wall at the side of the building. Opening the dictionary from the back, he discovered the index, which was nearly as thick as a regular-sized book. Flicking through a couple of pages, he quickly found 'Az' and then saw it – Azidothymidine (AZT). *Thump. Thump.* He pulled the medicine jar from his pocket to double-check, then placed it back. He glanced over his shoulder while keeping his finger on the page; the librarian had moved closer, holding a piece of paper as she scanned a bookshelf. *Thump.* Andy turned to the correct page and found the small subheading:

Azidothymidine (AZT). *AZT was developed in the 1960s as a treatment for cancer.*

So there it was – cancer. Andy felt a strange sense of relief; not because his mum was undergoing treatment for cancer but because it made life clearer to have it confirmed. The librarian walked past the back of his chair, casting a sideways glance over his shoulder. He instinctively covered the page with his hand. *Thump. Thump.* Andy returned to the page, his eyes scanning further down. But then he felt his pulse quicken; things no longer seemed so straightforward:

Although the treatment was initially thought to be ineffective and subsequently shelved, AZT was recently found to have some success during trials with patients suffering from AIDS. While it can cause severe side effects such as nausea, vomiting, headaches, dizziness, and stomach complaints, AZT has been identified as the only drug currently capable of slowing the progress of the AIDS virus and is being trialled in both the US and the UK.

Thump. Thump. THUMP. Andy's hand trembled as he flipped back through the *A* section and found *AIDS*. On the page was a grainy black-and-white photograph of a man, his skin marred by several dark blemishes on his arms and face. The caption read: *One of the symptoms of HIV and AIDS is the telltale patches of Kaposi's sarcoma.*

AIDS: A disease caused by the human immunodeficiency virus (HIV). Individuals infected with Acquired Immunodeficiency Syndrome (AIDS) suffer from a compromised immune system, rendering their bodies increasingly unable to fight off opportunistic infections. Symptoms can be wide-ranging and may include unexplained weight loss, fever, fatigue, recurrent infections, and pneumonia. Originally referred to as the 'Gay disease' or GRID (Gay-Related Immune Deficiency), the first cases emerged in the early 1980s. However, the term GRID was deemed misleading once it became clear that AIDS was not limited to the gay community. AIDS can develop at different rates and there is currently no known cure; patients may deteriorate quickly after their initial diagnosis.

Andy shoved the chair back, sending it crashing to the floor and stared down at the medical dictionary in disbelief. He was livid. His mum's evasiveness about her health, her reaction to Mrs Silva, her never-ending foot injury and Mr Harris's abrupt change in behaviour were all beginning to make disturbing sense. The librarian walked by again. Stopping, she peered at the open book in front of him.

'What on earth is a young boy like you doing reading stuff like that?' she asked, her voice sharp. 'Does your mum know you're here? I think it's time you got back to school, don't you?'

Andy didn't even bother with the bus ride home. Instead, he strode the two miles in a daze. Schools were spilling out and the streets were thick with traffic, but he barely noticed. When he turned off the main road, he spotted Reggie across the way, kicking a stone down the pavement. Reggie's trousers were streaked with mud and one of his blazer pockets dangled by a thread. Debbie always said Reggie looked like he'd been dragged through a hedge backwards. Spotting Andy, Reggie grinned, calling out from across the road. Andy forced a small wave. He wanted to be alone – to march to the end of the road, turn into his own street and get back to his mum and grandparents. But deep down, he knew that once he did, the reality of their situation could not be brushed under the carpet any longer.

Reggie had been Andy's closest friend since their very first day in reception class, and Andy felt a close bond with him. Reggie wasn't the most academic child around but his heart was always in the right place. Andy crossed the road to join him.

'Alright, Andy, what's going on with you then? Why were you out of school this afternoon?'

'I … I just … my mum's not feeling too good at the moment. I came home to check she's OK.'

'I *thought* your mum was looking a bit ropey the other day. Mr Harris said at form time after lunch that you're not coming back for a while.'

'Oh,' said Andy, caught off guard. 'Did he?'

Just hearing Mr Harris's name felt like a kick to the stomach. It was as if someone had whipped the support from beneath him, like one of those tablecloth magic tricks – only this time, everything came crashing down.

'Reggie, can I tell you something? You can't tell anyone and I need you to promise,' Andy said, his voice low and urgent.

'Yeah, course, Andy. No worries. We've always had each other's backs.'

Andy flashed a look over his shoulder and checked both sides, making sure no one could overhear.

'I … I think it's AIDS. That's what my mum has. I'm scared that she's really ill, Reggie. I went to the library today and looked it up.'

Reggie stopped, his face twisted in bemusement.

'AIDS? That's for them gay people, Andy.'

Andy felt a flicker of irritation at Reggie's ignorance but forced himself to stay calm. 'No,' he replied quietly, 'anyone can get it. I found some of her medication in the kitchen. I think it's for AIDS.'

Reggie scratched his head and started walking again. 'Jeez, I mean blimey, Andy. Surely she would have told you – Mrs Townley, I mean. You *live* with her.'

'Maybe. I don't know …'

An older boy shouted Reggie's name from a distance.

'Sorry, Andy. I've got to go. I'm really sorry about your mum. But she wouldn't lie to you, would she? Your mum is sound; she wouldn't have that AIDS thing – no way. Don't worry, Andy. See you, mate.'

Reggie took off running, his usual style that looked like it required a lot of effort but didn't actually make him go any faster.

But she wouldn't lie to you, would she? As he approached his house, he noticed Mrs Silva's net curtain twitching. *But she wouldn't lie to you, would she?* Seconds later, her front door opened and she poked her head out. *But she wouldn't lie to you, would she?*

'Andy? You were home from school early today? Is everything OK? Is Debbie alright?'

Andy stared at his front door, hot tears welling in his eyes as his anger swelled. 'She *is* a liar,' he hissed through clenched teeth.

Mrs Silva dramatically cupped her ear, frowning. Andy felt like a shaken bottle of the cheap fizzy pop his mum sometimes bought, ready to explode if anyone dared to twist the cap off.

'Andy?' Mrs Silva nearly shouted. 'I am asking about Debbie.'

'She's a liar, she's a liar, SHE'S A LIAR!'

Mrs Silva clasped her chest and recoiled, shocked. 'Andy! She is your mother.'

A group of teenagers further up the road turned and laughed. The front door burst open and Pam stood before him, looking alarmed.

'Andy, what *is* wrong? What's all the shouting about? Get *inside*!'

Andy brushed past Pam and into the middle of the sitting room, pointing a shaky finger at Debbie, who was lying on the settee. Behind him, Pam said something to Mrs Silva then closed the door hastily.

'You're … you're a *liar*,' he spat again, struggling to contain his rage, though a vague sense that he shouldn't be too loud restrained him. 'You've got AIDS! Not cancer – AIDS!'

Debbie stared up at him, her eyes wide and frozen in shock. Pam stood beside the armchair where Brian was sitting, watching the scene unfold in utter confusion.

'Andy, what's this now? AIDS? Don't be silly. AIDS is what …' Pam glanced at Debbie for reassurance.

'Andy, stop talking to your mother like that! How *dare* you—' Brian's angry voice thundered, but the truth was written all over Debbie's face, halting everyone in their tracks. This empowered Andy to press his point home.

'You *lied* to me. You *lied* to all of us, over and over. How dare *you*. You said we were a team – you said that all the time!' Andy's chest rose and fell as outraged sobs threatened to break free. Debbie put both hands to her face and closed her eyes tight, looking as if she was praying, tears escaping down her cheeks. A deafening silence filled the room as three sets of eyes waited for Debbie to speak, willing her to deny everything.

'Andy … I … I'm sorry. It's not easy. It's *really* not that easy. You can't *tell* people you've got AIDS. We *are* a team – I couldn't do this without you. I *won't* be able to do any of this without you.'

Andy stood in the middle of the lounge, breathing heavily. Pam sank onto the arm of the chair beside Brian, both of them stunned.

'I didn't tell anyone because I'm terrified – terrified of how people would look at me, how they'd treat me – what my own family would think. I don't want to be someone people are afraid to be around or touch. I've been hoping, praying for a cure or even just a treatment so I wouldn't *have* to tell you, or worry you, or put you through any of this.'

'But … but AIDS, Debbie. I mean, *how*? I thought …' Pam shook her head, struggling to grasp what she was being told.

'I'm not sure how it happened. There were a few people after Tony – just some companionship, nothing serious … but I really don't know.' Debbie looked at Andy, pained at having to be so open. 'I'm sorry, love. You know, I kept getting sick – fevers and coughs. I had diarrhoea for months which I now understand was my body struggling to fight off infections. I was going to the bathroom so often that I ended up giving up my job, mostly out of embarrassment. The GP kept saying I was just tired and stressed from everything going on with Tony leaving but at the end of one appointment, he casually suggested we might as well do an AIDS test to rule things out. I didn't think much of it, so I went in for the results and they just came right out and told me. I've been in shock ever since. And … and every day, I cling to hope, selfishly wishing that the virus won't affect me like it has others – that I'll be OK.'

Pam wiped her nose with a tissue she'd pulled from her sleeve. Brian's gaze seemed distant, lost in thought. Andy stood awkwardly by the fireplace, acutely aware of the tension in the room.

'But what I can say is that what's happening out there is a disgrace,' Debbie continued, breaking the silence. 'Entire sections of the gay community are catching this disease and dying. I've sought support from some incredible gay organisations, and, my God, their communities are being devastated. And haemophiliacs are getting it from infected blood and no one seems to care because the media keeps labelling it a *gay plague*. Just the other day, one newspaper described the pandemic as a *cesspit of their own making*. It's horrific. Imagine knowing you're dying from a disease that seemed to appear out of nowhere – but also feeling lonely, isolated and shamed. It can affect anyone … gay, straight, whoever. We've *all* been thrown to the wolves. There are some incredible groups out there, raising awareness and knocking on the doors of governments around the world, but there's literally no support network for women with AIDS at all. Nothing. The stigma and the lack of treatment – *that's* why people stay silent.'

'Oh … Debbie,' Pam said, dabbing her nose again. 'But … you talk about gay people dying from AIDS, but if they're dying … so are you.' Andy wasn't sure if it was a question or a statement but until Debbie gave an answer, he clung to hope.

Debbie paused. 'As things stand, yes,' she replied.

Andy looked at her; her face was clammy and grey but she still resembled his mum – just an older version. There were more Kaposi's sarcoma lesions on her skin: a blemish above her right eye and another on her hand. As he opened his mouth to speak, Debbie shook her head sadly at him, almost pleading for him not to be angry. Instead, he took a couple of steps forward and collapsed against her, burying his head in her tummy and crying, soaking her blanket with his tears.

'I'm sorry, Mum. I'm sorry. I was just a bit shocked. I'll help you, I promise. I'm sorry,' he said through his sobs as Debbie stroked his hair.

Brian cleared his throat and stood up, straightening his trousers.

'Is … is he safe, doing that, Debbie? You know, getting so close? Are you sure he should be doing that?'

10

Late on Friday night, McKenzie sat back on his Chippendale sofa, the TV murmuring with *The Last Resort with Jonathan Ross*. Indifferent to the show, he sipped a Château Lafite-Rothschild 1982 – an impressive and self-indulgent choice of red wine for a guest list of … himself. Its legendary richness slid down easily, dulling his thoughts as the evening drifted on. Next to the fireplace, his Christmas tree stood twinkling in all its perfection, dressed in a flawless arrangement of red and gold tinsel, glass baubles catching the light. McKenzie couldn't take any credit for it – he'd sheepishly hired a professional service to come in and handle the decorating. He knew full well it was a ridiculously decadent move. After all, how hard could it be to decorate a tree? And the invoice had been eye-watering, a small fortune for something he could've done himself. It had stood there all December, gleaming brilliantly – a slightly embarrassing monument to his own laziness, more so as he was the only one who had laid eyes on it. The new year had come and gone, yet he still hadn't got around to calling the company to have the tree taken down.

Across the top of his fireplace stood the more important Christmas cards – the ones from people whose names, if glimpsed by a curious visitor, might prompt an impressed 'oooh'. This, of course, was precisely why McKenzie had displayed them so prominently, though he hadn't exactly been inundated with suitably impressed guests. There was one from Elton – *Happy Christmas, you old tart!* – another from Freddie – *Merry Christmas, dear!* – and even one from Billy Ocean – *When the going gets tough, the tough have a great Christmas!* It was a veritable Who's Who of Christmas cards. McKenzie had bought the five-bedroom townhouse in Kensington over a decade ago, thanks to the royalty cheque from his breakthrough album – a cool £125,000 back then. It was probably worth five times that now. Why he'd opted for five bedrooms was anyone's guess; he rarely had guests and the vast, empty spaces often left him feeling slightly overwhelmed, rattling around in a house far too large for him. He'd never quite felt fully at home there and often found himself wishing for a cosy two-bedroom apartment instead. Before hitting the big time, when he first moved to London, McKenzie had rented a tiny bedsit in Clapham – a modest space with a bed, an armchair and a temperamental stove. Yet, bizarrely, he still pined for the simplicity of those days.

McKenzie was surprised to find he missed the overbearing presence of his Rottweiler of a manager. Atkinson had been laid low with a persistent does of flu, reluctantly confining himself to bed to recover – though not without loudly and vociferously blaming McKenzie-induced stress for his condition. With the European tour behind him and absolutely no desire to touch a guitar,

McKenzie found himself growing restless in the long, dark January evenings, unexpectedly adrift without Atkinson's relentless demands filling his days.

McKenzie was *so* bored that, a couple of days earlier – spurred on by a few glasses of early evening wine (a more reasonable Guigal Côtes du Rhône, that time) – he'd decided to be 'helpful' and stock Atkinson's fridge and cupboards with a few essentials. He hadn't set foot in a grocery store in at least a decade, but since Atkinson only lived a mile away, down Kensington High Street, McKenzie pulled a woolly hat over his unruly mop of hair and ventured out, feeling particularly saintly as he braved the aisles as an ordinary bloke. He stopped at the local mini-market, completely clueless about what Atkinson might want in his fridge, aside from milk. Staring at the price labels on the shelves, he was taken aback to discover that a pint of milk now cost 21p and bread was 40p. Despite being a millionaire, he still couldn't help but feel shocked at the price hikes over the past decade. As he mulled this over, McKenzie had no idea he was being 'papped' while picking up a tin of Heinz baked beans (24p!). The next day's headlines were inevitable: *The Sun* was particularly pleased with itself with *Bean Shopping, Mack?* while *The Mirror* opted for *Mini-Mart Mack.* Through his flu-ridden moans and groans, Atkinson insisted it was solid gold publicity following the 'Rock Around the Clock' debacle.

McKenzie leaned back against the settee and squeezed his eyes shut, the humiliating memory flooding back and making him physically cringe. He had been trying to record one of the few new songs he had managed to come up with during a particularly frustrating period of creative block.

'Time for Rock and Roll' wasn't exactly a McKenzie McCall classic, but it felt good to be working on something, anything, especially since they had nearly finished laying down the track. That's when Snakes, who was scurrying around the studio tuning guitars and making cups of tea, suggested that it bore a striking resemblance to the Bill Haley classic from thirty years earlier – 'Rock Around the Clock'. At that moment, McKenzie could have literally strangled him for bursting his rather brittle bubble. Without Atkinson's direct control to rein him in and fuelled by more Jack Daniels than ever should be consumed, McKenzie began to jam, belting out 'Rock Around the Clock' with reckless gusto. The band quickly joined in and suddenly they were electric together again – completely in sync, gelling and on fire, just like the old days. In the control booth, Charley leaned forward, pushing buttons and moving sliders, her head bobbing to the rhythm as she adjusted the mixing desk.

Snakes grabbed a camcorder to capture the magic, realising that McKenzie hadn't sounded this good in ages. They were rocking with a pulsing energy. When McKenzie listened to the playback, a rush of excitement surged through him; he was absolutely convinced they had captured something truly magical, a track that deserved to be heard by a wider audience.

'I can see it now, Mack,' Charley said, her eyes shining with enthusiasm.

'What can you see?' McKenzie replied, trying to keep his words steady and avoid slurring.

'When Atkinson phoned me, I thought you were a washed-up has-been. Then you started talking about me producing teenyboppers and I thought you were an old, arrogant dinosaur. But you've still got it, Mack. We need to find the right song and you'll be right back up there again – you're bloody good when you get going.'

McKenzie ran his hand over his stubble, his eyes bloodshot and his face red and blotchy from the sudden exertion. 'Well, thanks … I think. Can you mix this – make it into something presentable that still has a rough edge but polished enough to release? I need to chat with Atkinson.'

Twenty minutes later, McKenzie found himself leaning against Atkinson's door, slightly worse for wear, singing Slade's 'Merry Xmas Everybody' into the doorbell as he waited to be buzzed in. When the door finally opened, he stepped inside to find Atkinson sprawled out on his huge king-size bed, surrounded by tiger-print rugs and walls adorned with what could only be described as cow-patterned wallpaper. McKenzie couldn't help but think that for all the money he had made Atkinson, it certainly hadn't bought him any taste. The garish decor was a reflection of Atkinson's personality – loud, flashy, and utterly lacking in subtlety or decorum. McKenzie implored Atkinson to contact the record company and quickly release the song, suggesting that the video could simply be Snakes's camcorder footage interspersed with clips from a live concert earlier in the year. The best part was that there was a Christmas tree up in the studio, adding a festive touch that could help them challenge The Housemartins and Europe for the Christmas number one spot. He was determined to give 'The Final Countdown' a run for its money.

'Absolutely *not*, Mack. I will not allow this,' barked a nasally Atkinson, propped up in bed in black silk pyjamas, with paracetamol packets and snotty tissues scattered around him. 'One, if you hadn't noticed, I'm on my deathbed here – this is the worst flu I've ever had and your ridiculousness is most certainly not helping. Two, releasing a cover version will cheapen you and only advertise the fact that you're out of ideas. Stop drinking so much, Mack. Go on holiday for Christmas and come back ready to write your own songs!'

'Rock Around the Clock' was released two weeks later, just in time for Christmas and to McKenzie's utter dismay, it didn't even crack the top forty, peaking at a dismal number forty-six. Radio 1 wouldn't add it to their playlist, a blow that stung more than he cared to admit. What's more, the video merely highlighted that McKenzie, wearing his crumpled studio T-shirt and jeans, really *did* look like a washed-up has-been compared to the competition, like a toned Europe in their tight leathers. McKenzie winced at his unmistakable belly and uncomfortably bloated, sweaty look. He was hammered in the press, with headlines like *McKenzie Misses the Mark* and *McKenzie's a Mess* splashed across the tabloids. The entire affair had been a complete disaster, leaving McKenzie feeling lost. One thing was for certain: he wasn't going to trust himself to make any more decisions.

Atkinson was absolutely apoplectic, chastising McKenzie for taking advantage of his illness. He bawled down the phone, declaring that McKenzie was throwing his career down the pan and that everything was going pear-shaped. 'We're in a right old pickle now!' he shouted. As McKenzie listened, he couldn't help but wonder how many idioms Atkinson could shoehorn into one expletive-ridden rant. McKenzie wouldn't mind the tirade if it weren't for the fact that just the previous year, Atkinson had taken a call from Bob Geldof about a charity concert for Ethiopia he was organising at Wembley Stadium. Would McKenzie like to take part? He could go on after Status Quo, getting the show underway with a bang with two music veterans, one after the other.

'I told Geldof where to get off, Mack. He's on another planet – he'll never pull this off and we'll all end up with egg on our faces. What a bloody ego!' McKenzie vividly remembered Atkinson saying.

So, a couple of months later, McKenzie found himself watching the perfectly organised Live Aid concert from his settee with the reality of his missed opportunity sinking in as he realised he could have performed in front of a worldwide audience of billions. Bands like Queen reminded the world just how brilliant they were, rejuvenating their career as all their old albums surged back into the charts. They went on to sell out Wembley for two nights running and played Knebworth. Meanwhile, Bob Geldof was knighted – something Atkinson still smarted over. It's funny how *that* blunder had been quietly forgotten.

The European tour that autumn had been a welcome distraction, but McKenzie couldn't help but notice that the audience looked a bit thinner on the ground some evenings. While he would always please the die-hard fans with the old hits, he had nothing new to offer. With Atkinson slowly recovering, McKenzie felt adrift. He *was* a mess. Jonathan Ross was interviewing Donald Sutherland and McKenzie sighed, wishing he possessed the same effortless charisma. He considered heading down to the music room in the basement to strum a few chords and see what might come of it, but as he passed the fridge, something else proved more enticing – another bottle of beer and a sausage roll.

11

ndy's eyes flickered slightly before slowly opening. He took a moment to adjust and focus on the Madonna poster on the wall. Below it, on his desk, sat his prized possession: a ZX Spectrum home computer, the ultimate gaming machine. While more powerful home computers existed, none had the same charm as the Spectrum, with its 48 kilobytes of memory, which seemed to open up a world of possibility at his fingertips. Andy took full advantage, spending countless hours immersed in games like *Jet Set Willy* and *Football Manager*. Closing his eyes, Andy welcomed the gentle pull of drifting back to sleep, only to snap them open again. What was that noise? A peculiar squeaking, rubbing, scratching sound – was it coming from outside, or maybe downstairs? In the room next to him, Andy heard Debbie shifting in bed, padding across the floor before opening her bedroom door – he did the same. Debbie was dressed in shorts and a jumper, pulling a dressing gown over her shoulders. Her legs were pencil-thin, her knees prominent. She stood awkwardly, resting her right foot on its heel to avoid putting any pressure on it and Andy caught a glimpse of a scabby wound on the sole of her foot – still not healing.

The squeaking stopped and they both frowned at each other across the small landing, mirroring each other's confusion. Then the noise started again, prompting them to turn towards the front door at the bottom of the stairs. Through the small frosted pane of glass, they saw a shadow moving back and forth,

'What the …?' Debbie began, hobbling down the stairs while clinging to both banisters for support.

'Mum, careful …' Andy called after her, following in his pyjamas as the noise of the squeaking increased.

Debbie undid the latch, swung the front door open and stepped out into the crisp February morning. She hesitated for a moment before calling out, 'Mrs Silva, what are you doing …?' She paused between two cars parked at the kerb, her eyes fixed on the house. Debbie gasped, raising her hands to her mouth. Andy followed her out of the front door, arriving to stand beside her. Mrs Silva was perched on a small step ladder, clad in yellow rubber gloves and a flowery pink apron, a sponge in one hand and a bucket of water on the pavement below.

'Do not look, Debbie! Andy, go back inside. I will get rid of this!'

Mrs Silva stretched her arms out wide in a vain attempt to hide the red spray paint daubed across the front window and brickwork – a crude skull and crossbones, accompanied by hastily sprayed writing: *AIDS House!*

Curtains twitched in nearby homes and there was a cackle of laughter behind them.

Andy turned, shaken, to see Reggie with his brothers and some other boys from the street, sniggering and mock-tutting at the paintwork. As they swaggered off, one of the boys screamed, 'Don't go near them!' and they ran off shrieking with laughter. Reggie turned back, shrugged, and mouthed 'sorry', pulling a face that suggested blabbing had been out of his control and the consequences were somehow a shock to everyone. The betrayal sent Andy reeling. But worst of all, *he* had betrayed his mum.

'I'm going to be sick ...' Debbie spluttered, clasping her stomach with both arms before limping hastily back inside.

'I will get rid of this, Andy! You go inside,' Mrs Silva repeated from the ladder.

***

'It's just the AZT – it makes me feel as sick as a dog,' Debbie explained, her voice strained after emptying the contents of her stomach. 'I'm on a trial and they told me it's either AZT or a placebo. But I know full well I'm on the real thing; the side effects make me want to throw the bottle out the back door and let nature take its course!'

She sipped cautiously from the cup of tea Andy had made her, testing its effect on her stomach before drinking more. She had red sores around her mouth and nose, and a slight shiver ran through her, despite the gas fire radiating warmth. The central heating was turned up so high that Andy found himself wandering around the house in just a T-shirt.

'Mum, they're going to find a cure,' Andy said firmly. He *hated* it when she spoke like that. He was determined to care for Debbie, to do everything possible to keep her as healthy as he could and he had to believe that scientists around the world would come together and find a treatment soon.

'It was always going to get out somehow,' Debbie said, referring to the graffiti. 'I think we might need to keep an open mind about moving. Your gran and grandad … they're taking a bit of time to absorb everything but I'm sure they will have us. There's so much misinformation out there, Andy. It's just so frustrating – I'm not toxic. It's only if I bleed that people need to be careful. The newspapers are whipping up a hate storm and I don't want you to get bullied, or worse…'

The postman was whistling 'I Want to Wake Up With You' as he made his way down the street, letter boxes clanging as he pushed post through them. His whistling stopped abruptly as he got to their house – Mrs Silva had scrubbed and scrubbed and removed much of the spray paint but some remained. They heard him gingerly poke the letter through the letter box – like he was trying to make as little contact with their door as possible.

'Go and get that, love. Let's hope it's not another utility bill – I know I'm heating the house like the Sahara Desert but I just can't get warm.'

Andy handed her the letter and she tore it open, scanning the contents with a frown. He caught the slight twitch in her eyes and the imperceptible shake of her head. Folding the letter briskly, she shoved it down the side of the settee. Picking up her cup from the arm of the chair, she cradled it in both hands, drawing warmth from it.

'Just house stuff – I'll sort it,' Debbie said.

Andy's instinct told him he needed to see the letter. 'Let me have a look – maybe I can help.'

'Andy, it's noth—'

'Mum, let me see the letter,' Andy repeated firmly, his hand outstretched and unmoving. A year ago, Debbie would have told him exactly where to get off with a joke and a ruffle of his hair, but now, in her weakened state, she hesitated before finally holding it out.

'OK, but don't overreact,' she instructed. 'We'll think through what we're going to do. We're not going to act on our emotions.'

Andy took the letter from her hand and unfolded it, his stomach tightening as he read. It was short, to the point and utterly devoid of warmth. Under the school's letterhead, a formal paragraph typed on an office typewriter informed Debbie that she was to keep Andy home from school due to her 'current condition'. The school was working hard to implement measures to guarantee the safety of the other children, as Andy was now considered 'high risk'. It mentioned that these measures might require periods of isolation for Andy to limit his contact with other children, but the school was considering all options to ensure he was still included. They would send work for him to complete in the post. Shaking his head in disbelief, he held the letter in the air, unable to find the words. Debbie took another tentative sip of her tea.

'How can they do this? They can't stop someone from going to school. I've already missed quite a few weeks. This is literally … it's … disgusting.' Andy wanted to swear, but he'd never done so in front of his mum. 'They can't treat us like this. This is like … like … medieval times.'

As he finished remonstrating, two splattering thuds hit the window. Through the net curtain, they could see a mess of yellow gunk and fragments of eggshell sliding down the glass. They heard Mrs Silva's voice ring out from an upstairs window: 'Leave them alone, go away! What a mess! Hooligans!'

Over the next three days, nine eggs struck the house. Andy kept a mental tally, joking darkly to Debbie that the last three of the dozen must have gone into an omelette, sparing them an even bigger mess. Within minutes, Mrs Silva would appear to wipe the window, tutting and grumbling loudly. Afterwards, Debbie would knock on the kitchen wall and shout her thanks.

'They are horrible!' Mr Silva would shout back.

At night, there were shouts and taunts directed at the house. A firework was shoved through the letter box, where it ricocheted wildly around the narrow hallway, leaving scorch marks on the carpet. Occasionally, the phone would ring, only for the caller to hang up as soon as Debbie answered – or they'd yell, 'AIDS house!' before slamming the receiver down. Debbie spent more and more time curled up on the settee, wrapped in a blanket with her knees drawn tightly to her chest. She was still enduring bouts of severe diarrhoea and stomach cramps, but she managed to find the strength to seal the letter box with gaffer tape she'd unearthed in the kitchen cupboard, determined to stop anything else from being forced through. Andy knew Debbie could see how frightened and miserable he was, and he feared that his distress was only making it harder for her.

More days passed with no word from school. Debbie called a few times, but each time was told that Mr Dean was in a meeting, so she left messages that went unreturned. Andy spent his days reading whatever books they had in the house and looking after Debbie as best he could. On a day when Debbie felt a little stronger, they went into Manchester and bought some text books from WH Smith and committed to doing at least an hour's work together each day. Andy was furious that they'd been abandoned – a problem no one seemed willing to address. The two of them hunkered down and for a while, things almost felt normal. They watched their favourite TV shows – *Beadle's About*, *Blankety Blank* and *Hi-de-Hi!* – laughing together in their little bubble. Andy would have gladly stayed like this forever, just him and Debbie, keeping her comfortable and making her endless cups of tea. Unfortunately, two pressing issues loomed on the horizon: Debbie had an upcoming doctor's appointment and they were running low on food.

'The Co-Op is ten minutes away and I'll come straight back. We just need a few things – tea bags, milk, a loaf of bread, some cheese. Maybe I can make us some toasted cheese sandwiches?' Andy was eager for Debbie to eat. There was toast on a plate on the floor from lunchtime that she had said she might return to when she felt hungrier, but it remained untouched.

'Sorry, love,' Debbie said, handing him a £5 note from her purse. 'My mouth isn't much fun at the moment – everything feels like swallowing razor blades.' She opened her lips and Andy saw a furry white coating on her tongue and angry sores stretching deep inside. She started coughing and quickly closed her mouth again.

Andy rode to the local shop on the high street and secured his bike to the lamppost with a chain before heading inside to pick up his provisions. He knew Debbie was struggling with money, but he couldn't resist slipping a chocolate bar into his basket. It took him ages to decide – Marathon, Curly Wurly, Picnic, Flake, Dairy Milk – but he finally settled on a Mars Bar. The TV advert showed people in all sorts of energetic situations as they enjoyed the bar, and he hoped it would have the same invigorating effect on Debbie. After all, *a Mars a day helps you work, rest, and play.* Outside the shop, Andy fumbled absentmindedly with the combination lock, then looped the carrier bag handles over his bike's handlebars. Swinging a leg over the seat, he froze at a sudden burst of shouts from behind him.

'OY! AIDS ANDY!'

'PLAGUE BOY! WAIT!'

Holy crap. Andy's heart nearly jumped out of his chest. It was fight or flight and the choice on this occasion was most definitely flight. Pushing off, he wobbled slightly, causing the carrier bag to slip off the handlebars and hit the ground, sending the Mars Bar bouncing into the road. He quickly stopped, dismounted his bike and scooped up the fallen items. The fate of the Mars Bar felt disproportionately important as the four teenagers sprinted towards him. A car rolled past, squashing it flat. Andy had endured a lot over the past couple of weeks, but *that* was a hard blow to take. Whimpering as he reattached the bag minus the Mars Bar, Andy tried again and pushed off shakily. As he wobbled, trying to pick up speed, the bag banged against his legs and the sound of the boys' trainers pounding the tarmac grew closer.

'HEY, PLAGUE BOY!'

Please God, Andy thought, *let them throw eggs at the house but please don't let them catch me now.* His prayers seemed to be answered by a gentle slope in the road, giving him a little burst of momentum. Then, from his left, someone shot out from one of the adjoining roads and for a moment, Andy thought he was done for. A blur of red – a Liverpool football tracksuit … it was Reggie on his BMX, decked out with matching red wheels, saddle and handlebars. That tracksuit was impossible to miss – bright red from neck to toe – and Reggie wore it with pride. He rounded the T-junction and, with a sharp look to his right, quickly grasped what was happening.

'Andy, follow me, OK? Follow me!'

Reggie sped ahead and Andy was momentarily taken aback to see him moving so swiftly. Reggie darted to the right, jumped up a kerb and rode along the pavement for a short distance before swerving into a cobbled alleyway nestled between two sets of backyards and rows of terraced houses. If this had been the Manchester version of E.T., they'd have soared gracefully into the sky to safety, gliding over rooftops and alleyways to the rousing strains of a John Williams soundtrack. Instead, Andy stuck doggedly behind Reggie, his legs flailing off the pedals as he stuck them out straight for balance, teetering wildly around the corner at speed and wailing involuntarily at the thought of careering straight into someone's back wall.

Reggie swerved around a dustbin and an old punctured football, expertly navigating the obstacles in their path with a newly discovered finesse.

'THAT WAY!' came a shout from behind Andy. Reggie skidded to a halt outside a gate and leapt off his bike in one fluid motion, reaching over to slide the bolt and open it.

'Andy!' Reggie beckoned, thumbing towards his backyard. Andy's brakes let out a squeal of protest as he screeched to a less than dignified stop. He swung his legs off the bike and ran the last few yards, wrestling it through the gate, along with his carrier bag. Reggie slammed it shut and slid the lock back into place. They slumped down with their backs against the gate, panting.

From the cobbles behind them, they heard feet clattering against the stones.

'Lost him!'

'Damn it!'

'Hey, let's get some more eggs!'

'What about flour too? I've heard that makes a kind of gunge.'

There was laughter as the voices faded away back up the alleyway. Andy and Reggie listened until they were gone completely.

'The thing I don't get,' Andy said eventually, still catching his breath, 'is that no one wants to be near me. They all think they're going to catch AIDS from me – so what were they planning to do if they actually caught up with me? Dance around me, pretending to beat me up?'

Reggie shrugged. 'I'm sorry, Andy. I mean, I told my brother about your mum because I was worried, but I didn't think all this would happen. It just kind of slipped out. I know AIDS is bad because it's on TV all the time, but it's an illness. I don't really understand why people are being so horrible about it. My mum said I'm not to play with you, just in case.'

'It's OK, Reggie,' Andy replied. 'I think we might have to move. Mum doesn't think it's safe and she's finding things really hard. She won't say it, but I can see it.'

Reggie nodded. 'Mr Harris said he doesn't think you'll be back. He told the class you'd made the decision to stay home because of some family stuff and that he felt sorry for you.'

It had been a couple of months, but it still pained Andy to think of Mr Harris.

He'd loved Mr Harris and his heart lifted slightly with hope – perhaps Mr Harris was secretly fighting for him but had to maintain a professional front to support the headteacher?

'Some of the parents are talking about fundraising in case there's a legal challenge and you're allowed back into school. They want to be ready to fight it. Mr Harris met with them to help,' Reggie continued.

And all hope was *crushed.*

'I'm going to come back, Reggie. I am. They can fight it all they want. I'm going to come back to school.'

***

Waiting in line at the medical centre with Debbie, Andy felt a strange sense of calm. It was frightening looking after his mum, watching her become thinner, losing energy and ageing in front of him. Visiting the medical centre together was a positive step that gave him some optimism.

'There'll be some treatment soon, Andy,' Debbie kept telling him whenever he suggested more medical assistance. 'I just need to get through the next few years and it'll be hopeful – they're bound to find something. I just need to hang on in there.' But her cheeks were becoming more sunken and her cough – her painful, hacking cough – seemed to be worsening. She was always cold. It wasn't a freezing winter day by any means but Debbie was bundled up in gloves, a scarf, a heavy coat and several jumpers underneath. Much of the time he felt helpless. Yet here in the medical centre were people who could help – a doctor who could deliver news of new medicines or treatments available in the hospital.

'Take a seat and the doctor will call you. There's a bit of a wait I'm afraid,' the receptionist, an old-ish lady with greying hair and wearing a brown cardigan, told the man in front.

'Hi, it's Debbie Townley. Ten-thirty with Dr Richards,' Debbie said, stepping forward.

The receptionist nodded at Debbie and then smiled at Andy. She reached for her glasses, which were dangling around her neck on black string, and looked down at a large book in front of her, tracing her finger down the page.

'Let's have a look, shall we? Ah, yes, here you are, Mrs T—'

The lady's face twitched, her whole body tensing as though someone had pressed an invisible button on her chair, sending an electric shock through her. Andy caught a fleeting glimpse of something written in red pen – capital letters underlined several times – before she swiftly moved her hand to cover the book.

'If you … if you can just stand to one side, over there in the corner, a nurse will come straight away to … to get you,' she stammered.

'Oh … OK,' said Debbie, glancing behind her at the corner of the surgery where a potted plant stood on the floor. 'We just … stand by that plant?'

'Yes, please. The nurse will be with you as soon as possible.'

From the corner of the waiting area, Andy and Debbie watched the receptionist turn and whisper to another woman in a nurse's uniform who was studying a clipboard. They both cast a quick look at Andy and Debbie. Debbie had her arms tightly folded across her body and was hunched over slightly, battling a sudden stomach cramp.

'I don't see why we can't just sit in the waiting room. They're looking at us like we're about to rob the place,' she said breathlessly, grimacing as she spoke. 'My stomach's killing – maybe we should've just stayed at home.'

'No, Mum,' Andy whispered. 'We need to hear if there's anything they can—'

Just then, the door swung open ahead of them. The nurse emerged, like someone stepping into a forensic crime scene, wearing a surgical face mask, long rubber gloves and an apron.

'Christ,' Debbie muttered out of the corner of her mouth. 'She looks like she's found asbestos somewhere.'

The nurse walked towards them through the waiting area, causing heads to turn. 'Mrs Townley?' she said crisply from behind the mask. 'Follow me, please. Try not to … let's try to be quick. This way!'

Andy and Debbie followed her down the corridor at the side of the medical centre. They were shepherded into a room barely bigger than a stockroom. Floor-to-ceiling shelves lined the walls, filled with little see-through drawer units packed with dressings and other medical supplies. The room was gloomy and the nurse flicked on a light. At the far end of the room, a single chair waited.

'There's just the one chair, sorry. We presumed you'd be alone, Mrs Townley. Dr Richards will be here in a minute,' the nurse said. Closing the door behind her, she exited the room, her imposing shadow visible through the frosted glass. Debbie lowered herself into the chair and shivered while Andy stood behind her shoulder.

'I feel like I'm here for an inquisition. I hope they're going to let us go. Maybe it's a task and we have to escape,' Debbie said, coughing as she tried to laugh.

There was a knock at the door and the nurse entered again.

'Mrs Townley is right here, Dr Richards,' she said, turning to the figure behind her.

'It's Debbie,' Debbie replied, her voice steady.

Dr Richards entered the room. He was a tall, older gentleman wearing a white coat and grey trousers, with gold-rimmed half-moon glasses perched on his nose. Closing the door, he and the nurse remained as close to it as possible. This was ridiculous, Andy thought; they were looking at his mum like she was some kind of alien lifeform. They were medical professionals – surely they *knew* AIDS was difficult to transmit. Dr Richards had a stethoscope around his neck and a torch in his chest pocket but he made no attempt to use either on Debbie. Andy's faith ebbed away with every matter-of-fact word the doctor spoke during their brief three-and-a-half minute appointment in what amounted to a cupboard. There were no significant advances in medication for AIDS that Dr Richards was aware of. Debbie could try taking a higher dose of the AZT if she could manage the side effects, or reduce her dosage if she couldn't. He ordered more blood tests and advised her to present herself at the hospital if her condition worsened, where they now had a ward for people like her – *for people with her condition*, he corrected himself. When they finished, Debbie stood up, thanked them and strode towards the door with measured dignity. The nurse panicked and fumbled for the handle.

'We'll get a taxi home, Andy,' Debbie said as they walked from the medical centre through the shopping precinct. It was bustling with shoppers and activity. 'I found a couple of quid in the pocket of this coat. It'll drop us off right at the front door. I don't fancy walking home – those bovver boys might bovver us.' She was joking, but her jaw clenched, betraying her unease.

'Should we warn the taxi driver that you've …' Andy caught the immediate flash of hurt in Debbie's eyes and his heart sank. 'I'm sorry, Mum. It's just the way everyone talks about this illness; it's hard not to let that wear off on me.'

As they walked past Radio Rentals, where a bank of TVs flickered in the window, Andy's frustration simmered beneath the surface at their experience in the medical centre. He had caught an early morning debate programme on TV the previous day as he flicked through the channels. A vicar, a *vicar*, was arguing that people with AIDS were being punished by God for their lifestyle. An MP, an *MP*, was also in the audience and chimed in that people with AIDS spread the disease because of their deviant lives. The Prime Minister, the *Prime Minister*, was going into a general election year promising to ban any mention of the word 'gay' in schools. What hope did anyone have in a world like this? The people in charge – the government – were supposed to care for the citizens of the country, yet they seemed to be actively stirring up ignorance and hatred.

This played on Andy's mind as they had a quick browse through the records at Our Price. To lift their spirits, Debbie bought the single 'I Knew You Were Waiting (For Me)' by Aretha Franklin and George Michael. She loved George Michael. As they left the shop, Debbie stopped in her tracks. Andy spotted it immediately as well. A sandwich board outside the newsagents across the street displayed a poster with the local newspaper's latest headline: *AIDS Boy Banned from School.*

'Oh God, Andy,' Debbie said, her voice trembling. 'I just … this is like a horrible nightmare. I'm so sorry … for everything.'

It was her tone that hit Andy the hardest – a hint of defeat. He was stunned. He had no desire to read the article; perhaps it was filled with compassion, but how could any adult with a heart write such a headline? He wasn't the one with AIDS; he was caring for someone who did – someone who happened to be an extraordinary woman … his mum. They knew exactly what they were doing … exploiting their situation with a misleading headline for some cheap shock value.

When Andy and Debbie got home, there was more graffiti on the front door. 'PLAGE!' The culprit couldn't even spell. As Debbie put the key in the door, Mrs Silva slid open her living room window.

'Debbie? What did the doctor say? I am here if you need my help to bob round and do anything you need.'

Andy looked at his mum. She was pale and shaky, and he knew the AZT was making her head foggy. She forced a faint smile but there was a noticeable tremble in her voice when she spoke.

'You're kind, Mrs Silva,' she managed softly. She paused, struggling to keep her composure. 'It's better if you keep your distance. If you knew … if you *really* understood, you wouldn't want to be involved. Really, it's fine. You can just leave me be … so I can try to get better.'

Mrs Silva shook her head and she closed her window. For a moment, Andy thought she'd taken Debbie's words to heart. But a second later, her front door opened and she stepped out onto the pavement, Mr Silva following close behind in his slippers. Mrs Silva's expression was firm, a hint of indignation in her eyes as she looked directly at Debbie.

'I *do* understand, Debbie. I am not stupid,' she said, nodding towards the newspaper in Mr Silva's hand. 'People can be horrid – *we* understand.' She took a small step forward. 'We are neighbours and we will help!'

***

Andy carefully removed Debbie's boots, cleaned her foot and re-dressed the wound. Then he handed her a hot water bottle, which she hugged to her chest as she lay back on the sofa, finally able to relax a little under his watchful eye.

'Sorry, Andy. I feel pretty useless. I can't bend down – I've got swollen glands in places I never even knew I had glands.'

She closed her eyes and put her head back on a cushion. Andy placed a blanket over her.

'Have you contacted school, Mum, about me going back – have you spoken to them?'

'We need to talk about it, Andy. Mr Dean said they've made progress with some risk assessment for you but it's got to go through the governors yet. The governors don't meet until next Thursday evening, apparently. He said they have the support of the Council and they are acting appropriately – what can we do? They might get you home-schooled or find a way where you kind of phone into lessons and listen in. There's a boy in America who does that. They're going to post you more work to do.'

'Mum, this is all wrong. They're just stalling because they don't want me there. Why don't they get the governors together now? They've read *The Daily Mail* and get their dodgy facts from there like everyone else!'

Debbie opened her eyes, lifted her head, then grimaced and rubbed her neck.

'I know, love. Why don't you wait and see what the governors have to say? I worry about you being there, Andy, with all those teenagers – who's there to protect you? The teachers? Some of them are worse than the kids.'

Andy sat down in the armchair by the window. A photo of Debbie and Tony smiled at him from the top of the TV.

'Where's Dad?' he asked softly, instinctively lowering his voice, as if a louder tone might somehow strain Debbie's body even more. 'He could come with me to school, to support me – I know he would. And where are Gran and Grandad? We need them … we need them all to help us fight. Who's *actually* helping us?'

The fire in his mum seemed to be fading. She used to be a fighter – stronger than most. Pam always called her a tough cookie. Left to raise him on her own, she managed it all with humour and patience, even when she must have been heartbroken inside. He wasn't even sure it was the AIDS that was killing her spirit; it felt like *people* were grinding her down. Everywhere she went, she was met with the same attitudes and it was sapping her self-worth.

'They can't treat us like this, Mum. There has to be someone out there who cares. They can't stop me from going to school. I'm going back on Monday, whether they like it or not. It's Thursday today – you can call them first thing tomorrow and warn them to expect me on Monday.'

'Andy, you can't just …'

'No, Mum. What's happening is a disgrace. I'm going to let everyone know what I think of the school, what I think of the Council, what I think of the government … and Maggie Thatcher!'

The next morning, Debbie still hadn't woken. So much for fighting *anything*, Andy thought, though he was content to let her sleep; he was exhausted himself. Debbie had no idea that Andy had developed the habit of sleeping lightly, regularly creeping to her doorway throughout the night to check on her. He would listen for the soft rhythm of her breathing and watch her duvet rise and fall. She looked almost childlike, always wearing a tracksuit top over her pyjamas to keep warm. The weather had turned colder and Andy couldn't help but worry about the effect it might have on her – cold weather was particularly hard on AIDS patients. Andy had risen feeling restless. Heading downstairs early, he switched on the television and caught a bit of TV-am; breakfast TV still felt like a novelty. Anne Diamond was discussing the heavy snowfall in some parts of the country. The programme ended at 9.25 a.m., followed by a local news bulletin. Andy watched as a reporter stood in an old people's home, where residents were knitting hats for newborn babies at the local hospital. He could see the reporter struggling to make the story sound more engaging, padding out the couple of minutes of airtime they'd been given. Must be a slow news week, Andy thought. He sat staring at the TV, no longer paying attention to what type of wool the old ladies were using. *A slow news week.* Taking his plate and mug to the kitchen sink, he returned to the sitting room, deep in thought. Reaching for the telephone book under the coffee table, he flipped through the pages for a minute before surprisingly finding what he was looking for. Picking up the phone, he placed a finger in the dial, hesitated, and then began to turn it.

12

McKenzie's arm slipped off the settee and his hand thudded against the polished wooden floor of his sitting room. He woke with a gasp and slowly manoeuvred into a hunched sitting position, blinking heavily as he rubbed his throbbing head. His ears were still ringing from the thumping music at the party he'd attended the night before. What day was it? Sunday? No, the party last night was on Sunday – he remembered because it was unusual for him to be out on a Sunday night, unlike the old days when he'd be out on the town every night. Ten years ago, he would have already bounced out of the door, heading to the studio, meeting friends for lunch or even playing a game of tennis. *Tennis*! His recovery time from a night out had increased pitifully and there was no chance he'd be serving any aces today, either metaphorically or physically. McKenzie dragged his arm across his mouth; it tasted like the contents of a kitchen bin. He needed water. His mind rewound to the previous evening, accompanied by a sinking feeling that was becoming all too common.

It had started so well – a party invite to an up-and-coming band's album launch at The Camden Palace. The

Predators had been his support band a couple of years ago on tour and he'd championed them in several interviews. He'd even helped them with their current single, which they wrote while touring with him. He advised them to rearrange the song to make it punchier and strummed a slight change to the melody that made it more hummable. Really, he could have demanded a writing credit but he was happy to help. The Predators quickly gained momentum, becoming too big to support anyone and headlining their own shows. McKenzie kept in touch, sending friendly faxes to their manager expressing how pleased he was with their success. They mentioned him a few times in interviews too, acknowledging his influence. Knowing the party would be filled with trendy musicians – The Pet Shop Boys, Mel and Kim, Bananarama, Curiosity Killed the Cat and a whole host of young acts he hadn't even heard of – McKenzie had made an effort to dress up. He'd asked his occasional stylist, Aldo (a fiery and wonderfully flamboyant young Italian) to come over with some fashion options. McKenzie settled on a pair of ripped jeans, which Aldo referred to as 'strategically distressed'. For a moment, he wasn't sure if Aldo was talking about the jeans or McKenzie's own life. A white shirt and navy waistcoat completed the look, along with his usual cowboy boots, much to Aldo's dismay:

'Ma dai, davvero! Is this a spaghetti western? Someone tell Clint Eastwood over here to leave the saloon boots at home!'

The Camden Palace was a pulsing haven for London's avant-garde crowd, its cavernous dance floor drenched in neon lights and dry ice, overlooked by a shadowy balcony where VIPs would observe the hedonistic antics of the wild crowd below. McKenzie usually hated these parties; always at risk of being seen as trying too hard to be hip. But surprisingly, he'd relaxed and enjoyed the younger musicians stopping to tell him that listening to his albums had been a part of their teenage years. Atkinson was also there, back to his brash self. He'd even lost a bit of weight after spending a couple of weeks laid up in bed.

'Gives me an excuse to eat and drink to excess and pile it back on again,' he shouted at McKenzie with a wide smile as they stood at the bar. 'I'd better enjoy those steaks while I can, Mack. At this rate, I'll be dining on a soggy burger at the local Wimpy the way your sales are plummeting!'

It was strangely comforting to have Atkinson back on his obnoxiously offensive form. Charley was there too; she had produced some of The Predators' early demos and was clearly chummy with them – especially their lead singer. As McKenzie watched them chatting, a slight pang of what could only be interpreted as jealousy caught him by surprise. Maybe she was networking and seeking publicity for herself as well – it wouldn't hurt her to be photographed with a singer currently in the spotlight. Perhaps she was just playing the game like everyone else, trying to get a leg up in this business. The whole industry was one big charade.

McKenzie remembered that at some point during the evening, The Predators climbed up on a makeshift stage and jammed a few songs to the delight of the party guests. He was savvy enough to realise that doing 'spontaneous' things like this made it far more likely for the event to hit the gossip columns and generate publicity – it would have been thoroughly planned and rehearsed. McKenzie was enjoying their 'unprompted' mini-set, until halfway through when the singer spotted him and grinned, pointing at McKenzie between songs. *Oh crap.*

'Hey, let's hear it for McKenzie McCall!' The audience cheered, although McKenzie couldn't help noticing the slightly half-hearted whoops. A spotlight swept around the crowd on the dance floor, eventually falling on McKenzie's face and his frozen smile. He felt uneasy with the sudden attention, especially after indulging in far too much complimentary champagne. 'You'll be supporting us on our next tour now, Mack! As we go up the charts, you're going down – we're literally passing each other!' A few people cackled and McKenzie felt the pity in their eyes. 'Mack knows I'm only joking, he was one of the first to get behind us. What a legend!'

There was a smattering of applause and McKenzie raised his glass in the direction of the stage before the guitarist struck the first chord of their latest single. The attention on McKenzie evaporated as the guests went wild, returning their focus to the band. He shot a sideways look at Atkinson, perched on a stool at the far end of the long, metallic bar. Atkinson was pestering a record executive, who looked thoroughly uninterested and was clearly desperate to escape and listen to the gig. Atkinson offered a shrug back to McKenzie that seemed to say 'What can you do?'

Even he appeared to be giving up on McKenzie's image.

For the rest of the evening, McKenzie hid at a table in the corner, sipping at complimentary margaritas the waitresses brought around on trays. At this point, it was fair to say he was feeling tipsy – well, drunk. Very drunk. Room-swirlingly drunk. He recalled Charley coming over at some unidentifiable point.

'He's an arrogant sod, my cousin,' she said, sitting down next to McKenzie.

'Who?'

'Joey Adams, the lead singer of The Predators – he's my cousin. We'll be having words over the dinner table next time he turns up for a Sunday lunch at my mum's, assuming he's not too high and mighty to bless us with his presence.'

'Ahh, he's your cousin,' McKenzie said, his mood lifting. 'Well, he's not wrong in what he said, but I'd have preferred his banter to be a bit more discreet – ideally not in front of two hundred of the most influential people in the music business.'

McKenzie stirred his margarita with a cocktail stick.

'I keep telling you, Mack,' Charley said, 'you only need one song – one song to get you back up there. It'll come.'

McKenzie teetered in that dangerous zone where alcohol made his head spin, muddling the part of his brain that controlled his speech. People drifted by for a chat, but he had no recollection of who they were or what they talked about. Eventually, Atkinson had bundled him into a taxi. He had no memory of getting home, cooking a pizza, or leaving the charred remains on the glass coffee table in front of him – where it still sat barely touched.

Putting his face in his hands, McKenzie groaned a long, loud groan, willing himself to get up. The TV was blaring; it must have been 1 p.m. because it was the news bulletin and Margaret Thatcher was being interviewed about a potential spring general election.

'Right now, even I'd vote for you if you could take away this banging head, Maggie,' McKenzie muttered at the screen.

There was a half-drunk bottle of beer on the coffee table, surrounded by a number of old takeaway boxes, a few dirty mugs and yesterday's newspapers. Taking a swig from the bottle, McKenzie grimaced at the flat beer he now had to swallow. Rock bottom – that's where he was. He edged forward on the settee, preparing himself for a courageous attempt to stand up and stumble to the kitchen for a glass of water. He gazed at the TV through bleary eyes, not quite ready to make a move as he tried to quell the nausea bubbling in his stomach with some deep breaths. There appeared to be a news item – a boy and a lady were striding up a path towards some school gates, the picture wobbling as the camera operator struggled to keep up. The woman looked a little unkempt, with what appeared to be pyjamas peeking out from beneath her jeans. She had her arm linked with the boy as they marched forward. A reporter was jogging breathlessly beside them, a large red microphone in hand, commentating as she went. The path was lined with excitable teenagers in school uniforms; some looked angry and were jeering, while others laughed and jostled one another, pulling faces at the camera and holding up rabbit ears over their friends' heads.

McKenzie made quick judgements from his, admittedly, privileged position – it looked like some small-town drama that he had absolutely no time for. Hauling himself up, he rubbed the back of his neck and a wave of dizziness forced him to abort an attempted stretch. His eyes were drawn to the TV again and he couldn't help watching the news item unfold before him. The boy and his mother now approached the steps leading to the main entrance of the high school. Another boy appeared from the chaos, dressed in a red Liverpool tracksuit top, and gave the first boy a pat on the back. What *was* this? The boy and his mum started climbing the stairs towards the school. McKenzie found himself strangely transfixed by the surreal goings-on – as if it were something straight out of *Adrian Mole*. A line of teachers stood across the top of the stairs, sleeves rolled up and arms folded – the body language of gruff nightclub bouncers.

When the boy reached the top of the steps, he stopped. His mum wobbled slightly, stepping down a step, then up again, clinging to the boy's arm a bit harder. There seemed to be a strange stand-off, with a brief exchange between the boy and the tallest teacher in the middle – a balding guy with tattoos on his forearms. Crowds of teenagers gathered at the bottom of the stairs, no doubt thrilled by the drama unfolding and the unexpected delay to their usual lessons. The tough-looking teacher in the middle shook his head and stood firm – you wouldn't mess with him, McKenzie thought. The mother pulled at the boy to leave and he reluctantly followed. The crowd of teenagers parted to let them pass. Suddenly, the scene cut to an interview with the boy at the school gates. McKenzie reached for the remote and turned the volume up, now strangely invested in whatever was going on.

'I just want to go to school but they won't let me in, that's why I contacted you – people should see what is happening to us,' the boy said. There was a crowd of people behind them and someone shouted at him to go home. His mum darted an anxious look back over her shoulder.

'The school has said they've acted appropriately and reasonably and they've communicated to both of you that they need time to carry out a full risk assessment. What's your response to that?' the reporter asked, pushing the microphone back towards the boy.

'My mum's got an illness, like lots of people do. There's no reason I shouldn't be able to go to school. I'm fine; there'd be very little risk anyway.'

The reporter turned to the mum. 'And you, Mrs Townley – how do you feel about your son's actions today?'

McKenzie thought the mum looked like she was shivering – or maybe just jittery. Her hair was thin, her eyes were sunken and a large red blotch marked the side of her forehead.

'I'm proud of him. He just wants to go to school and my … my condition shouldn't stop that.'

Next to be interviewed was the man who had been shaking his head – a tall figure with a Welsh accent and a rugby club tie. He stood outside the main entrance to the school. A caption flashed up on the screen: *Mr J. Harris, Deputy Head.*

'The fact of the matter is, Mrs Townley has got AIDS. We have been handling this matter discreetly, striving to avoid drawing attention to the family's plight. We cannot expose other children or staff to the risk of infection from an incurable disease. If we simply allowed Andy to return, many parents have indicated they would withdraw their children from the school. We have the full backing of the school community to act – sensitively, of course, but also in a responsible manner – in the face of this very challenging situation. All we have asked of the family is a little time to establish a solution that is in the best interest of everyone involved.'

The news report cut back to the studio, where Michael Buerk sat poised at the desk. 'In other news …'

McKenzie pointed the remote at the TV and pressed the mute button. What *the hell* had he just seen? Rubbing three days' worth of stubble on his cheek, he wandered to the kitchen. The kitchen was his pride and joy – expensive dark woods, marble worktops and gleaming gold handles. A set of patio doors opened to steps that led down to a narrow garden, where an ornate summer house stood proudly at the bottom. Placing a glass on the kitchen surface, McKenzie opened a cupboard. As he rummaged, packets of paracetamol, ibuprofen and vitamins tumbled out and he swore at them for their unwarranted insolence. Finally laying his hands on the Alka-Seltzer, he popped two tablets from the packet and dropped them into the glass of water. They fizzed and bubbled, creating a satisfying sound. Leaning on the work surface with both hands, he propped himself up, waiting for the tablets to dissolve. *So the boy was being kept from school because of AIDS – not even because he had it, but because of his poor mum?* McKenzie couldn't shake Mrs Townley's haunted expression from his mind; he had seen that look before. There had been a few guys in the London music industry who had suddenly started looking unwell, their vibrant energy diminishing as they went from outgoing and bubbly to cautious and concerned, then disappearing altogether. One minute, they were there – a hive of creativity, joy and brilliance; the next, they had simply gone. Everyone knew what was happening and whispers of AIDS circulated, but the men were quietly forgotten, rarely mentioned again. These were healthy, carefree young men in the prime of their lives, achieving their dreams in the music industry, suddenly struck down by an illness that wreaked havoc on their bodies.

With the tablets now dissolved, McKenzie gulped down the water, spilling some on the T-shirt he still wore from the night before, joining a large margarita stain on the front. He spluttered on the grainy remnants of the tablets at the bottom of the glass before returning to the sitting room and sinking into the couch. *Pebble Mill,* an afternoon talk show, was now on the TV – it was featuring The Predators as they promoted their latest single. McKenzie couldn't get away from them, rubbing his nose in their sudden success.

He sat for a while, staring at the screen, lost in thought. Sod The Predators. Actually, sod Atkinson and the bloody superficial music industry. He reached for the phone on the side table at the end of the settee. It was vintage black and his finger hovered over the gold dial. Atkinson was *definitely* not the person to contact in this situation; McKenzie knew that Atkinson would go nuts if he found out what he was about to do. So he called his PR company for help instead, making it clear they'd be sacked if Atkinson caught wind of what he was asking.

13

The phone rang while Andy watched *Grange Hill* and Debbie busied herself in the kitchen, preparing him some tea: Findus Crispy Pancakes, potato waffles and baked beans. The sounds of her pottering about – soft clinks and thuds as she opened cupboards and the oven door – were comforting. To their relief, there had been no immediate backlash from the TV news report. There was a lull in the egg throwing; maybe it was becoming an expensive hobby, with parents starting to complain about eggs vanishing mysteriously from their kitchens – and the sudden shortage ruining their morning fry-ups. Perhaps egg production across Massleforth needed to be ramped up to meet the booming demand.

Andy had been to the shop earlier that afternoon, enduring the usual ignorance from a customer who loudly insisted that everything he touched should be disinfected. It was becoming routine for cashiers to refuse to handle the money he placed on the counter until after he'd left – presumably so they could put on rubber gloves or spray it with something.

The phone continued to ring and Andy went to get up.

'I'll get it, love,' Debbie called, making her way slowly across the lounge. It was the little things Andy noticed about how their lives had changed. Debbie used to be a whirlwind around the house. If the phone rang, she would dash to answer it, trilling a cheerful hello and often bursting into squealing laughter with one of her friends on the other end. Remaining there for the next half hour, she would be shrieking about the latest gossip. It drove Andy up the wall, especially when he was trying to watch something. Now, it was more of a shuffle and a pause, answering in a hesitant, wheezy whisper like she was running out of batteries. Debbie's voice used to fill the house. Andy remembered smiling when his dad winked at him and pretended to turn an invisible volume knob down behind her back whenever she was singing. But now the volume had turned down for real.

'I'm sorry, who?' Debbie said, picking up the receiver and trying to untangle the spiral cord, briefly looking towards the kitchen where the crispy pancakes had been left under the grill.

'McKenzie? We don't know a McKen ... McKenzie McCall? I think you've got the wrong ... wait a minute ... the singer?' Debbie frowned, rolling her eyes at Andy. 'That's a good one. McKenzie McCall! You could have at least pretended to be someone who's actually been *in* the charts recently. Now leave us alone. It's an improvement from eggs at the window but this is still pretty pathetic.'

Slamming the phone down, she turned back to the kitchen, her expression hardening.

'Someone's having a laugh. I bet it's one of the neighbours,' Debbie muttered, returning to the kitchen to pull the food from under the grill. 'Unfortunately, the news reporter warned us we might get unwanted attention after being on TV.'

The phone rang again.

'Just leave it, love. Honestly, there are some strange people about – just let it ring or pull the cord from the wall.'

Andy glanced from the phone to the TV, where a character called Roly was being shouted at by a terrifying teacher called Mr Bronson. Ignoring Debbie's advice, he reached for the receiver and answered the phone.

'Hello?'

'Oh, hi … hello … erm, Andy? I was just speaking to your mum, I think. It's … erm … McKenzie McCall here. You know, I do a bit of singing sometimes – though, as your mum pointed out, not currently in the charts … sadly.' He gave a nervous chuckle. 'I … erm … don't think your mum believed it was me, which is understandable, I guess. I mean, why would McKenzie McCall call your house at quarter past five on a Tuesday evening?'

'Andy, tea is ready and plated up …' Debbie called, appearing at the doorway. 'I *told* you not to answer it!'

'Hold on,' Andy muttered into the phone, covering the mouthpiece with his hand. 'Mum, I think it actually *is* McKenzie McCall. It sounds like him. I mean, I only know from when he's been on *Saturday Superstore*, but … I *think* it's him.'

Debbie came over to stand beside him, wiping her hands on a tea towel and frowning.

'Don't be silly, Andy … well …' She hesitated. 'Maybe ask him something McKenzie McCall would know, if you think it's really him.'

Andy contemplated this. His knowledge of McKenzie's back catalogue was sketchy, but like most people he'd hummed along to some of the well-known tunes. He put the receiver back to his mouth and narrowed his eyes.

'McKenzie? Erm … what chart position did "Red Redemption" get to?'

McKenzie answered without missing a beat. 'Hmm, that was one of the better ones – number six in the UK and it even managed to climb to number twelve in the United States. It was from the album *New York Summer Heat*, which was actually recorded in Wales … in the cold … and the rain, but we were trying to appeal to the American market. It did particularly well in Scandinavia and went to number one in Denmark.'

'Thank you … one moment,' Andy replied, covering the phone again to consider the response. Trouble was, he had no idea if any of what he'd been told was true.

'I think it really is him, Mum,' he whispered. 'He said it went to number one in Denmark. Either that, or it's someone who can make up McKenzie McCall facts pretty quickly.'

Debbie shrugged, bemused. 'Well, then, you'd better ask why he's calling us. But if it sounds dodgy, just hang up, hear me?'

'Hello? Yes, erm … why are … is there … why are you calling, please?' Andy stammered.

'Ahh, well, er … I'm not really sure,' McKenzie replied, his voice uncertain.

Andy covered the phone and mouthed to Debbie in a dramatic whisper, 'He says he doesn't know *why* he's phoning.'

Debbie grimaced. 'Oh that's just great, so now we've got an international rock star on the phone who dialled the wrong number. Ask him if there's anything we can help with or if we can get back to our crispy pancakes?'

Andy couldn't help but smile at the absurdity of it all.

'Erm … well, Mum says our tea is ready. Is there anything we can help with, or, erm … is that everything?' Andy asked again, cringing at himself.

'Well, Andy, I guess I'm kind of calling because … I saw the thing on the news and I thought it was a brave thing to do. I wanted to know how you both are.'

Andy relayed this to his mum as discreetly as possible. 'He says he wants to know how we are.'

'Oh, we're marvellous,' Debbie replied, mock indignantly. 'Never been better. My body is pretty much giving up on me and we've been egged so many times our house looks like the world's biggest plate of scrambled eggs.'

'Erm, Andy, I can hear your mum and I appreciate that this is a bit of a surprise,' McKenzie continued.

'Shhh, he can hear you,' Andy whispered, shaking his head at Debbie.

'I admired that you both took a stand like that, you know, at school. I'd like to help. I'm not quite sure how, but maybe … maybe I could come and see you both and take it from there. I just … I'd rather you didn't mention it to anyone, not right now.'

'One sec,' Andy replied, turning back to his mum. 'He wants to meet us but doesn't want us to tell anyone.'

'Of *course* he doesn't,' Debbie replied. 'And when is this meeting going to take place?'

'Maybe tomorrow?' McKenzie offered, though Andy caught the doubt lurking in his voice.

**

Perhaps more to his own surprise than anyone else's, McKenzie found himself trundling up the motorway in his old silver Golf GTi. He loved this car. Over ten years old, it was the first car he'd bought when his music began to make him some real money. He'd grown so attached to it that he'd never had the heart to part with it.

These days, he rarely drove. A driver was always on call with a burgundy-red Bentley – a sleek status symbol dripping with success, one that Atkinson wholeheartedly approved of. The Bentley was designed to turn heads, ensuring McKenzie was noticed whenever he arrived somewhere, luring the paparazzi and fuelling the next day's gossip columns. McKenzie had been relying on an old AA road map, pulling over several times to rest it on the steering wheel and try to figure out where he was and how to get to Massleforth. Heading north felt strange – he'd grown up in Cheshire, not far from where Andy and Debbie lived, just twenty miles or so away. As he drew closer, memories of his childhood flooded his thoughts, with vivid images of his mum and dad at the forefront. They'd both been older when they had him, each on their second marriage and as their cherished only child, his whims were often indulged. One summer day, after watching The Beatles perform at a local town carnival, McKenzie decided he *must* own a guitar. The date was forever etched on his memory: July 6th, 1963 – Verdin Park, Northwich. The Beatles were on the brink of stardom. They had already amassed a fanatical following around the North West 'Mersey Beat' circuit, but were virtually unknown nationally – just four excitable young guys from Liverpool. The stage was squeezed just to the left of the funfair, a modest setting for a band destined to redefine music. As girls around him screamed their names, a young McKenzie was transfixed by the band's instruments – watching Harrison and Lennon strum with intensity, while McCartney plucked at his iconic violin bass with his signature head-bobbing. At the back, almost hidden by his drum kit, Ringo Starr played with an unmistakable grin on his face, clearly having the time of his life.

After their set, McKenzie had watched in awe as they crowned the Carnival Queen. Dressed in leather jackets, they exuded effortless cool. The experience left a lasting impression on a young Michael McCall, so much so that he went home and begged his dad for an acoustic guitar. Perhaps to keep his son from becoming too spoiled, Mr McCall insisted Michael take on chores for ten Saturdays to earn pocket money for the guitar. After a painful wait – and with a beautifully waxed car in the driveway – they went together to buy a guitar. After choosing one, young Michael held it, marvelling, and uttered the immortal words that would later inspire its famous nickname: 'It's just so … special!' The guitar was to become known across the globe as the *Old Special*. It was so precious to McKenzie that whenever he flew, he'd pay for a seat for it next to him rather than have it put in the cargo hold. McKenzie missed his parents' guidance with all his heart. Perhaps that was why he showed such unfathomable patience with Atkinson who, despite his shortcomings, had become like family – a flawed blend of mother, father and brother all rolled into one.

Sitting alone in the café of a department store in Manchester, McKenzie felt a pang of anxiety he hadn't experienced in years. Being out in the 'real world' was unnerving – he was just another person, unrecognised, yet strangely exposed. Dressed in jeans and a denim jacket, with a baseball cap shadowing his face and a beard grown mostly out of laziness, he hoped he looked unremarkable. Still, he'd been dismayed that morning to notice a few grey whiskers in his beard. Atkinson would have him booked into a salon for a full dye job in a heartbeat if he spotted them. But Atkinson was two hundred and twenty miles away, clueless that McKenzie had fibbed, claiming he was spending a quiet day at home.

'I've got meetings with your record label, Mack. Trying to convince them you still exist. Get that guitar out and start strumming the damn thing – after you've blown off the dust and cobwebs! We need a song, Mack – more than ever. I need to be able to tell them something positive, anything,' Atkinson had barked down the phone during his usual morning call.

Not a single person had bothered McKenzie – no one had recognised the former winner of a 1978 Album of the Year and Ivor Novello award, not even when he'd stopped at Keele Services for the loo. Back in his London days, he used to take the Tube, blending in effortlessly – no one batted an eyelid. Despite this, he couldn't shake the feeling that he *must* have protection: a driver, security, the works. Once he had lived in a tight security bubble, it was hard to step outside of it and he wasn't sure he could cope without that protection. This act of rash independence had been a shock to his system. Sitting in the corner of the café, waiting for Andy and Debbie, his leg bounced up and down. Wishing he had a steadying glass of wine within reach, McKenzie clasped his hands in front of him, then placed them on his lap. Shifting restlessly in his seat, he was already regretting getting involved. What on earth would Atkinson say? He'd think he'd gone even madder than he already believed. And the press? What if they found out he was here, meeting someone with AIDS? He could already imagine the headlines: *Mack Makes AIDS Friend*. The thought made him shudder.

Just as he was about to make a run for it, McKenzie spotted two figures – a boy and a woman – winding their way across the shop floor through the racks of clothes. The boy smiled sheepishly when he noticed McKenzie and whispered something to his mother. He wore stonewash jeans and a denim jacket, similar to McKenzie's, though probably not the same fashion label. The mother also wore jeans and a thick coat, along with a cream hat, scarf, and gloves; a polo neck jumper covered her neck. Despite her efforts with make-up and the layers of clothing, she was very thin. Her prominent cheekbones and grey, lumpy complexion painted a stark picture of someone struggling. This made McKenzie nervy. What would he say? He hadn't even considered that. What do you say to someone with an illness like this? He was rubbish in these kinds of situations at the best of times. Standing up, he attempted a smile as they approached. He was used to sipping drinks in Claridge's and The Groucho Club, rubbing shoulders with music heavyweights like Mick Jagger, Rod Stewart and Errol Brown – not drinking a mug of Tetley tea in C&A. Once, on a night out in London, he had briefly shared a table with Diana Ross and Tina Turner, who had actually told him she liked his song 'The Magic of Midnight'. He felt like he'd died and gone to heaven.

McKenzie held out his hand then quickly withdrew it, opting for a shy little wave instead.

'Hi! Sit down. How are you? You OK? You look gr— I mean, how are you doing?' Bloody hell, McKenzie thought. Why was he so bad at being normal? *So Bad at Being Normal* – now that would be a great song title, he had to remember that when he got back to London.

'Hi, McKenzie!' Debbie said brightly, settling into her seat and nodding for Andy to sit beside her. 'Sorry we're late. For some reason, I lost the use of my right arm for a bit and we thought we might have to bail on you. Then my head felt like it was on fire but after a quick rest, it eased up a little – so here we are.'

McKenzie opened his mouth to speak but was completely unable to think of any response that hit the right tone.

'That's probably not the best way to greet an international rock star, on reflection,' said Debbie, removing the scarf from round her neck but keeping the coat and hat on.

'Allow me to, erm, get you something,' said McKenzie, realising he was under Andy's starstruck scrutiny and acutely aware of the crushing disappointment it so often invited. 'Tea?'

'We'll both have a tea, thank you,' replied Debbie, adjusting her turtleneck and pulling it higher around her neck, giving a small shiver.

'Could I have an iced bun, please?' Andy asked, the normality of discussing cups of tea settling him.

'Yeah, course, would you like one too?' McKenzie asked Debbie, who pulled a face.

'No thanks, I tend to find things taste a bit like gravy granules at the moment what with the AZT medication I'm taking – my mouth is in pretty much a state of constant agony too.' She opened her mouth just enough for McKenzie to catch a glimpse of red and white sores on her tongue and he recoiled slightly, which Debbie ignored. 'I have to drink these awful protein shakes to keep going, and – well, let's just say they're not great for the old flatulence.' She chuckled lightly. 'I think I'm oversharing – it's the nerves. You go get the teas, McKenzie,' she added. For a moment, McKenzie glimpsed the young, beautiful woman she was.

'Righto,' said Mack, standing up and glancing around. 'I'll just, erm …'

Debbie looked at his bewildered face and laughed.

'Not something you do often, is it?' she asked with a grin, thumbing behind her. 'You get a brown tray from the pile there. You join the queue and slide your tray along the rail and someone will eventually ask you what you want. They'll get it ready for you and you move along to the till. Hey presto, they'll hand you the teas and iced bun and then you bring it back to the table … after paying, of course.'

McKenzie's eyes widened.

'You don't have any money on you, do you?' Debbie sighed, rolling her eyes as she fished into her purse and handed him a couple of pound coins. McKenzie felt foolish – he almost never had to carry cash. Out shopping, his security minder or Atkinson would handle payment.

As McKenzie wandered towards the brown trays, following Debbie's instructions, he overheard them whispering behind him.

'Mum, we're buying McKenzie McCall a cup of tea!'

'Yes, we are … did I *really* just discuss my wind issues with a world-famous rock star?'

When McKenzie returned to the table, there were a few minutes of awkwardness while they arranged the milk and sugar for their teas. They had a small jug of milk and a bowl of sugar to share between them. Debbie added a spoonful of sugar to both her tea and Andy's then poured in some milk.

McKenzie reached for the milk jug and then hesitated. Andy caught his eye.

'You can't catch it from touching things, you know?' Andy said, a little more sharply than McKenzie thought necessary. 'Or from toilets, or swimming pools, or petrol pumps, or cutlery, or anywhere else people say.'

'Andy, that's a bit rude,' Debbie chided gently.

McKenzie smiled apologetically.

'I know, Andy and I'm sorry.' He picked up the milk jug, adding a drop to his tea. 'I'm not trying to offend you by skipping the sugar. *The Daily Express* keeps pointing out I'm getting a bit of a rotund belly so I'll give it a miss. Sadly, my manager agrees and wants me on a crash diet.' He chuckled. 'You know that woman who does all the energetic keep-fit routines on breakfast TV? Atkinson thinks I should don a Lycra jumpsuit and legwarmers and join in with her stretches in the sitting room every morning.'

To McKenzie's relief, Andy and Debbie laughed. With the ice broken, Andy began quizzing McKenzie about life as a rock star. Andy asked if McKenzie was a millionaire and what it was like to go on *Top of the Pops*. Debbie, aside from punctuating the conversation with a hacking cough, was content to let Andy chatter away, smiling affectionately at him now and then.

'Do you know Duran Duran? Or Wham!?' Andy asked, his face full of wonder.

McKenzie smiled. 'Yes, I've met them a few times.'

'And … are they nice in real life?'

'Of course – they're just young guys living a dream life and loving it. It's quite endearing, actually.'

Andy's eyes lit up. 'Have you ever met Freddie Mercury or Elton John?'

'Freddie, yes. Elton, no – but I'd love to. He's a genius.'

'What was Freddie like?'

'Surprisingly small, shy and private for someone with such a huge, amazing stage presence … but the nicest, funniest guy.'

McKenzie laughed when Andy asked why he hadn't been in the charts for a while.

'Well, the songs don't come as easily once you're a bit older and past your best,' he said, with a slightly forced chuckle. 'People think songs just happen when you're a musician. I say to them, try writing one and see how you get on.'

There was a slight shift in mood and Debbie leant forwards.

'Why are you here, McKenzie? You said you wanted to help. So what is it? What do you want to do?'

McKenzie's anxiety flared again as he looked around the café. Leaning forward, he lowered his voice. 'I … I don't really know. I was thinking on the way here, maybe I could kind of sponsor you … you know, from a distance. I mean, from London. I could provide you with some funds to go to a private doctor. Atkinson will know someone. Maybe I could make a donation to a charity or a support group you use? Maybe I could provide Andy with a home tutor, or even send him to a private school who … who will have him – so he doesn't miss out on too much of his education. Maybe I could just ease any financial pressures.'

Debbie, looking unimpressed, blew her nose into a tissue with a bit more force than necessary and leaned in, almost daring McKenzie to move back.

'That's awfully generous of you, McKenzie. Really, it is.' Debbie's voice was steady, her gaze unwavering. 'But even if you found me the best private doctor in the world, the outcome is the same. The reason I'm taking this stuff – the AZT – the reason I'm enduring these horrific side effects? It's not for me. It's for the next people with AIDS who are coming after me. It's for those who come next.' She paused, her tone hardening. 'We need to find treatments. We need to test things, to find what works. We need to trial medicines that might save lives, even if it's too late for me. This disease is a death sentence. The moment you hear that test result is positive, that's it – you know what's going to happen.'

'Mum …' Andy murmured, his voice small. Debbie immediately put her arm around him, pulling him close. She kissed his head softly, holding him as if to shield him. 'I'm sorry, love.' Then she looked back at McKenzie with intensity. 'More importantly, we need to change attitudes. The truth is, no one cares. They think it's some "gay disease" and that people with AIDS deserve it. AIDS has given anyone who doesn't like gay people a chance to stick the boot in and say "I told you so – it's what we said all along". So the gay community is just being left to pretty much deal with it and it's shocking. But there are haemophiliacs and straight people getting it too, all over the world, right now.' She paused. 'Look at me – I'm a woman. But here I am getting a taste of what the gay community is going through. They're not seen as "innocent victims", and that's disgraceful. This disease should rock the world to its foundations. But no one is listening.'

McKenzie moved uncomfortably in his seat, rolling the mug between his hands. The exit looked inviting – this wasn't what he'd expected at all. He'd come to help a lady and her son, to be the hero. He'd imagined himself rolling up like a knight in shining armour, paying some healthcare bills, receiving their gratitude and heading back to London feeling better about himself. But now she seemed angry and he was starting to wonder if he'd misjudged everything. He shifted in his seat again, realising Debbie wasn't finished yet.

'So while I appreciate your offer of help, McKenzie – and I do, honestly – I need you to understand what we really need.' Debbie's voice was unflinching. 'What we need is for someone in your position, someone with influence, to stand up and be counted. To campaign with us for more research, more medical funding. We need to make politicians listen. There are some amazing groups, inspirational people in the gay community, coming together to raise awareness, to put pressure on governments to support the medical world, to invest in research. We need to give those who are dying a dignified death. And we need to find a cure for those who have a chance – or for all those in the future who will be infected. Mark my words, there's going to be lots more. We need someone to get this message out there.' She paused, searching his face. 'Haven't you seen the headlines? Can you imagine how it feels, not only to be dying, but to read *them* while you're dying?'

'Mum …' Andy attempted again with pained expression. He placed his hand over hers and clung to it, clearly willing her to stop.

He knew it was shameful and cowardly, but McKenzie needed to escape. He longed to be anywhere else – talking with Atkinson about the next song, the next album, the next party – anything. Did she honestly think he was going to go on TV and start talking about AIDS? The papers would tear him apart; his career would be over.

'I'm sorry. I … I shouldn't have come,' he stammered. 'I was trying to do the right thing, but I'm … out of my depth. I made a mistake.' He forced himself to look at her, though his voice barely held. 'If … if you need help with a doctor or a tutor, I'll sort it. Just contact my publicity team, but please don't mention … please don't say—'

'That you know someone with AIDS?' Debbie interrupted. She leaned back, folding her arms as she let her words sink in.

McKenzie flushed. Sheepishly, he got up, tugging his cap lower and pulling his car keys from his pocket, feeling the weight of her gaze.

'I'm sorry. I'm really sorry. It's just … difficult. I want things to be OK for you.' He hesitated, grasping at anything that might help. 'Your ex-husband? Couldn't you … contact him? Get him back on the scene for support?'

Debbie shook her head, her stare drifting past him to the window. She bit her lip, pausing before speaking, as if gathering the strength to answer. '*Unbelievable*,' she said quietly, shaking her head. 'An international rock star drives two hundred miles from London to grace us with his holy presence, only to give us the same bloody advice everyone else does.'

'*Mum …*' Andy murmured, for what felt like the hundredth time.

'I'm really sorry,' McKenzie repeated. 'I shouldn't have

got your hopes up. I'm … pretty useless, really. Bye, Andy. Bye, Debbie.'

As he turned away, the self-loathing washed over him. He was a shallow, entitled fraud. But as he headed to the door, relief flooded through him. He had to curb his impulsiveness and learn to leave certain things well alone.

***

In the bath that evening, Andy sat with his knees drawn to his chest, letting the shower rain down over his head. He remembered his mum and dad decorating the bathroom: the peach walls paired with the avocado toilet, sink and bath. His dad had laid the flooring himself – brown tile-effect lino – and they'd been so proud of it. The memory was crystal clear: the radio blaring, Mike Reid on Radio 1, his parents singing along to the Eurythmics. There was laughter through the wall as Andy played *JetPac* on his Spectrum in his bedroom. Suddenly, a shriek, a thump, silence – and then an explosion of laughter. Andy jumped up from his joystick and dashed to the bathroom door. There he'd found Debbie lying in a heap in the bath where she'd slipped, with Tony flailing as he tried to pull her out. They'd looked up at Andy in the doorway and burst into giggles again. Andy smiled at the memory – it was three years ago, yet it seemed like a lifetime.

When Andy returned downstairs to the sitting room, he found Debbie on the edge of the settee, a tissue in hand and tears streaming down her face.

'What's wrong?' he asked, sitting beside her.

'That,' she said, nodding at the TV, 'is how you make a difference. Look at her.'

On the screen, Princess Diana was chatting with a line of nurses, spring sunshine streaming into the building. She looked radiant in a blue dress and perfectly coiffed hair. She was visiting an AIDS ward at a hospital in Middlesex and the reporter explained how she had shaken hands with every patient. It was the first positive story they'd ever seen about AIDS. It felt momentous.

'She really understands what people with AIDS are going through,' Debbie said, sniffing. 'And she knows that her being there will make a difference to people's attitudes. It's so brave. But you know what's a tragedy, Andy? None of those patients would show their faces on TV – not even with Princess Diana there. They're scared of what might happen; they feel they have to protect their families. We've got such a long way to go.'

Andy nodded. 'Mum, I don't really understand. Why do they call it HIV sometimes and AIDS other times?'

He had so many questions he'd wanted to ask, but for fear of upsetting his mum further, he had always avoided them. Now, though, this felt like a good opportunity.

'Well,' Debbie began gently, 'some people are HIV positive, which means they have the virus, but they might only have mild symptoms – or sometimes none at all. They could have just suspected they'd come into close contact with someone carrying HIV, so they got tested. When the test shows they have the virus, we say they're HIV positive. But when the virus has done more damage and people start to get very poorly, that's when we call it full-blown AIDS.'

Andy contemplated this for a moment. 'And … you have full-blown AIDS?'

Debbie nodded hesitantly. 'I think so, love. Yes.'

'The virus is in your blood? So … why can't they just

change your blood? Like a transfusion? Replace it with someone else's healthy blood.'

Debbie gave a sad smile. 'I wish it were that simple. The virus is in my blood, yes, but it's also in my muscles, my organs … everywhere, really.'

Andy nodded thoughtfully. They both turned to watch as Princess Diana, at the end of her visit, delivered a speech: '*HIV does not make people dangerous to know. You can shake their hands and give them a hug. Heaven knows they need it.*'

14

It was mid-morning and McKenzie perched on a bar stool at his kitchen island, a newspaper spread out before him, though his thoughts lingered on his evening with Charley. They'd had a relaxed, informal meal at Bibendum – a large, trendy restaurant with a sparkling atmosphere. The pretext had been to discuss the direction of his aimless new album but McKenzie found himself genuinely enjoying Charley's no-nonsense attitude. He respected her knack for balancing support with honesty – a refreshing change after years of listening to Atkinson.

While gossiping about the music business, Charley shared a few insider stories. One was about a famous band she'd worked with, whose lead singer would routinely halt recording sessions to check his hair in a hand mirror tucked into his jacket pocket. Another tale was about a band who looked fantastic but weren't exactly the most talented musicians. After their recording session, the producer quietly brought in session players to overdub sections and polish the track. Later, as the band smugly mimed along to their hit on *Top of the Pops*, they remained blissfully unaware, marvelling at how incredible they sounded. Towards the end of the evening, Charley clearly had something to say and placed her hand gently on his and broke the news: she was being reassigned from producing his album to other projects. The change, she assured him, was temporary – just until he had more songs ready. Spring was always a hectic season for recording studios, with record companies urging their acts to begin new albums in time for autumn releases, perfectly timed for the Christmas market. McKenzie, not helped by the wine he'd consumed, found himself more intrigued by the flutter of something inside him as Charley held his hand for those fleeting seconds than by what her words actually meant for his career.

Later in the evening, after McKenzie had regaled Charley with some of the funniest moments from his decade of touring, the inevitable happened: he was approached by a fan. This irritated him. He was a sitting duck – tucked under a table, unable to escape. And this was the worst kind of fan: drunk, male and convinced that McKenzie owed him something because he'd bought his first album twelve years ago. The fans who had been with him from the start were often the trickiest – feeling they had the divine right to offer McKenzie opinions, or worse, advice. McKenzie patiently signed the man's restaurant menu, hoping that would be enough to appease him. But no, the man wanted to chat.

'So when's the next hit coming, Mack? You've been pretty quiet. Are things drying up for you?' He guffawed, his level of familiarity raising McKenzie's hackles. The man wore an oversized black suit with silvery flecks, sleeves rolled up. His hair was voluminous, the result of far too much blow-drying and hairspray. Standing with his hands in his pockets, he exuded an arrogance that made McKenzie think he was probably a city trader with more money than brains. His jacket pocket bulged with what looked like a large Filofax. In McKenzie's experience, the bigger the Filofax, the more pleased with themself the person appeared – just look at Atkinson. McKenzie hated the *when's the next song coming?* question, as if churning out a top ten hit was as easy as flicking a switch.

'Oh, you know, I'll probably write one tomorrow after *TV-am* finishes and before my mid-morning cup of tea. I'll fire out another after the one o'clock news. Before my evening meal, I was thinking of giving Elton a call to see if he wants to duet, or maybe David Bowie – he did "Under Pressure" with Queen, so I fancy my chances.'

The man smiled, unsure how to take McKenzie, but he didn't move.

'Who's ya bird? One of your groupies? You rock stars get all the dolly birds chasing ya!' He guffawed again, winking at Charley. McKenzie hadn't looked up at the man once and a wave of weariness washed over him.

'You've got your autograph. Now you can get back to enjoying your meal.'

'Eh?' The man's smirk faltered. Clearly believing the conversation was going better than it was, his posture shifted to something more defensive.

'You can go back to your meal now,' McKenzie repeated, keeping his eyes on his glass of wine on the table.

'Well, there's no need to be like that! I've got all your albums – even the last one, which was crap. You celebrities are all the s—'

As the man continued to speak, McKenzie and Charley shared a quick nod, silently confirming they were on the same page.

'GO AWAY!' they bellowed in unison.

The man straightened, fiddled with his tie knot, shrugged his suit a few times and then stormed off. McKenzie laughed it off but the man's words echoed in his mind … *things drying up for you*? You hit the nail on the head, Mr Filofax man. So, after his driver dropped Charley off, McKenzie spent longer than he should have overanalysing the peck on the cheek she'd given him. Then, filled with defiant determination and the man's words ringing in his ears, he headed home. He'd ventured down to the basement with purpose, pulled out his trusty old guitar and wrote a bloody cracking song. Actually, he hadn't. He'd opened another bottle of wine, sat alone and sulked.

The phone rang shrilly on the wall on the other side of the kitchen, making McKenzie jump, snort and almost topple off the bar stool all at once. Springing to his feet, he forgot his head was still spinning from the wine the night before. His legs gave way and he stumbled feebly to his knees. Wiping a dry mouth with his forearm, McKenzie paused, contemplating his next move. For a moment, he thought he might have to crawl across the marble kitchen tiles like a wind-up Action Man figure. Using the side of the kitchen island for support, he pushed himself up and lumbered towards the phone – a far cry from *any* Action Man heroics.

'Hello?' he croaked, knowing full well it was Atkinson.

'Well, we're up the goddamn canal with a broken arrow now!' Atkinson boomed, forcing McKenzie to move the receiver six inches from his ear and wince. 'Dropped, Mack – your record label has dropped you. Let that sink in. You've been sitting around scratching your balls while the music scene has moved on. "Rock Around the Clock" was the last straw for just about everyone. You're lucky I'm still hanging in there with you – but only just, Mack! Only *bloody* just! They're going to love this in the press. They're already hammering you. *Mack's a Mess* – did you see that headline, Mack? Did you?'

McKenzie heard Atkinson pause to take a drag of his cigar before continuing, slightly calmer. 'We'll need some damage control – get a statement out there first stating it's you who has decided to move on. We'll say they wanted you to churn out the same old boring albums and you were desperate for the freedom of more creativity … something like that. I'll think of something – we'll sort it, Mack. Mack? Are you even listening?'

McKenzie knew from experience that, in times of crisis, it was best to say little. Atkinson would soon be firing off solutions within minutes of a meltdown. Of course being dropped hurt. McKenzie had been with his record company for thirteen years. He still remembered the exhilaration of being signed by a global label and, until recently, being one of their prestige stars. Life in the music business was thrilling on the way up – everyone wanted to be your friend – but on the way down, those same people were all too eager to kick you into the gutter. While Atkinson swung into action, attempting to manipulate the narrative in their favour, McKenzie spent the next few days in his home, unable to face the outside world. Reflecting on his success as a musician, he realised that the overriding feeling he had experienced was one of boredom. The thought of leaving the house and being recognised overwhelmed him, so he simply didn't go out as much. Much of his life felt confined to a series of enclosed spaces – a tour bus, hotel room, music studio, TV studio, backstage dressing room – leaving him with little sense of freedom.

Atkinson called morning, afternoon and evening to update McKenzie. In Atkinson's own humble opinion, he had done a commendable job with the press. Atkinson had planted a few quotes from 'a friend close to the star' with loyal journalists, claiming that McKenzie was, of course, disappointed to be without a record label (*true*), that he was incredibly excited about what the future held (*false*) and that there was already a fierce bidding war for McKenzie's signature from other labels (*very false*). With his newfound freedom, McKenzie was now holed up in the studio putting the finishing touches to some fresh new sounds which they hoped would be released in the near future (*literally could not be further from the truth*).

McKenzie flicked through *Number One* music magazine, the TV chatting away to itself in the background. For the first time in years, he noticed he hadn't received a single mention in its pages and a wave of depression washed over him. As he scanned the articles covering bands like A-ha – blessed with chiselled good looks and a cutting-edge sound – he felt older and more out of touch than ever. When Michael Jackson recorded an album, he had the luxury of choosing from the best songwriters from across the globe, narrowing down hundreds of potential tracks to just ten. How could McKenzie compete with that? He had only his battered *Old Special* to rely on. Over thirteen years, he'd released eight albums. The early ones came easily with success following quickly. Simply picking up his guitar inspired the songs to flow. He had the magic touch: the first six albums all hit the top ten, catapulting him from playing in pubs to sold-out theatres and, eventually, arenas. He released a song called

Rustic Charm, a Harry Belafonte homage with a calypso rhythm and even *that* reached the top twenty. Driven by his childhood memories of his mum playing Belafonte records, he had written it more for her than for anyone else.

McKenzie had never been one for interviews. A natural introvert, he preferred to keep to himself. He was aware that he could come across as standoffish in front of a camera, but this had only added to his mystique – the moody, silent type who let the music do the talking. He had achieved everything he ever set out to do and more. Maybe he just needed to accept that he had reached his peak and this was his natural decline; he had basked in the limelight longer than he had any right to. This was nature's way of nudging him towards a more normal life, away from the spotlight. Atkinson was right: he *was* losing his desire. If Atkinson hadn't been pulling the strings, McKenzie would have jacked it all in and retired to a quiet fishing village on the coast, fading into obscurity. Maybe it was time to let Atkinson go and put them all out of their misery.

McKenzie reached for the TV remote and turned the volume up – it was nearly eight o'clock. The commercial break was on, sandwiched between *Coronation Street* and *The Bill*. After a brash advert for Daz washing powder finished, the atmosphere shifted dramatically. On the screen, a volcano erupted, spewing flashes of fire and tumbling rocks. A man chiselling granite sent blue sparks flying, accompanied by the foreboding tolling of a church bell with each strike of the hammer. It was more like a lavishly produced horror film than the usual cheerful adverts for Fairy Liquid, Smith's crisps, Gold Blend coffee or the Yorkie chocolate bar that typically filled this time slot. The voiceover, which McKenzie immediately recognised as John Hurt – an actor he admired and had met a few times on the London social scene – spoke ominously. 'There is now a danger that threatens us all …' it began. 'It's a deadly disease and there is no known cure.' Like millions across the country, McKenzie couldn't tear his eyes away from the screen. 'Anyone can get it – man or woman …' the voiceover continued, '… and it's spreading.' A tombstone crashed to the ground, the word 'AIDS' chiselled into it, as the voiceover concluded, '… if you ignore AIDS, it could be the death of you – so don't die of ignorance.' McKenzie stared at the TV. He understood the government's intention: to keep people safe, to encourage them to protect themselves and to halt the spread of this deadly disease. But for someone already living with AIDS, or for those close to someone with it, this message must have been extraordinarily difficult to watch. And at the back of his mind, there they were again – Debbie and Andy.

McKenzie's letterbox was built into the gatepost at the front of his house. The next day, he retrieved his usual stack of fan mail from behind the tall wooden gates of his driveway. It was the usual mix – some flattering, some asking for things like money, autographs, or appearances at random village fetes and a few downright unsettling ones. Along with that, there was the business correspondence, which he routinely forwarded to Atkinson's office. At the bottom of the pile was a leaflet, identical to the one landing on front doormats across the country that day: *AIDS – Don't Die of Ignorance.* McKenzie wasn't sure what to do with it, so he left it on the kitchen counter, an uneasy reminder of what he had walked away from in Manchester.

Inevitably, discussions filled the newspapers and

dominated television airtime for the next few days, making it impossible to escape a creeping sense of guilt. There was the usual homophobia, along with the predictable bile from the press – headlines like *AIDS Timebomb: Would You Go Near Someone with AIDS?* and *Nation at Risk Causing Government to Act.* But there was also real anger from resolute AIDS campaigners, who were rightly gaining a larger platform – how could a government claim to care while simultaneously proposing a law like Section 28, which would ban any mention of the word 'gay' in schools? McKenzie found the febrile atmosphere unsettling. The trouble was, he had very few people to talk it through with. True acquaintances were rare. In the music business, forming genuine friendships was hard; everyone always seemed to want something from him.

When Atkinson called that night, he updated McKenzie on his progress in finding a new record label, urging him once again to pick up his guitar. 'Just play some chords, Mack. Try a few combinations and see what happens, for goodness' sake.'

But McKenzie was preoccupied.

'Have you seen all this stuff about AIDS, Atkinson? They're saying fifty thousand people in the UK will be infected with HIV by the end of the year. Within a couple of years, most of them will have full-blown AIDS. There's no treatment and hardly anywhere with proper hospital space for them.'

There was silence on the other end. For a moment, McKenzie thought Atkinson was quietly absorbing the sheer gravity of it all.

'Am I hearing this right? I am *absolutely* speechless, Mack. Here I am, trying to save your sausage and your response is to give me an information bulletin about a disease. People make choices, Mack. They can't go crying over spilt tea when those choices come back to bite them. Speechless, honestly!'

More than anything, McKenzie wished that, for once, Atkinson truly *was* unable to speak. He gently placed the receiver down on the side table and wandered off. The image of Atkinson still ranting away to an empty line brought him a small sense of satisfaction. McKenzie strolled through the quiet house, his mind drifting. Eventually, he made his way down to the basement, where his guitars waited. He ran his hand along his *Old Special*. The worn wood beneath his fingers stirred a pang of longing – he missed his dad. Leaving the basement, he wandered into the conservatory, pausing to take in the room's long, beautifully polished table. He could almost hear the laughter and conversation of the countless dinner parties he'd hosted there over the years. A few years back, Freddie Mercury had been one of the guests. At the time, the newspapers were buzzing with rumours that Queen was on the verge of splitting up. Between shots of Stolichnaya vodka, Freddie had leaned over with his trademark sardonic grin and assured McKenzie, 'Oh, it's absolute nonsense, darling. We'll be together until I bloody well die.' The memory made McKenzie smile. It had been a while since he'd seen Freddie out on the town and he missed bumping into him. With his impromptu tour of the house complete, McKenzie found himself back in the sitting room. The plush carpet was soft beneath his feet and the large bay-fronted window cast a pale light across the room. He picked up the phone, ensured Atkinson was gone from the other end of the line, and dialled.

'Andy? It's McKenzie … again. I'm just checking everything is OK?'

15

ndy felt a surge of relief that someone had called, even if it was a self-absorbed, narcissistic rock star from London who'd let his mum down when she'd needed help. Taking a steadying breath, he was determined not to break down, but his voice trembled.

'Mum's in hospital – she collapsed. She got up off the settee and went into the kitchen, I heard her saying she was seeing lights. I didn't understand so I followed her and … she was lying there on the kitchen floor. Her eyes were kind of bulging, rolling back and she was jerking all over. I had to call an ambulance but it took ages for one to come. I think it's because I told them she had AIDS. They asked if I could drive her myself – I told them I was twelve. I had to sit with her and she started saying strange things that didn't make sense.'

Andy told McKenzie how, as the paramedics loaded Debbie into the back of the ambulance, a small crowd gathered across the street, watching in silence. Not one of them stepped forward to check if Andy was OK. When the ambulance doors finally slammed shut, he stood motionless as it pulled away, lights flashing, before disappearing around the corner. Reggie appeared beside him, clutching a battered Liverpool FC football he'd been playing with at the park in the early evening sunshine. 'Sorry, Andy – hope your mum's OK,' he'd murmured, giving him a quick, awkward pat on the back. 'I'm just off for my tea, hope she comes back soon.'

A heavy silence hung on the other end of the line. Andy could almost feel McKenzie's panic through the receiver. There was no simple 'everything's fine' – nothing to let McKenzie off the hook. No easy way for him to step back now.

'OK, Andy, don't worry.' It seemed that McKenzie's voice was trying for reassurance, but Andy suspected it wasn't a role he was used to. 'First things first: is there anyone with you?'

'Yes,' Andy replied, 'Mrs Silva, my next-door neighbour.'

Mrs Silva appeared in the doorway, wearing a self-knitted cardigan over a plain dress, a floral headscarf tied under her chin and a pair of bright yellow rubber gloves.

'Andy!' she barked. 'Who is this on the phone? Tell them you are alone and you need help!'

'OK, that's good … she sounds a bit scary though,' McKenzie said.

'She's fine,' Andy reassured him. 'She's kind, just loud. You get used to it. She's cleaning the kitchen and she's cooking some tea for me.'

'Top lady,' McKenzie replied. 'Now, have you contacted anyone else?'

'No,' Andy replied, his voice shaky. 'I called the hospital but there's a delay with Mum being admitted to a ward – they didn't seem to know what was going on and told me to call back later.'

'It sounds like you're doing great, Andy. Can you get in touch with your grandparents? I think you need to. And your dad, maybe it's time to contact him? He should be involved, don't you think?'

Andy could feel the tears threatening to spill. He was scared – utterly overwhelmed. He thought about Reggie, playing football on the field, then sitting down to eat his tea. Afterwards, he'd probably head out to play again or spend an hour on his Spectrum. Andy envied that simplicity – just kicking a ball around with nothing else on his mind. No worries about how his mum was doing, where his dad was, or how many eggs would be thrown at his house that evening. Andy just wanted to be a child for an hour. Somewhere in a hospital, his mum was lying on a trolley and he didn't even know if she was being properly cared for, or if they were just leaving her to it because she had the 'wrong' illness. He had lost faith in everyone – well, everyone but Mrs Silva, who was stretching to reach the ceiling with a feather duster and tutting loudly at a cobweb.

'I'll contact Gran and Grandad. But I don't know where Dad is or how to reach him. I wish I did.'

There was a brief silence on the other end of the line. They both knew that what McKenzie said next could change everything between them.

'I'm going to pack a bag and drive up,' McKenzie said. 'When I get within about ten miles – maybe somewhere like Knutsford Services – I'll stop and find a payphone. Hopefully you'll have more information by then. It's half five now, so that'll be around eight o'clock. If you've already gone to the hospital, will you leave instructions with Mrs Silva on where I can find you? Is that alright?'

'Yes, I think so,' Andy replied, his voice small. Then, quietly, he added, 'I feel sick.'

'It's stress and worry,' McKenzie said gently. 'It's understandable. Sometimes when I go on stage, my stomach's all over the place and I have to run to the toilet. You need to take care of yourself, Andy, so you're strong for your mum. We need to look after you too. You can start by eating Mrs Silva's tea. I just need your address, Andy ...'

***

After McKenzie hung up the phone, he took one last look around the sitting room before stepping back into the real world again. Above the fireplace hung his first shiny gold disc, proudly framed. A little further along the wall, in a sleek montage, were photos with some of his heroes: nearly cheek to cheek with George Michael backstage at Wembley; striking a mutual respect pose with Nile Rodgers, both pointing at each other; and laughing with David Bowie at Annabel's. McKenzie could easily have spent the rest of his life within the four walls of this living room, surrounded by these extraordinary memories. For a moment, he wondered if he had been too hasty, if he could let Andy and Debbie down again. But this time, it wasn't about them – it was the anxiety of the unknown, the discomfort of stepping out of his familiar, cosseted world. Spontaneous, independent actions weren't natural to him. His life had always been scheduled by Atkinson. In the early days, he used to joke about having his every move timetabled: 'Don't forget, I'll need a number two at 0800 hours, Atkinson, right after breakfast – if we can fit it in.'

McKenzie was in charge now. He'd need to pack a bag, leave a note for the housekeeper and give her direct instructions to lie through her teeth to Atkinson if he called. Turning to his little phone number index, he slid the dial down to *C*, then pressed a button. The list of handwritten numbers appeared, all the people he knew under that letter. Holding the phone receiver between his shoulder and ear, he dialled. When a voice answered, he spoke quickly.

'Hey, it's McKenzie. I need some advice. I just need to explain a few things first …'

***

McKenzie was driving up the M6 with Charley and Gary. Charley was easy enough to explain – he'd called her for a quick pep talk and some moral support before heading north, but Charley had taken it a step further.

'I'll be standing at the end of Landsdown Road in ten minutes,' she had said after McKenzie gave her a frantic, thirty-second summary of his situation.

'You'll be at the … what do you mean?' McKenzie had asked, confused.

'I'm coming with you, Mack. You can't do this on your own. You're clearly going to mess this up again,' Charley replied bluntly.

Charley lived just a six or seven-minute drive away in Notting Hill, and within twenty minutes they were heading out of London in McKenzie's ageing Golf GTI. As they neared the M40 slip road, they spotted a young man standing by the roadside, a backpack at his feet. His thumb was raised in the universal sign for a lift and a piece of cardboard in his hands had *Manchester* crudely scrawled on it.

'Oh, Mack, stop for that guy – we're literally heading where he needs to be,' Charley said.

'Absolutely not a chance in hell,' McKenzie replied, shocked at the very suggestion. 'Do you have any idea what Atkinson would say if I started pottering around the country picking up potential serial killers?'

'You mean you've never once hitchhiked, Mack? I don't believe it. He might be going home to see his mum or a sick relative – all he needs is someone to stop.'

McKenzie's thoughts drifted back to a warm summer night in 1973, just as he was on the verge of hitting the big time. Penniless, he had thumbed a lift to Birmingham to see Slade at the Town Hall, riding in an HGV lorry driven by an unsettling man called Neville. Neville spent the entire journey talking about his love of taxidermy, describing in disturbing detail how he preserved every creature that crossed his path. Without that ride with Neville, McKenzie never would have witnessed an astonishingly raw and loud performance by one of his favourite bands. He remembered it vividly: Slade played with electrifying intensity, driving the crowd into a frenzy – until, in a shocking and unexpected moment, drummer Don Powell suddenly collapsed. The aftereffects of a terrible car crash earlier that year had taken their toll.

McKenzie slammed on the brakes and pulled over just past the entrance to the slip road. Pumping his fist at this small victory, the man clumsily slung his bag over his shoulder and began half-running towards the car, the weight of the load slowing him down. He wore denim shorts and a T-shirt emblazoned with a Wham!-inspired *Choose Life* slogan across the front.

'Hi!' he said, throwing his bag into the back seat before clambering in beside it. 'Thank you so … hey, you look like McKenzie McCall!'

'Yes, it has been mentioned before,' McKenzie replied.

For the next two hours, they were regaled with Gary's life story, including his London-based girlfriend, whom his northern family disapproved of. He'd lied about attending a culinary exhibition at Earl's Court (Gary was a restaurant pot washer who dreamed of becoming a chef, much to his family's pride) to spend a steamy two nights with her, about which he went into *far* too much detail. His endless chatter was punctuated every few minutes with, 'You really *do* look like McKenzie McCall, you know?' When Gary was dropped off at the roadside somewhere near Manchester, he waved cheerfully, offering a final word of encouragement: McKenzie should consider a career as a McKenzie McCall look-alike, as he'd make an absolute packet. 'You might need to lose a bit of weight though, mate,' he added helpfully.

'At least you've got something to fall back on if you really can't come up with another album,' Charley said, smiling as she stared straight ahead.

As McKenzie turned onto Andy's street, he slowed to a crawl.

'Number fifteen – watch for it. Odds are on the left,' he said as they inched down the narrow, terraced road.

'Is it that one? No, that's eleven … it must be – oh …' Charley's voice trailed off as McKenzie stopped in the middle of the street. Ahead of them stood a house that looked like it had been in a fight. The windows were streaked with smears of food, remnants of eggs or worse, splattered across the glass. Graffiti marred the walls and door, with scrubbed patches on the door where someone had tried – and failed – to clean it off, leaving parts starkly white against the grime.

'What in actual hell?' Charley breathed, staring in disbelief. 'What is happening in this country? That poor mum and her boy.'

'Toxic media, fuelling it,' McKenzie muttered. 'I'll go and see if he's in – hopefully I won't get torn to pieces by some local rabid mob.'

Leaving the engine running, McKenzie slipped out of the car and made his way to the battered front door. As he knocked, a door to his right shot open.

'You are Michael. Debbie's friend,' Mrs Silva said, more a statement than a question. McKenzie hesitated, then realised Andy must've given her a fake name. Smart kid, he thought.

'Ahh, yes, just on the way to the hospital now. We just need—'

'She is at hospital.' Mrs Silva said.

'Yes,' said McKenzie. 'We're on our way now. We just need—'

'Bridgewater Cross Hospital, it is an emergency. Ward 14A. Andy is there now. He will require people to support him.'

'Yes,' said McKenzie, turning and pointing to the car with the engine running and door open in the middle of the road. Charley gave a wave from the passenger seat. 'We're just going now.'

'You should get there quick,' said Mrs Silva, still looking him up and down.

'We're just going n—'

'Wait here!' Mrs Silva barked, turning around and closing the door, leaving McKenzie standing in the street. A moment later, the door opened again.

'Take these – for all of you, while you're waiting on news about Debbie.' She handed McKenzie a small Tupperware box filled with homemade biscuits.

'Thank you, that's … really kind,' said McKenzie. 'We'll get going now.'

'You need to be quick!' shouted Mrs Silva.

As McKenzie puffed back around to the driver's side, a blue Ford Transit van pulled up behind him, blaring its horn. A burly man leaned out of the open window, his arm waving impatiently as he glared at McKenzie through the windshield.

'Sorry!' McKenzie called, giving an apologetic salute towards the van. He wasn't used to dealing with actual members of the public – real, everyday people, not just fans he occasionally ran into – and for a moment, he wondered if the man might actually get out and punch him. Mouthing, 'Going now!' he gestured up the road with a thumb.

'Oi, mate … aren't you McKenzie McCall?' the man called, the irritation fading from his face. Dressed in typical builder's gear and a flat cap, he leaned out of his window with a wide, toothy grin. 'Well, I'll be! What are you doing driving a banger like that in this neck of the woods?'

'Yes, yes, that's me,' McKenzie replied with a forced grin. 'Just … out for a spin in my trusty Golf. Still does nought to sixty in nine seconds – not rusted at all, really. Reliable old thing.' He gave an awkward double thumbs-up. 'Anyway … have a pleasant evening!' He quickly ducked back into the car, collapsing into the driver's seat and passing Charley the

Tupperware. He sat gripping the wheel, staring straight ahead, momentarily replaying the entire cringeworthy exchange.

'Well, that was embarrassing,' Charley commented matter-of-factly. She had slouched so far down in her seat that her woolly bucket hat practically covered her entire face.

McKenzie accelerated to the end of the road and turned around. On the way back up, they passed the van again, now parked and the man gave an enthusiastic beep and waved as if they were old friends.

'It's funny, isn't it?' McKenzie mused, as they pulled back onto the main road. 'A horn always makes the same sound, but sometimes it comes across as friendly and other times as angry. How does that work?'

'Fascinating, Mack. Truly,' Charley replied, rolling her eyes and reaching into the Tupperware box. 'How about we focus on finding Andy and Debbie and leave that one to the horn experts … oh my, these biscuits are divine!'

When McKenzie and Charley arrived at the hospital car park, it was peak visiting hour and not a single space was in sight. They circled a few times, passing through the barrier, then back out and in again.

'There's one, Mack!' Charley cried, pointing ahead.

As they approached the space – clearly first – another car, a red Austin Metro complete with fluffy dice dangling from the rear-view mirror, rounded the corner from a line of parked vehicles and accelerated toward it.

'No chance, lady. That space is ours,' McKenzie said, gripping the steering wheel tightly.

Both cars came to a halt, facing off, inching forward in a tense game of chicken. The driver of the other car was a young woman with crimped hair, 'Nothing's Gonna Stop

Us Now' blaring from her radio. She leaned forward, her face set with determination. But then her mouth fell open. Recognition dawned as she realised she was having a stand-off with an international rock star – his jaw clenched, eyes focused and not about to back down.

'I'll just, erm, park up. That OK?' McKenzie mouthed, pointing politely toward the space.

The young woman nodded slowly, staring at him in disbelief.

When Charley and McKenzie got out of the car, locking the door with the key, the young woman was still sitting there. Her hands clutched the steering wheel and her mouth remained slightly open.

'Thank you!' McKenzie called cheerfully, giving her a quick wave.

Her wide eyes followed them, unblinking, as they strolled across the car park. The sun was setting behind the hospital, casting a watery orange glow across the sky. At the main entrance, a cluster of uncomfortable-looking patients in various plaster casts were smoking outside. McKenzie and Charley joined the queue at the reception desk.

'Yes?' said a stern-looking older woman, peering over a pair of wire-framed glasses. She eyed McKenzie and Charley as if they'd wandered into the hospital solely to test her patience.

McKenzie stepped forward. 'Ahh, *good evening*,' he replied in the pointed way people do when they feel a greeting offered to them wasn't friendly enough. Charley nudged him in the ribs. 'We're here to visit a friend of ours – Ward 14A. If you'd be so kind as to point us in the right direction, it would be frightfully appreciated.'

Charley stepped on his foot. 'You really aren't used to talking to normal people, are you?' she whispered. 'What's going on with your voice?'

'Ward 14A?' the woman replied briskly, shaking her head as she flipped through a large book in front of her. 'We don't use letters in our ward numbers.'

'I've been informed it's most certainly 14A,' McKenzie insisted.

Charley shot him another look. Even McKenzie wasn't entirely sure where the tone of solemn formality had appeared from. The lady's finger hovered over something in her book and her eyebrows raised.

'Ah, I see,' she said crisply, glaring at them over her glasses before lowering her voice. 'Head to Ward 14. Through these doors and to the right, you'll find a sign for 14A. It's… a *new* ward.'

'Great, thanks ever so much,' replied McKenzie. He found himself strangely enjoying these interactions with the general public – the variety of personalities was unexpectedly refreshing and he fancied he was getting better at it with each exchange.

Winding through long corridors with gleaming tiled floors and the unmistakable scent of disinfectant hanging in the air, they went in search of Andy and Debbie. After a turn into yet another corridor, they finally reached Ward 14 at the end. Through the large double doors, they could see a team of nurses bustling around a large, curved wooden desk. An elderly woman clunked past with a walking frame and one of the nurses came around to gently guide her by the elbow, leading her out of view.

'Alright, so that's Ward 14… but where's 14A?' McKenzie

said, pressing his face against the glass panel in the doors and squinting down the ward.

'It's here, Mack. Look …' Charley pointed to a plain wooden door to their right. Two sheets of A4 paper, with a *14* and an *A* crudely printed on them, were blue-tacked above it. The *A* had slipped, so it was hanging at an angle.

'Well, that's a welcoming entrance to a ward,' McKenzie muttered.

Charley opened the door, peeking around before swinging it wider. 'Come on, Mack, it's through here.'

They stepped into a dim, narrow corridor which felt like an abandoned office area. The walls were bare and the harsh glow of fluorescent tubes overhead did little to lift the gloom. Ahead was a small, battered table that looked like a leftover school desk, cluttered with clipboards. Two nurses stood over it, absorbed in the paperwork. Doors lined both sides of the corridor, leading to small rooms.

Just as McKenzie and Charley started towards the nurses, a gentleman shuffled out from one of the rooms. He wore a thick dressing gown over checked pyjamas and a crutch supported his hunched frame. A bony ankle protruded over his slippers. The man paused to cough, his hand lifting to his mouth, showing dark purple lesions on his thin, sallow skin. His face was gaunt and he had wisps of hair barely covering his scalp. A few days of stubble dusted his jaw and his skin had a slight yellowish hue. When his coughing fit subsided, he nodded at McKenzie and Charley before slowly hobbling up the corridor, the crutch wedged firmly under his arm.

'I can't do this, Charley,' McKenzie said, his voice faltering. 'I don't have the skills – I don't have the … I don't know, the experience to handle this. I won't know what to say. I'll just sit there, in the way, like some big, insensitive lump.'

Charley rolled her eyes at him for the fourth time in two hours. 'Don't be ridiculous, Mack. What, you're just going to turn around and go home now that we're here? You know you're not going to do that. Come on.'

One of the nurses looked up and smiled at Charley, then did a noticeable double-take when her eyes landed on McKenzie. She was young, dressed in a navy blue uniform, with brown hair neatly pinned into a bun beneath a white nursing cap.

'Hi! Andy mentioned you'd be coming. We didn't really know what to believe but he was adamant that McKenzie McCall would be visiting – made us swear we wouldn't tell anyone. I'm Angie,' she said with a smile.

The man was now at the end of the corridor, still coughing and breathless, his face turning red. The second nurse put down her clipboard and hurried to his side, gently patting his back.

'Yes, I was keen to come, you know, for Andy and Debbie. Andy said she wasn't very well and we're here to wish her a speedy recovery and hope she's home soon. But I don't really know what to expect … is that old gent OK?' McKenzie asked, still watching as the nurse tried to help the struggling patient.

'Old gentleman?' Angie replied, glancing back. 'He's thirty-seven. Bad chest – pneumonia. It's pretty common for patients here. Let's get you to Debbie.'

As they walked, Angie spoke in a gentle tone.

'We find that honesty is the best policy around here. I'm not sure Debbie will be going home, McKenzie. Do you know what the plan is for Andy?'

'She won't be allowed home?' McKenzie asked, taken aback.

'Not many AIDS patients come here and then go home,' she explained calmly. 'By the time they reach us, their bodies are usually weak. We're here to provide end-of-life care.'

McKenzie and Charley locked eyes briefly.

'You OK?' she asked.

'I guess I just…' McKenzie shook his head and gave a small, lost shrug.

'This isn't just some grand gesture, is it, Mack? Not just a rock-star stunt, where you get to play the role of saviour?'

McKenzie looked at the floor. She was right. He was coming to realise he was properly invested.

He turned to Angie. 'I understand, sorry,' he replied, flustered. 'I don't really know what Debbie wants for Andy … we haven't had that kind of conversation. I mean, they're not really my responsibility.'

McKenzie was panicking, caught up in something that felt too heavy, too personal – something he didn't have to be a part of. But he heard how that must have sounded and added quickly, 'I mean, I'm not family, but we'll try to talk to Debbie.'

'We're here for them – we'll do what it takes,' Charley chipped in, slightly more reassuringly.

'That's good,' replied Angie. 'I don't know what your relationship to them is, but they are going to need all the support they can get.'

The three of them reached the door to Debbie's room. Through the glass panel, McKenzie could see Andy sitting on the bed, one knee drawn up and the other leg dangling over the edge. He looked so young as he held Debbie's hand, his eyes fixed on her sleeping face. Looking small and fragile in the hospital bed, Debbie's frame was even thinner than McKenzie remembered. In the corner, Pam was tidying the bedside table, gently lifting a cup to wipe underneath then carefully rearranging a few belongings on top.

'She had a seizure today,' Angie explained. 'She's been vomiting so much that her body hasn't been able to absorb enough sugar, causing her blood sugar levels to drop dramatically. From Debbie's medical notes, we can see she's chosen to stop her AZT medication. It's a common choice – sometimes the side effects are too overwhelming. At this point, though, our focus is on managing her pain and keeping her as comfortable as possible.'

'You mean this could be it?' McKenzie asked, struggling to take it in.

Angie nodded gently. 'It could be days, maybe weeks. From experience, we believe she'll likely fade, but sometimes patients surprise us. Occasionally, they rally and there's an improvement.' She paused, apparently searching for the right words. 'The reality is, her body is shutting down, weakened by the virus. Her organs will start failing. But for so many of these patients, their hearts are still young, strong, built to last decades longer. And that heart keeps on trying, making it difficult to let go.'

Her voice faltered and to McKenzie's shock, he saw tears welling up in her eyes as she tried to steady herself. Charley reached over, placing a comforting hand on her arm, quietly grounding them all.

Angie gave a weary smile. 'I've seen so many young men pass through here. Debbie is the first woman I've treated. But they're all in their prime, full of life and creativity.

The world is losing people who could've done even more amazing things. Sometimes it feels like we're all alone here. This was just a cluster of admin offices before they hurriedly converted it into an AIDS ward. Then they left us to pretty much manage on our own. My boyfriend thinks I'm crazy for staying but so few staff volunteered to work here. When AIDS patients first started coming in, I saw how they were treated – suddenly there'd be no beds, no one willing to do a scan. People didn't want to be near them. At least here, we can show a little humanity.' She paused again, her voice tinged with tiredness. 'But I go home in tears after most shifts. The exhaustion, the frustration … it can be a lot to take.'

They all paused a moment longer, gazing through the small glass panel. Inside, Pam noticed them standing by the door and Angie gave a soft knock before opening it. 'Hi Andy, hi Pam! Well, you promised me McKenzie McCall and here he is,' she said with a smile, holding the door open. 'Come on in, McKenzie – and Charley too.'

There was a brief, awkward silence as McKenzie realised both Charley and Angie were waiting for him to speak first.

'Hi, Andy … and, um, Pam,' McKenzie began, clearing his throat. 'We just thought we'd stop by, you know, to say hi. Pam – Debbie and Andy have become, well … friends, and I was talking with Andy earlier. He mentioned Debbie wasn't feeling too well tonight so I thought I'd come by and check in on everyone.' He paused, feeling slightly unsure. 'Oh, and this is Charley. She, um, works for … she works with me sometimes.'

Andy beamed up at him, casting a hopeful look back to see if Debbie might wake. Pam, meanwhile, calmly folded a cardigan, draped it over the back of a chair and looked mildly puzzled by the presence of a past-his-prime rock star in the room.

'It's nice of you to come. Andy's been telling me you've made a few pop records and have been in the hit parade in the past – it all sounds fascinating. There's not much to do right now; Debbie's sleeping and she's had quite a strong dose of pain relief. I'll make a coffee and call Brian – Andy's grandad. He … he wasn't quite ready to visit tonight but he'll need to come by later to take me and Andy home. Can I get you anything?'

McKenzie and Charley both shook their heads, thanking her as Charley opened the door for her to pass through. She nodded and gave them a sad smile as she passed, leaving them alone with Andy. He tenderly stroked Debbie's hand, like a loyal guard dog. McKenzie felt useless again – he was hopeless in situations like this. He'd never really known how to talk to children – never had to.

'How you doing, Andy?' he asked, his voice unsure. 'I mean, I know things *aren't* great, but … are you OK? I know you're *not* OK, but …'

Charley sat down next to Andy at the end of the bed.

'It's a good job he sings better than he talks, isn't it, Andy?' she said. Andy smiled and McKenzie gave an exaggerated yes-I'm-rubbish-at-this-kind-of-thing shrug. McKenzie walked round to the other side of the bed and sank into a plastic chair. The window was beside him and it was darkening outside – but it was a summery dark, with the sky holding on to a touch of light.

Charley chatted with Andy about a variety of topics, putting him at ease. Slowly, Andy's initial shyness faded and he began to open up in return. McKenzie silently thanked God for Charley's presence and admired how naturally she could do this – bringing conversation effortlessly. Andy shared stories about school, how he'd been banned from going and how Mr Harris had changed so suddenly. Angie popped in to check on Debbie's temperature and pulse. Debbie stirred, her eyes flickering open. She asked for some water and Andy sprang into action, pouring it from a jug on the bedside unit. She gave a sleepy nod in McKenzie and Charley's direction.

'You came back,' she murmured to McKenzie. 'I knew you would.'

She apologised for being so tired before quickly drifting back to sleep.

Pam re-entered the room. 'Andy, we should start getting ready to go. Grandad's coming to pick us up,' she said.

Andy nodded, but his face crumpled. 'I don't want to leave her,' he said, tears welling up. 'I don't want her to be alone.'

'I know, Andy,' Pam replied, rubbing his shoulders. 'I don't want to leave her either but she's sleeping and she'd want you to have some rest. We'll come back tomorrow. After a good night's sleep, she might feel a little better.'

Andy stroked his mum's hand again before getting up to kiss her on the cheek.

'We can come back too, if that's OK with you, Andy?' Charley asked, shooting McKenzie a quick look. He nodded uncertainly. Andy looked at Pam, who gave him an agreeing shrug. Nodding eagerly, he wiped away a tear that had escaped his eye.

McKenzie and Charley strolled through the hospital corridors. Charley paused at a kiosk to buy a packet of

Pacers and a Marathon. As they reached the entrance hall, McKenzie gestured towards the payphones.

'Shall we call a hotel and book in, rather than drive back to London?' he asked. 'Can you call the operator and get The Quayside's number? You're so much better at this stuff than me.'

Charley considered this for a moment as she sucked on a Pacer, then nodded.

'I always book under the name Martin Heade,' McKenzie said.

Charley raised an eyebrow.

'He was an underrated painter in the 1800s. Liked to keep himself to himself – but I love his work,' McKenzie explained.

'You know, McKenzie, you're more cultured than you let on.' Charley paused, then added with a wink, 'We can share a room, but two beds – and no funny business.'

McKenzie smiled, struck by the way her large brown eyes sparkled with mischief.

16

ndy slept soundly at his gran's house. On his way downstairs, he paused halfway, drawn in by the smell of bacon, sausages and toast. He could hear Pam and Brian talking in the kitchen.

'… for goodness' sake, Brian, she's your daughter and she's seriously ill. They don't even know if she'll …' His gran's voice trembled and trailed off.

'I can't tell anyone what she's got, Pam. Imagine what they'd say at the club. "Where's your daughter been, eh, Brian?" It's embarrassing. None of it makes sense. For God's sake, look at the newspaper today – it's full of this bloody AIDS stuff.'

Pam was washing a few items in the sink, crockery clinking sharply as she made her frustration clear. Andy shifted on the stairs and they creaked beneath him.

'Quiet now, Brian. Here's Andy.'

Pam had gone all out with breakfast, insisting that Andy was too thin and needed to eat more, since he was a growing lad. Brian sat at the table, hidden behind his newspaper but Andy could feel the tension between his grandparents. After breakfast, Andy made his way to Manchester by bus, a five-pound note from his gran tucked into his pocket. He headed straight for Superdrug, having decided Debbie needed a little pampering. After some consideration, he dropped a tube of Nivea hand cream into his basket, followed by some shampoo. Debbie's lips had looked dry, so he added a small tin of Vaseline. Finally, he picked out a soft sponge and a fruity bar of soap that looked – and smelled – good enough to eat. It felt liberating to be doing something positive, to have a purpose for the morning and Andy walked with a bounce in his step.

At the checkout, the young girl behind the counter eyed him curiously. She tapped the price of each item into the register, then placed the items in a bag. Her name badge read *Julie* and she chewed gum as she worked.

'That'll be £2.80. I think I saw you on the news? They wouldn't let you in school because your mum's ill?'

Andy's heart sank, his bubble bursting. Keeping his head down, he nodded, feeling himself shrink back. He waited for the inevitable ignorant remark.

'I felt really sorry for you,' she said finally. 'What a horrible way to treat you and your mum, especially when she's unwell. This country's going down the pan, if you ask me. I blame Maggie.'

Andy looked up, a faint smile flickering across his face. He held out his five-pound note. The girl looked at it briefly before taking it from him. She handed Andy his change.

'I saw Princess Di on the telly talking to people with that illness. I hope you and your mum keep fighting,' she said with a determined nod, then leaned back, twirling her hair as she watched him walk away.

Next, Andy headed to Woolworths to pick up a few treats for his mum, just in case she felt up to enjoying them – a Curly Wurly chocolate bar and some pick 'n' mix. As he browsed, he spotted a small decorative wicker basket on display and decided to add it to his purchases, thinking it would be a nice way to arrange everything.

Finally, he stopped at a greengrocer's shop near Piccadilly Station and picked up a bunch of grapes – soft and hydrating, something he thought might be soothing for his mum. Feeling pleased with his thoughtful choices, Andy made his way back to the bus stop, eager to get back to his gran's and head to the hospital with his little basket of treats.

***

Spending the day at the hotel, McKenzie and Charley savoured the rare quietness and freedom away from the bustle of London life. McKenzie had always liked hotels – he was recognised, of course, but people generally left him in peace. By early afternoon, with a sense of purpose, he stepped through the reception area and headed towards the entrance.

'Would sir like me to call a chauffeur?' asked the doorman, dressed smartly in a long navy coat with gold buttons and a bowler hat.

'No, no, that's fine – just popping out for a bit, thank you,' McKenzie replied with a nod.

He strolled the streets until he found a corner shop, where he picked up a few items for Debbie – a box of Cadbury's Milk Tray and a couple of bottles of wine. McKenzie made sure to always have a bit of cash on him after the café humiliation, recognising that maybe he was growing as a person. On his way back, he spotted a florist, ducked inside and asked them to put together a bouquet.

'Sorry if I'm mistaken, but aren't you McKenzie McCall? What brings you to Manchester? You touring?' asked the lady behind the counter as she tied the flowers together, wrapping them carefully in clear plastic.

'God, *no*,' McKenzie replied instinctively, but then offered a friendly smile. 'I'm just up from London for a few days, running some errands. It's non-stop sometimes, isn't it?'

After signing a few autographs and agreeing to a request to have a quick chat with the florist's mother, who needed proof he was really McKenzie McCall and wouldn't believe it until he sang a few lines, McKenzie was delayed a little longer than expected. Finally, he returned to the hotel room where Charley was waiting.

'The flowers are a nice touch, Mack, but wine? What were you thinking? You can't take wine to a hospital,' Charley said, shaking her head with a half-smile.

'Well, I thought the flowers would brighten up the place,' McKenzie replied, unruffled. 'And the wine? If she does rally, she might want a sneaky glass when the nurses aren't looking.'

Charley laughed. 'You're a real softie, aren't you? But two bottles? That's pushing it.'

'Who said the other bottle was for her?' McKenzie grinned. 'I can't face another awkward chat with Andy without a bit of help.' He paused, then added, 'I'd better ring Atkinson – he's probably tearing his hair out by now, well, if he had any.' With a small flourish, McKenzie produced a single white rose from behind his back. 'Oh, and this one's for you. To say thank you.'

Charley took the rose, her eyes lighting up as she lifted it to her nose. McKenzie smiled and picked up the hotel phone between their beds to call Atkinson.

'Atkinson? McKenzie!' he said, mimicking Atkinson's usual tone and giving Charley a playful smirk.

'McKenzie, where in God's name are you?' Atkinson's voice crackled with irritation. 'I called the house and your housekeeper told me you were holed up in the basement with your guitars. Well, I knew *that* was a lie straight away!'

'I just nipped out, buying flowers,' McKenzie replied, with a trace of innocence in his tone.

'Flowers! Who on earth are you buying flowers for? Don't be a loose cannon and get us into more trouble, Mack. Sometimes I think I don't even know who you are any more. *Flowers?* Right, listen to me – I'm going to need a couple more days. I'm close to landing you a new record deal. It's a smaller label, but they're keen to get a big name on their books, even if it's a big name on the slide. We're in negotiations but there are a few kinks to work out. They can't have it all their own way, even if you are damaged goods. I'll fax over the paperwork once it's finalised – I don't want you claiming later that I'd *coerced* you into it. I know how you like to toss these accusations around willy-nilly. Just give me two more days, Mack, and then we'll hit the ground running with a proper strategy. We'll sort it, Mack.'

'Two more days, Atkinson? Perfect,' McKenzie replied.

17

When McKenzie and Charley arrived at Ward 14A that evening, the atmosphere was noticeably different – charged with an energy that felt out of place. Once the door shut behind them, it was as if this ward existed in its own universe, a place where the usual hospital rules and routines didn't apply.

'Nothing to do with me!' Angie quipped playfully, raising her hands in mock innocence as McKenzie and Charley passed the makeshift desk. As they made their way down the corridor, each room was unusually full. Young men and women crowded around the beds, filling the air with low, excited chatter. As McKenzie approached a room on the right, he caught a whispered, 'He's coming. It's him!' followed by a flurry of giggles. Inside, faces turned eagerly, grins spreading as heads craned back, eager for a glimpse of McKenzie McCall.

McKenzie could never quite shake the feeling that he was an unlikely source of fascination. Yet news of his appearance the previous night had clearly swept through the patients' families and friends, drawing every possible visitor all at once. But there was something else, too. The usual sombre quietness had lifted, replaced by a lively buzz of laughter and chatter that softened the sterile walls of the ward, making it feel strangely comforting and homely.

As McKenzie and Charley reached Debbie's open door, Andy was perched on the bed in almost the exact same way as yesterday. This time, Debbie was sitting up, looking thin but alert, her eyes bright. Both she and Andy turned to greet their guests with warm smiles as McKenzie manoeuvred through the doorway, juggling the bouquet of flowers and the bag.

'Well, look who it is – McKenzie McCall! Clearly no one was expecting *you* tonight,' Debbie deadpanned. She nodded towards the flowers. 'Are those for me? Anyone would think I was on death's door in a hospital. Thank you, McKenzie – they're really lovely.'

McKenzie put the flowers on the bedside table.

'Nice to see you, Debbie. Uh … I brought this too.' McKenzie leaned in to kiss her cheek, then meekly handed her the carrier bag. Debbie pulled out a wine bottle, turning it to inspect the label before letting out a low whistle.

'McKenzie, that's naughty,' she said, feigning disapproval. 'This is a hospital – you can't just bring in bottles of fine French wine.'

Charley stepped forward, extending her hand, which Debbie shook with a warm smile.

'Hi, I'm Charley, a friend of Mack's. I warned him about the wine but he wouldn't listen. Here's something a little more sensible – chocolates.'

'Oh, nonsense!' Debbie replied with a grin. 'Hand me one of those plastic cups, Andy. I'm having some now! This looks like a nice bottle – beats the stuff I usually get from Kwik Save. Now, the question is, how are we getting this cork out?'

'She's not just a friend,' McKenzie felt compelled to clarify. 'Charley here is a famous, in-demand record producer – she's got three songs in the top twenty right now, all produced by her. This is one talented woman.' He paused as Andy and Debbie glanced between him and Charley quizzically as he patted his pockets fruitlessly. 'Oh, pants – I didn't think to bring a corkscrew!'

Angie appeared in the doorway. McKenzie quickly shifted to block her view of the wine bottle.

'Everything OK, Debbie?' Angie asked, ignoring the four guilty-looking faces.

'All good here, Angie, thanks! We, uh … just need a corkscrew. You know, for some, um, juice …'

'Debbie!' Angie mock-scolded, eyebrows raised. 'This is a hospital – why on earth would we have a corkscrew lying around?'

'Well, that's that, then,' Debbie muttered when they were alone again. But a moment later, Angie reappeared, holding a corkscrew in the air.

'One of the young lads in the other room had one on his key ring. Here you go,' she said, winking. 'And I haven't seen that bottle. Got it?'

Debbie sat contentedly sipping her wine, chatting animatedly about how Andy had been spoiling her with his basket of gifts. An IV drip was hooked up beside her and bruising mottled her arm.

'He's a good lad, isn't he?' Charley said, playfully ruffling Andy's hair.

'Should I take this back to them?' Andy asked, holding up the corkscrew.

'I'll do it,' McKenzie volunteered, prompting Charley to raise an amused eyebrow; it was nice to see him looking more relaxed and down-to-earth. McKenzie strolled out of the room and moments later, whoops and cheers echoed down the corridor. His arrival in the other room was clearly a hit.

'Are you two an item?' Debbie asked Charley with zero subtlety, nodding towards the door McKenzie had just exited. Charley smiled.

'Nooo, nothing like that. I worked with him for a bit but we paused because … well, sometimes it happens with writing albums. But he is an amazing songwriter and honestly, he's a nice guy under that cool, gruff exterior.'

'So, that's a yes, then,' Debbie quipped. Andy grinned and nodded in agreement.

McKenzie didn't return for a good ten minutes and when he finally reappeared, he paused in the doorway. 'So, I'm in Matthew's room with some friends – Matthew's the guy we saw in the corridor yesterday. They want me to grab my old guitar,' he said, shaking his head as if to say, *and I have no idea how they talked me into it*. He tossed Charley his car key. 'It's in the boot. I'm actually in the middle of a card game. Would you mind? Thanks so much.'

All three of them raised their eyebrows this time. Charley went to retrieve McKenzie's guitar, scolding him for keeping something so valuable tossed in the boot of his car. McKenzie shrugged, pointing out that no one would bother with his old, rusty Golf – and besides, he liked keeping the guitar close by. As Charley crossed the hospital car park, it struck her that she was holding one of the world's most iconic musical instruments: the *Old Special*. Returning to Matthew's room, she found McKenzie seated with about seven other visitors, all gathered in a loose circle around Matthew's bed. Matthew looked incredibly poorly – his skin discoloured and his face puffy from the medication, with the rest of his body alarmingly underweight. Despite it all, he beamed with unrestrained delight at the sight of the guitar.

Wrapped in a blanket, Debbie sat on a chair with her legs tucked up to her body, a plastic cup of wine in hand. A few more bottles had appeared from people's bags, adding to the casual, makeshift atmosphere. Someone placed their cards down in a fan shape on the bed, a satisfied smile on their face and a cheer went up to celebrate the winner. Charley handed McKenzie his guitar from its case, and the room fell silent. He strummed a few chords, listening intently, adjusting the tuning on the neck before strumming again – ever the professional, even for this intimate gathering. A couple more people entered the room, standing by the door expectantly and another patient was wheeled in by Angie. McKenzie glanced around at the expectant faces.

'This is the scariest gig of my life,' he said, prompting laughter.

McKenzie strummed the opening chords of one of his few ballads released as a single, 'When We Met'. His voice felt out of shape – he hadn't sung in a while and the effects of too many drinks in recent weeks were evident. The first verse was shaky but as he continued, he started to find his rhythm, the warmth of the music slowly returning. The song seemed to fit the mood of the room and when he finished, a burst of applause followed. A few of the young visitors wiped tears from their eyes.

'Well, that was self-indulgent, doing one of my own,' he joked. 'Maybe something a little livelier – a song from my old mate, Freddie?'

Cheers erupted and McKenzie stood up, launching into the upbeat opening chords of 'Crazy Little Thing Called Love'. He laughed as the visitors stood up and began clapping along. Flicking the hair out of his eyes, McKenzie caught Charley's gaze. It had been happening more often lately and she gave him a playful giggle, raising her cup in a silent toast. After Queen, he played Elton John's 'I'm Still Standing', followed by The Drifters' timeless classic 'Save the Last Dance for Me'. By this point, McKenzie was strolling up and down the corridor with his guitar, the crowd of visitors and patients clapping in rhythm. Andy danced behind him enthusiastically, adding to the impromptu celebration.

Eventually, after a string of '70s and '80s classics, McKenzie, Charley, Andy, and Debbie found themselves back in Matthew's room. The visitors had started to drift away, leaving them chatting with Matthew and another man who had remained by the bed, his hand resting gently on top of Matthew's. Up close, Matthew wasn't just thin – he was skeletal. Propped up in bed, he seemed too weak to lift his head from the pillow. On a table next to him was a framed holiday photo of two tall, muscular young men in shorts and vests, their bronzed physiques on full display as they stood with their arms around each other's shoulders. Charley pointed towards the picture.

'Are those your brothers, Matthew?'

Matthew turned his neck slowly towards the photo.

'Brothers? That's us two, on holiday last year. Me and Mark,' he said, gesturing to the man beside him.

Charley's face fell. 'Oh my gosh, I'm so sorry,' she said, her voice filled with regret. 'I just … I'm so sorry.'

'I've got AIDS too,' Mark said quietly. 'Matthew's has progressed a little faster than mine. I want to do everything I can for him while I still feel well enough myself.'

'I'm so sorry,' Charley said again, her voice barely above a whisper.

'I was an architect,' Matthew said, still gazing at the photo. 'I was handsome wasn't I? I lived a pretty wild life in the early eighties, burning the candle at both ends – things were so good. My career was really taking off; I designed some of the new buildings you see around Manchester City Centre. Then I met Mark here. He was an architect too and we just hit it off. I was so happy. I finally had a reason to slow down and settle.' He paused, taking a breath before continuing. 'But within the first year of our relationship, we were both diagnosed with HIV. I started becoming forgetful, making mistakes I wouldn't normally make. And then the Kaposi lesions started to show. I think my co-workers at the firm began to suspect. I was called into the boss's office and he told me that they were restructuring the workforce and my services were no longer required.'

'That's loyalty for you,' Debbie remarked from her chair, shaking her head. 'But you *are* architects, not *were*. Don't let them take that from you.'

Later that evening, after Matthew had nodded off and Debbie had returned to bed too, McKenzie, Charley and Andy sat around her as she slept. McKenzie still had the guitar resting on his knee, his arms draped over it. Andy yawned.

'We need to contact your gran to pick you up. You must be shattered, Andy,' Charley said.

Andy nodded, his eyes watering from the strain of yawning. 'Thank you for coming. I know you have to go back to London soon but you won't forget about us this time, will you?'

The addition of 'this time' hit McKenzie like a punch to the stomach.

'No, Andy. We're not going to forget about you,' McKenzie said, his voice firm. 'You can have my number and we'll stay in touch with Pam. That's a promise.'

McKenzie wasn't sure he wanted to return to his life as a fading rock star in London. The people on this ward – the communities and families affected, the nurses working tirelessly to support patients in their final days, all while facing prejudice – were in a *real* struggle against the world. There was something here that mattered, something he couldn't ignore. A silent struggle, hidden from the world – *a silent struggle*. McKenzie strummed his guitar again, a couple of minor chords creating a melancholic effect, followed by a few major chords.

'I'll phone your gran, Andy,' Charley said, getting up and leaving the room. She glanced at McKenzie and his guitar and he caught something in her expression. *A silent struggle*. He strummed again, then started humming along with the chords. The humming slowly shifted into random words, then full lines as he stared out the window, his eyes distant. McKenzie adjusted the melody as he went, the way he always did when a song was beginning to take shape. He reached into the pocket of his jacket, which was hanging over the back of the chair and pulled out his Dictaphone.

It had been a while since he'd done this. Pressing the record button, he placed the device on the table in front of him and began experimenting with the chords again. He repeated each line a few times, refining it as he went along.

In the hours before midnight, when the light is gone,
There's a silent struggle, a fight battling on.
Faces wear a painted smile, hiding pain beneath,
There's a silent struggle …

McKenzie paused, his eyes drifting to Debbie, who lay asleep in the bed in front of him.

'*… of hope but also grief?*' Andy finished the line. McKenzie looked at him, nodding, his fingers still gently strumming. For the first time in a long while, something clicked inside him. He could feel Andy's eyes on him, his expectation, and it spurred him on.

Charley returned to the room and paused as she heard McKenzie playing and singing softly. She glanced at them both. McKenzie adjusted the chord sequence for the chorus and Andy chimed in with some lyrics.

Every step, every mile of voices left unheard,
There's a silent struggle, a fight with unspoken words.
Through the darkness, they carry the flame,
There's a silent struggle, seeking justice, not to blame.

Charley stood quietly, watching the moment unfold.

'Well, you two *have* been busy, haven't you? I was only gone a few minutes. Andy, your gran will be here in twenty. I suggest we get the rest done while we're on a roll,' Charley said, sitting on the edge of her seat. McKenzie nodded. Charley was always alert to the potential of a song.

McKenzie shifted the key and strummed a few chords. Now, his instinct was kicking in – the familiar creative flow, the way it used to be when he wrote songs.

'Silent struggle,' he sang.

'… with dreams that fade away,' Charley echoed.

'Silent struggle …' he repeated, letting the words linger in the quiet.

'… when the night turns to day,' Andy added, his face lighting up with a huge smile.

In the next twenty minutes, they wrote two more verses, repeated the chorus and McKenzie had just begun experimenting with a bridge section when Andy's gran arrived to collect him.

We stand together – in the silence we confide.
We stand together – the truth we mustn't hide.
We stand together – our tears that fall unseen.
We stand together – we live, we fight, we dream.

As the final line hung in the air, McKenzie looked at Charley and Andy, a sense of startled accomplishment settling between them. Pam stuck her head through the doorway.

'How's the patient? I hear she's had a good day. You ready, Andy?'

Debbie stirred, opening her eyes. 'I'd be even better if he hadn't been strumming that bloody guitar for the last thirty minutes. There's people trying to sleep round here.'

18

Driving back down a nearly deserted motorway under a purple sky, McKenzie and Charley sat in companionable silence, both bracing themselves for a return to their 'normal' lives.

'You know what we have to do tomorrow, don't you?' Charley said at last, looking over at McKenzie, who kept his eyes on the road. He knew exactly what she meant. 'Silent Struggle', sitting on the tiny tape in his Dictaphone, was crying out for completion. Yet already, his thoughts were leaping ahead, swirling with fragments of a new song. 'A Shadow of Hope' was taking shape in his mind and for the first time in ages, he felt a surge of confidence – more songs would come. Words were waiting, ready to find their match in melody; chords were forming, eager to bring those lyrics to life.

The next day, Charley, McKenzie and his band assembled in the studio. McKenzie had slept less than four hours – a common occurrence when the spark of creativity struck him. But rather than feeling drained, he felt energised, his body buzzing with a rare vitality. In the early hours, he'd added 'Darkest Days' to his Dictaphone demos, quickly followed by the more uplifting, rock-infused 'Born to Soar'. Now, presenting four songs to the band, he was seasoned enough to read their reactions. Their immediate enthusiasm confirmed it: these were strong tracks.

'What do you mean you're in the studio?' Atkinson barked. 'I haven't booked you a studio. What studio? Where? Who with? Mack?' McKenzie swung on the chair in the control room, enjoying Atkinson's meltdown as he realised he wasn't in charge of whatever was happening.

'We're just putting some tracks together, you know, ones I wrote…' McKenzie replied, casually twisting the coiled phone cord around his finger and exchanging a silent laugh with Charley.

'Tracks? What tracks? This is out of order, Mack. You're becoming more reckless by the day. One minute you disappear off the face of the planet and the next you're laying down tracks. I am supposed to be your—'

'Atkinson, just close your mouth for a second and listen. Just *listen*. This is 'Silent Struggle'. I wrote it with some friends – it's still rough, but Charley's about to mix it into something a bit more polished.'

'Friends? What friends? "Silent Struggle" … sounds a bit limp, Mack. Like I said, I'm your manager—'

'Just *listen*, Atkinson,' McKenzie interrupted, keeping his voice steady. He held the phone receiver out and nodded to Charley, who pressed a white button which illuminated. The first chords rang out, soon joined by the bass and drums, building a subtle, steady rhythm. Then McKenzie's voice cut through, strong and clear:

In the hours before midnight, when the light is gone,
There's a silent struggle, a fight battling on.
Faces wear a painted smile, hiding pain beneath,
There's a silent struggle of hope, but also grief.

Every step, every mile of voices left unheard,
There's a silent struggle, a fight with unspoken words.
Through the darkness, they carry the flame,
There's a silent struggle, seeking justice, not to blame.

Silent Struggle – with dreams that fade away.
Silent Struggle – when the night turns into day.
Silent Struggle – they're carrying the light,
Silent Struggle – fighting the fight.

In the quiet whispers, hearts are torn apart,
There's a silent struggle, thoughts that won't depart.
With every tear, there's a story untold,
There's a silent struggle, in the shadows they hold.

The world may turn its eyes away,
There's a silent struggle happening today.
With courage, they rise and take a stand,
There's a silent struggle, hand in hand.

Silent Struggle – with dreams that fade away.
Silent Struggle – when the night turns into day.
Silent Struggle – they're carrying the light,
Silent Struggle – fighting the fight.

We stand together – in the silence we confide.

We stand together – the truth we mustn't hide.

We stand together – our tears that fall unseen.

We stand together – we live, we fight, we dream.

McKenzie and Charley exchanged a look as they listened. Charley tilted her head slightly, her trained ear catching any rough edges to smooth in the mix. As the last chord faded, McKenzie lifted the receiver back to his ear.

'Atkinson?'

Silence followed, presumably while Atkinson either picked his jaw up from the floor or blinked the pound signs from his eyes as his business instincts kicked in.

'Right, Mack, listen up. You're going to tell Charley she's not leaving that studio until the track is mixed – even if she needs to stay all night. We're pressing it to vinyl tomorrow and releasing it next week. We might even get it on a compact disc – your first CD single, Mack. We'll throw together a quick video with some old concert footage of you singing the slower songs, spliced with something poignant … maybe people looking sad in a park. I'll figure something out. I'm calling the record company – oh, and I got you the deal, by the way. It's sitting on your fax machine, but apparently you've been out buying flowers, so you might have missed it. We need a gig lined up as soon as the single drops. We'll sort it, Mack. This is going to be big. Now, finish those tracks and write some more – we need an album, ASAP.'

'Yes, Atkinson,' McKenzie replied and he meant it this time. He knew he could pull it off.

'Mack?' Atkinson barked.

'Yes, Atkinson?'

'I mean *now*, Mack. Get them finished *now!*'

'Yes, Atkinson.'

McKenzie put the phone down and Charley gave him a bemused frown.

'I think he liked the song,' McKenzie said.

***

With Charley's expert mixing touch, coupled with extra backing vocals from McKenzie and the band, the song was finally ready for release. Charley layered the vocals to create a choir effect of multi-tracked voices, giving the track a rousing finish. For the cover of the single, Atkinson chose an image taken a few years ago: McKenzie sitting on a stool, one leg on the floor, the other resting on one of the stool's bars. He was gazing down, appearing lost in sombre thought, illuminated by a single spotlight against a black background. Atkinson claimed there wasn't time to take a new cover shot, but McKenzie suspected it was because he was looking a bit trimmer back then. Months of indulging in Fortnum and Mason pork pies, crisps and red wine – combined with the creeping betrayal of a late-thirties metabolism – had left McKenzie carrying more padding than ever before.

McKenzie and Charley had spent nearly a week together, including some all-nighters, and had developed a strong creative bond. They made several trips to Manchester to visit Andy and Debbie on the ward. Debbie was looking brighter and had more energy and Andy eagerly shared the news that she might be allowed home.

'She's rallying,' Angie said, her tone cautious. 'We often

see this – the body's confused by what's happening. When people are desperate to live, a bit of extra fight can kick in.'

McKenzie and Charley put the finishing touches to the album. The songs had poured out of McKenzie, driven by a whirlwind of despair, hope and hopelessness. Something within him had been unleashed and the words and melodies kept flowing. During downtime, he would listen to music on his Sony Walkman, pacing around the studio's sofa area while Charley beavered away, mixing what they had just recorded. His headphones were always over his head, volume cranked up high, as he absorbed an eclectic mix of his favourite artists – Chris de Burgh, The Drifters, Slade, The Kinks, The Doors, Smokie, Diana Ross, Elton John, The Bee Gees, and Tina Turner – playing them on repeat to keep the inspiration pumping.

As McKenzie listened to Cliff Richard's *I'm Nearly Famous* album – one of his favourites – he noticed Jack, the drummer, waving frantically at him and making a phone gesture with his thumb and little finger. McKenzie slid the headphones down around his neck and entered the control room, where he grabbed the receiver which had been left on the mixing desk.

'Mack? Atkinson! I've booked Wembley – next Sunday, a week from today. They had one night free, so I just went for it. I've also got you some rehearsal time at the Shaw Theatre next week – it's where Queen rehearsed their Live Aid slot, so if it's good enough for Freddie, it's good enough for you. My nose is on the chopping block, Mack – you might sell ten tickets and then the wheels will really come off the boat, but 'Silent Struggle' is going to be huge next week. I've got some of our loyal DJs spinning it on the airwaves this weekend – Kenny Everett says he's going to play it non-stop on Capital Radio. Let's pack the place and give them the comeback gig of all comeback gigs.'

'Wembley? You've booked Wembley Stadium?' McKenzie spluttered. Atkinson always did this – delivered a torrent of information so quickly that McKenzie didn't even know where to start with the questions.

'Don't be ridiculous, Mack. I'm good – no, scratch that – I'm bloody brilliant, but even I don't pull miracles out of thin air. Wembley Arena, next Sunday. I've got the crew lined up, we'll dust off the lighting rig from storage and away we go. How's the album coming along?'

He always did that too – quick subject changes.

'Well, we've got nine tracks in the can – Charley is pulling it all together. I just want one more.'

'Nine tracks is fine, Mack! All the big artists only do nine now. Decide on the order, figure out how many tracks you want on the A-side and let's get it pressed – none of your usual faffing about. You need an album title too – "Silent Struggle" to go with the song?'

'No,' McKenzie said, remembering something Debbie had said – the bravery of it had stayed with him. 'It's going to be called *For Those Who Come Next*.'

Atkinson fell silent.

'For Those Who Come Next. For Those Who Come Next,' Atkinson repeated to himself. 'I don't get it, Mack, but maybe that's a good thing – a bit of mystery. I like that. Alright – get that album finished and let's start rehearsing. Everything's going to explode in the next few days. I told you I'd get McKenzie McCall back on the map. I told you we'd sort it!'

McKenzie couldn't help but think, as he put the phone down, that he was pretty sure it was him who had just written the album.

That night, McKenzie's melancholy mood gave way to something deeply personal and self-indulgent – the tenth song for the album. Perhaps a period of pushing himself out of his comfort zone in unfamiliar ways had spurred some overdue self-reflection, particularly about the direction his life had taken over the past few years. He realised he had always felt more at ease alone, though he hadn't fully recognised it at the time. Gradually, and almost unconsciously, he had begun to embrace solitude. For years, he had forced himself to chase the sociable life he had always dreamed of – one filled with a large circle of friends and family. But the effort had left him anxious and drained. Despite this, he still wished things were different. People had let him down – some drawn to his fame and fortune – but it went deeper than that. He struggled to keep people in his life and couldn't quite understand why. Friendships seemed to slip through his fingers, leaving him wondering if he was destined to remain on the periphery. More than anything, he hoped things would be different with Charley. In the end, this realisation inspired the song 'I'm Withdrawing into Myself', a poignant contemplation on his journey towards finding peace in the quiet life he had once resisted.

I tried to chase the laughter, the glow of crowded rooms,
Wore a mask of confidence, to hide the quiet gloom.
But every word felt hollow, a role I couldn't keep,
Now I find my solace, in the company I seek.

I'm withdrawing into myself, where the silence feels like home,
No more chasing shadows, is it better I'm alone?
There's a peace within the stillness, though the world may never see,
I'm learning to embrace the quiet side of me.

The noise of expectation, it lingers in my ears,
A symphony of voices amplifies my fears.
I play the part they ask for, the smile they want to see,
But the quietness of solitude is what sets my spirit free.

I'm withdrawing into myself, where the silence feels like home,
No more chasing shadows, is it better I'm alone?
There's a peace within the stillness,
though the world may never see,
I'm learning to embrace the quiet side of me.

You hoped I'd find the courage to dance among the crowd,
To leave behind the quiet and live the joy out loud.
But I could never follow the life you dreamed for me,
And in letting go of others, I lost what we could be.

I'm withdrawing into myself, where the silence feels like home,
No more chasing shadows, is it better I'm alone?
There's a peace within the stillness,
though the world may never see,
I couldn't be the person you really wanted me to be.

The next evening, McKenzie and Charley were sitting in Debbie's room on Ward 14A. By now, McKenzie was less of a novelty – greeted like a regular, though still signing a few autograph books and old albums each visit.

'Mum can go home in the morning,' Andy announced with a smile. 'She's gained a bit of strength – the doctor said so, didn't he, Mum?'

Debbie nodded. 'My mum will visit each day to help,' she said, 'and Mrs Silva wrote to say she's stocked the freezer and fridge with all sorts of cooked meals, she's cleaned the house and washed all our bedding. I'm hoping we can get Andy back in school soon. Since Princess Di spoke out, attitudes seem to be changing a little, so maybe things will shift. But we need a Plan B if not; he can't miss any more education – it's playing on my mind. There's only so much we can do together at home.'

Debbie's newfound vibrancy – she seemed so much brighter, a spark of her old fight returning – was both heartening and bittersweet, a reminder of her resilience despite her illness. When there was a lull in the conversation, Charley reached into her bag.

'We want to show you both something,' she said. She pulled out a pre-release copy of the 'Silent Struggle' vinyl single. 'We've been working hard … well, McKenzie has. I've just been pushing buttons and turning knobs. But we wanted you to have this – it's the song we wrote together last week, Andy. It's being released on Monday. Atkinson doesn't mess around.'

Andy took the record, staring at it with wide eyes.

'What Charley said isn't strictly true,' McKenzie said. 'The song sounds, hopefully, pretty good because of her round-the-clock talent – she's mixed my suspect guitar and vocals into something half-decent. It's teamwork. We just hope you like it and don't mind that we went ahead and recorded it.'

'I can't believe it – when you're home tomorrow, Mum, we can play it straight away!' Andy said excitedly.

Debbie nodded her approval, weary but clearly savouring Andy's joy.

'That's the first copy off the press, Andy. Want us to sign it? It might be worth something someday – if people remember an old dinosaur like me,' McKenzie added with a grin. Andy nodded eagerly and McKenzie pulled a pen from his jacket, writing, *To Andy, from YOUR biggest fan, McKenzie.* He passed the record to Charley, who added her signature accompanied by a squiggled smiley face.

As they were preparing to leave, McKenzie ducked into Matthew's room for a quick chat. Matthew was lying with his head at an awkward angle so Mark got up to help him turn towards McKenzie. They sat together quietly for a while, but McKenzie could see that the effort of listening and trying to communicate was exhausting Matthew. As he got up to leave, McKenzie hesitated, reaching into his pocket for his autograph pen. He scribbled a number onto an old newspaper lying on the bedside unit. 'Mark, if you need someone, that's my number, OK? Please reach out if needed.'

Mark nodded in thanks, his face sad and lost, as a silent understanding passed between them that Matthew didn't have long.

***

'I don't think he's ever going to let go of that,' Debbie said to Charley, nodding towards Andy who was still clutching the record as they waited for McKenzie to return. 'Thank you … both of you,' Debbie continued. 'Please thank McKenzie for me, he's not always the easiest to read but we really appreciate everything.'

Charley smiled. 'He's a big softy, really. Hey, Andy, there's one more thing. Turn over the record and look closely.'

Andy flipped it over. The back cover was simple, showing a beam of light cutting through the darkness. He scanned the tiny print showing the track listing: Side One was 'Silent Struggle', and Side Two, the *B* side, was 'Rise Above' – a demo track that hadn't made the album cut.

'Look at the brackets after the song,' Charley said with a soft smile.

'Silent Struggle: McCall, Okorie, Townley,' he read slowly.

'Townley? You're *Townley*,' Debbie exclaimed. They both turned to Charley, who smiled again.

'McKenzie was adamant we all got a writing credit, Andy,' Charley explained. 'We wrote it together. Okorie – that's me. McCall, obviously McKenzie. Townley … that's you. You're a songwriter, Andy.'

Andy grinned, throwing his arms in the air in celebration, almost flinging the single across the room. 'That's amazing – how nice of him to do that. My name is on a *hit single*!' he cried.

'Here's hoping,' Charley replied with a wink. 'You know what else that means, don't you?' She looked at the faces of Andy and Debbie. 'You'll get your share of the royalties. Every time it's played on the radio or TV, you'll get something. If it sells well, you're going to get a nice chunk from this.'

'Silent Struggle' hit the airwaves as scheduled on Monday, instantly igniting a national buzz. For McKenzie, the surreal thrill of hearing his voice on the radio again and spotting his name splashed across headlines took some getting used to. This time, though, the chatter wasn't about his weight – it was all about his music. Critics and fans alike were unanimous: the track wasn't just good – it was a triumphant return to form, the kind of comeback that demands attention. *The Times* hailed it with a glowing review:

> *A heady mix of melancholy and poignancy, underpinned by an uplifting melody that will have you reaching for the needle to play again and again. This is McCall returning to his heyday and then some. A release which has caught the music world off guard, McKenzie McCall is back – and boy, did we miss him.*

It was different this time. As McKenzie listened to Atkinson's daily predictions about where 'Silent Struggle' was going to enter the chart, he struggled to find the same rush of excitement. Maybe he was just older now, with more on his mind.

'It's going top ten on Sunday, Mack, you mark my words,' Atkinson said confidently. 'By the time you step on stage on Sunday night, Bruno Brookes will have done his top forty countdown on Radio 1 and your audience will be in celebratory mood. It's perfect – you couldn't write it.'

With a new song creating a splash, it was inevitable the spotlight fell on McKenzie's life again. He had grown used to being the has-been, the musician whose star had long since dimmed. He had made his peace with slipping into the shadows; being thrust back into the public eye was a shock to the system. Charley was booked to work with an up-and-coming band and McKenzie found himself missing her.

Despite the busy schedule, they spoke on the phone regularly.

'I heard it on the radio four times this morning, Mack,' Charley said. 'Simon Bates and Mike Smith both called it the best thing they've played in ages. Do you think I got the mix right, though? There are a few areas I wish I'd spent more time on – the drums could've been raised a bit. Atkinson was rushing us. It's a whole different experience listening to it on the radio.'

'It's perfect, Charley,' McKenzie reassured her. 'You took a good song and turned it into something we can be proud of.'

McKenzie understood exactly how Charley felt. It was the same reason he avoided listening to his old songs – there was always something he wished he'd done differently. Finishing a song felt less like an accomplishment and more like a reluctant surrender. There was always one more thing to tweak: an extra backing vocal here, a new guitar part there. He would spend endless hours at the mixing desk, peeling back layers, recording and rerecording, chasing a perfection that always seemed just out of reach. In those moments, Atkinson's blunt candour became his anchor, forcing him to finally let go.

'Get a grip, Mack. Stop dithering around like some self-indulgent loon. The song is finished. It was finished three days ago. Get it on the album, or I'll tell the record company we're having to reschedule the release date – to 1998 or something.'

'How are Debbie and Andy?' Charley asked.

'I spoke to Andy this morning,' McKenzie replied. 'Mrs Silva answered the phone first. She gave me the full rundown – her life story, her husband's life story and a minute-by-minute account of Debbie's movements since she got home from the hospital. She's quite a force – if I ever need to replace Atkinson, I'm headhunting her. I'm planning to head up there tomorrow night – my last chance before Wembley. We'll be rehearsing almost non-stop Thursday, Friday and Saturday. Atkinson also has me booked for *Top of the Pops*, a few radio interviews and *Going Live* on Saturday morning.'

'Ah, Saturday morning TV,' Charley teased. 'I bet you're doing the kids' phone-in – the ultimate rock star nightmare. How are you feeling about it all?'

'I'm absolutely bloody dreading it. I'm still traumatised by children's TV and my *TISWAS* experience, back when I was starting out. They dumped a bucket of slime on my head right before I was about to perform "Heaven Sent". I had to sing one of my most emotional songs – written about the death of my pet dog, I'd like to point out – with slime dripping down my face and into my mouth. Even Atkinson said he started questioning whether all publicity is good publicity after that fiasco. Thank God there's no way to dig up old clips like that one – it's buried for good.'

Charley chuckled. 'I actually meant, how are you feeling about the gig? But thanks for reminding me about the *TISWAS* story!'

McKenzie laughed too. 'Yeah, fair play to Atkinson – he's pulled out all the stops and by all accounts, the tickets are selling. But I don't know … I feel like things don't matter as much any more.'

'I get that,' Charley said. 'This album I'm working on should be exciting, it's a young band and they're so pumped up, but I feel … distracted. Maybe after working with the legend that is Mack McCall, these teenyboppers just don't cut it.'

McKenzie laughed again. 'I wonder if you'll *ever* let me forget that teenybopper clanger. You only bring it up about three times a day!'

19

The next night, McKenzie drove up to Manchester, completely disregarding Atkinson's advice from just hours earlier:

'Mack, we're nearly there! Someone I know at Woolworths' head office says your single is selling like hot balloons – you're heading straight for number one. You're recording *Top of the Pops* tomorrow and I've got you on *BBC Breakfast* first thing. A car will pick you up at six a.m. Do *not* mess this up, Mack. It's a cosy interview with Selina Scott – they promised me her, not Frank Bough. They'll air thirty seconds of your video. Try to look like you actually want to be there for heaven's sake. One sarcastic comment from you and this whole comeback could go up in steam. You're rehearsing at the Shaw Theatre after *Top of the Pops* and you'll be there the rest of the day. Early to bed, Mack, no booze and eat something decent tonight. You need to be on top form going into Sunday – it's going to be a busy few days!'

McKenzie parked on a nearby street, slipped on his cap as a makeshift disguise and strolled over to Debbie and

Andy's house. As he raised his hand to knock, the door to his right opened and Mrs Silva peeked out.

'You are Mack?' she spat out, having evidently discovered his real name and now furious at this deception.

'Yes, that's right, sorry. Mack. McKenzie. But we're keeping it kind of quiet,' he said, glancing about and rearranging his cap.

Mrs Silva looked him up and down. McKenzie had taken to wearing Doc Martens rather than his usual signature cowboy boots when he visited Manchester.

'You do not look like a rock star, one bit. Debbie is tired, so please be mindful of this when you visit.'

To McKenzie's momentary relief the door swung open and Pam greeted him.

'Shoes off, McKenzie, I hoovered in here earlier,' she said firmly.

Mrs Silva looked again at McKenzie's footwear and gave Pam an approving nod. McKenzie stepped inside and wiped his feet on the mat, before sitting on the stairs and removing his boots. It was like entering a toy house. He was a tall man, used to a sprawling town house, but he liked it and it reminded him of the homely house he grew up in.

'I can't stay long, Pam. Atkinson's got me on a tight leash this week … new song, Sunday gig, a couple of TV spots … wants me in tip-top shape, you know. I … I hope Debbie's OK.'

Pam gave him a look that made it clear his rock 'n' roll life held little interest for her and then motioned for him to come through.

McKenzie, who had dined with international rock stars and mingled with royalty in at least three countries – royalty, he might add, that had specifically requested *his* company – suddenly felt very insignificant. He'd even once had a brief chat with Michael Jackson in the VIP lounge at Heathrow. Over canapés, Jackson had casually mentioned his lifelong dream of a duet with a British rock star. McKenzie knew, of course, that nothing would come of it – Jackson's team had swooped in like secret agents at the first hint he might inadvertently agree to something he'd regret. But still, he'd spoken with the King of Pop himself, the biggest-selling artist of the 1980s so far. Yet here with Pam, or under Mrs Silva's scrutiny, McKenzie was reduced to a quivering wreck.

'They've been getting letters in the post,' Pam said darkly. 'I don't know what Debbie was thinking, letting Andy go on TV like that. Some are supportive, encouraging them to keep fighting. There are even letters from others with this illness, saying how inspirational they are – but most are awful, McKenzie. One said they should do the right thing and leave the area to keep everyone else safe. Another called Debbie a selfish, terrible mother for keeping Andy here and threatened to report her to social services. They had one today that said they should watch their backs.'

Pam's face was drawn with worry and McKenzie could only mutter, 'Jesus,' with a shake of his head.

'Debbie's upstairs with Andy,' Pam went on. 'The hospital let us borrow a fold-up wheelchair and they made it out to the park this afternoon. She's tired, but it's been a good day and she's doing well. We're all hopeful she's over the worst of this latest dip. Maybe the AZT is starting to keep the AIDS at bay. She's been more like the old Debbie.'

Pam sounded upbeat but McKenzie could see that her body language didn't fully mirror her tone. He certainly wasn't going to mention that Debbie had stopped taking the AZT.

When McKenzie reached the bedroom, Andy was perched on the edge of Debbie's bed. Debbie still wore the make-up she'd applied for their outing, giving her face a touch of colour and hiding most of the blemishes, but her skin had a familiar yellow tinge. Her neck appeared stretched thin and her hair was sparse enough to reveal glimpses of her scalp.

As McKenzie stood in the doorway, Debbie squinted, closing her eyes tightly, then reopening them, waiting for them to adjust. His single was propped up beside the mirror on her dressing table.

'Hi, McKenzie,' Andy greeted him, smiling.

'Is this our pampered prince from London?' Debbie said, scrunching her eyes again. 'I'm surprised you've got time for us what with your triumphant new single – it's been on Piccadilly Radio about nine times today. I told Andy, I know you helped him write it, but there's only so much McKenzie McCall we can take.' Debbie's voice was hoarse. She laughed but the sound quickly morphed into a violent cough. She took several deep breaths, trying to regain control.

'I've always got time for my favourite Manchester people, even when they're rude about my musicianship,' McKenzie said, sitting down and giving Andy an affectionate punch on the arm.

Debbie was lying in bed, wrapped in a thick dressing gown over her pyjamas and T-shirt. Around them were scattered photo albums, each labelled with a year and Andy was flipping through one. As McKenzie sat on the bed, he picked up one of the albums and saw that beneath the photos, Debbie had written humorous captions, each one punctuated with plenty of exclamation marks.

When Andy fought a crab and lost!!

Debbie running away from a particularly angry wasp!!!

Christmas '84 – we're all frowning and looking impatient because Gran couldn't get the flash to work!

Tony realising he can't play tennis after spending the day telling us how good he was!

There was picture after picture of a young couple, happy and smiling – Debbie and Tony – blissfully content in that early stage of a relationship where everything feels effortless. You couldn't fake that kind of happiness. Love and companionship radiated from these photos, something McKenzie had never experienced with anyone, not properly. Tony, with his moustache and summer vests, exuded a rugged handsomeness, his eyes kind and full of life. Debbie, with Madonna-style hair, looked vibrant and beautiful, wearing denim dungarees paired with colourful T-shirts. You could almost feel her personality and charisma leap from the photos. There were BBQs, with both of them doting on a young Andy – Tony holding him on his shoulders, Andy shrieking in a mix of terror and delight. There were photos of them on sunbeds by swimming pools, playing in parks and at birthday parties. One particularly poignant picture showed the family standing in front of a Christmas tree, Tony with one arm around Debbie and the other holding a toddler Andy, who was clearly determined to grab Tony's moustache. With Tony attempting to pull his head away, their spontaneous laughter was captured. McKenzie, Debbie, and Andy spent a good half hour with the albums, pointing at the photos and chatting happily. Andy asked Debbie about some of the pictures. Some she spoke about vividly, while others left her blank, as though her memory flicked on and off.

'Here's one of us with Grandad and Gran on a tiny train!' Andy said, holding up the album. The photo showed the whole family squeezed into a small carriage of one of those miniature trains that run through parks. Toddler Andy sat between Brian and Pam, eating an ice cream, while Pam tried her best to clean him up for the photo but was clearly too late. Brian smiled at the camera with one arm around Andy and the other around Debbie, who was giggling beside him. Tony must have been behind the camera.

Debbie strained to look at the picture, a small smile forming on her lips. 'Ah, that was a nice day,' she said softly. 'It absolutely poured the moment we got off that little train. Mum went into a panic because you didn't have a coat and Dad wrapped you up in his and carried you. You loved it. He used to do the same with me when I was a child …'

Her eyes glistened for a moment before Andy closed the album and placed it back on the bed. Pam's voice called up the stairs, letting Andy know his tea was ready.

'Do you want some, McKenzie?' she yelled. 'There's a few spare sausages and probably enough mash?'

McKenzie couldn't help grinning – the thought of home cooked sausages and mash sounded great, but it was the ordinary domesticity that *really* appealed to him.

'No … no, thank you!' McKenzie called back in the direction of the stairs.

'Good grief, Mum, he's used to eating at The Ritz, he's not going to want to sample your charcoaled bangers!' Debbie croaked back. She breathed in with the exertion of trying to shout and her chest rattled.

'I was only asking,' Pam replied, wounded.

'Go on, love,' Debbie said to Andy. 'You go. McKenzie and I will … we'll carry on with the photos, and you can say goodbye before he heads back to London.'

'OK, Mum. Can I look at more later?'

'You bet. We've still got '85 and '86 to go through,' Debbie replied with a smile.

Andy pumped a fist and grinned, then swung himself down the stairs using the banister. From below, they heard Pam telling him to wash his hands before the kitchen door closed, leaving only the muffled voices drifting up through the ceiling.

An awkward silence settled over them. McKenzie shifted on the bed – moments like these made him miss Charley. She was brilliant at keeping the conversation going, leaving him to jump in now and then with a funny quip.

'It's really good to see you out of the hospital, Debbie. You're looking well … I'm really pleased,' he said, trying to channel the kind of warmth Charley would bring.

Debbie's expression was unreadable and for a moment he worried he'd annoyed her again with his inability to say the right thing.

'Something feels different, Mack,' Debbie said matter-of-factly, her voice thin and husky. 'There's been a shift – more weakness, more pain. I feel like every organ is aching. My eyes keep going fuzzy, I'm running high fevers at night and I feel so cold. My chest feels heavy. I've got a hernia that makes it hard even to walk or get up. My liver's acting up, my stomach's bloating … I'm fighting for Andy, but I'm tired. My body's giving up and it's getting harder to protect him from seeing it. There's constantly something new. This week it's these sores on my legs – look.'

She pulled one foot out from under the covers, revealing part of her shin. The skin was red and ulcerated, with white patches where it had broken open. McKenzie grimaced and recoiled.

'I'm sorry, McKenzie. I shouldn't have done that to you,' she whispered. 'I'm scared – scared for Andy and scared for my mum having to cope with all this. I'm scared I won't see Dad again, who can't even acknowledge I've got AIDS. And … and … I'm scared of dying. How did this happen, Mack? To me, to all of us, to everyone in the same boat with AIDS – how could this happen?' She paused, swallowing hard. 'I've tried to bury my head in the sand but I feel like I'm coming to the end point. I'm frightened, Mack.'

McKenzie opened his mouth to speak but the words didn't come. He didn't know *what* to say – he *was* a pampered prince, sheltered from the real world. Whenever he found himself in an uncomfortable situation, Atkinson was always there to smooth things over and deal with it. Atkinson had shielded him from reality for so long that McKenzie was now completely unprepared for it. In the absence of words, he reached for her hand and gave it a gentle squeeze.

'McKenzie, I need you to promise me something.' Debbie's voice took on a more businesslike tone. 'When I'm taken back to Ward 14A, that'll be it. That'll be the last time. I won't be coming home again. I need to ask if you and Charley will still be there for Andy. He'll go to my mum and dad but he'll need good people around him. You two could

… you could be like surrogate godparents. I know it's a big ask.' Panic flashed in Debbie's eyes as she leaned forward. 'I need to know he'll be OK, that he'll have people looking out for him.'

McKenzie's throat tightened. 'You don't need to ask, Debbie. We won't let him, or you, down. I promise. I'll be there for him.'

Debbie's expression relaxed and she settled back, though her eyes remained fixed on McKenzie. She was a woman who was running out of time.

'I've been thinking about something a lot. When I end up back in the hospital, there's something else I need you to do, McKenzie.'

'Of course, Debbie. We'll do what we can – shopping, talking to Andy's school … anything.'

Debbie didn't miss a beat. 'I want you to find Tony. Find him for Andy – for when I'm gone. I've got an address. Andy doesn't know but he sends money from time to time. When I'm back in the hospital, that'll be the time where my role is almost at an end – I want you to find him.'

20

The next few days were a whirlwind, reminiscent of McKenzie's early career – though now with creakier joints and noticeably less energy. After an awkward but acceptable appearance on breakfast TV, McKenzie headed to Elstree Studios for *Top of the Pops* to record a performance of 'Silent Struggle' with the band, to air on the show that night. The show was a staple of British television, the stage every musical act wanted to grace in hopes of nudging their latest song up the charts. McKenzie hated it. On the TV, the studio seemed to buzz with excitement, but in reality, it was a musical cattle market. Every artist, no matter their stature, was treated the same – herded around the studio like naughty teenagers at school. Endless waiting gave way to a coordinated chaos as acts were corralled onto a cheap stage that looked as if a stiff breeze might carry it away. When the show hit screens on Thursdays at 7 p.m., it gave the illusion of a packed studio buzzing with hundreds of adoring fans. In truth, it was about thirty teenagers, herded like hyperactive sheep from set to set, instructed to swarm the presenters and feign wild enthusiasm for the camera's benefit.

Elstree Studios had all the charm of a factory warehouse and McKenzie struggled to muster the enthusiasm to mime his songs convincingly. Aldo had been called in to style him again – casual jeans and a silvery blazer, aiming to keep it current without trying too hard to be cool. McKenzie felt out of place and old, but he muddled through the performance with a professionalism born of habit. Another job begrudgingly ticked off the list.

Between TV appearances, McKenzie and the band were rehearsing at the Shaw Theatre. After so many years performing together, they were like a well-oiled machine; each part moving in sync to create their famously tight sound. Some fans hadn't bought an album since the '70s but still showed up to watch McKenzie live, drawn by the band's polished, raw energy, driven by deep, resonant drums and bass guitar. The setlist came together quickly and they spent extra time rehearsing 'Silent Struggle' for its debut live performance. Around them, the crew hustled, assembling a mock stage and lighting rig.

'Blimey, Mack, we'd all taken bets you'd never be back,' Snakes called with a cheeky grin. 'I've been pulled off the Status Quo tour for this, but I wouldn't have missed your big comeback for the world. The Quo are furious I ditched them. I said to Rossi, "Calm it, Francis, you don't say no to Atkinson Stark."'

'Couldn't do it without you, Snakester,' McKenzie fired back with a wink.

Snakes leaned in with a glint in his eye. 'Oh, and guess what, Mack? Prince Charles got in touch through one of my royal contacts. All a bit hush-hush, mind you. He wanted to know if there were any spare tickets – Diana loves a good concert. I told him, "No chance, mate! This is the hottest ticket in town; there's not even room for a princess!"'

McKenzie was privately a little hurt that everyone kept calling this his 'comeback'. To him, it felt more of a reawakening – a rediscovery of who he had always been. When he tried to make this point to Atkinson during a break in rehearsals, Atkinson nearly spat out his champagne and choked on his cigar smoke.

'Don't be ridiculous, Mack. Your career was as dead as a bloody donut. I told you I'd keep grafting until I got you back where you belonged. I could've jumped ship when all these hot new acts were begging for management, but did I? No. I stuck by you, Mackie Boy, and now my hard work's paying off.'

McKenzie had managed to dodge Atkinson's relentless questions about his mysterious new writing partner, 'Townley', but he knew it was only a matter of time before he'd have to come clean – especially to ensure the legal side was sorted so that Andy and Debbie received their royalties. For now, though, it could wait.

'Whoever this Townley fella is,' Atkinson went on, 'we're bringing him on board for the next album – he's resurrected your career like some biblical miracle!'

The crew and band were pulling together and everyone seemed energised and grateful to be there – spirits were high. McKenzie, however, felt too nervous to fully enjoy it. He knew that if the gig went well, he'd look back on it with fond memories but he often found himself relishing the memories more than the event itself. There was so much riding on him.

On Friday, between fine-tuning a live 'Silent Struggle', McKenzie called Andy and Debbie's house.

'She's still tired from the park,' Pam said when she answered.

'The park? You mean they've been again today?' McKenzie replied, relieved. He thought that if Debbie could be OK, it would make the lead-up to his gig easier – but quickly dismissed the thought, realising how utterly selfish it sounded.

'No, from Tuesday,' Pam said, as if it were perfectly normal for Debbie to still be tired several days later. After chatting for a moment about McKenzie's upcoming gig, Pam added, for the umpteenth time, that McKenzie's life was beyond her comprehension. 'Hold on, Andy's just coming down the stairs.'

McKenzie heard her hold out the phone and quietly whisper his name to Andy.

'Hi, McKenzie,' Andy said. The sound of Andy's voice, carrying its usual hint of melancholy, stirred something protective and almost fatherly in McKenzie – a reminder that this was a boy bearing more worries than any child should.

'How's it going, kidder?' McKenzie asked, attempting an overly bright tone.

'*Kidder?*' Andy echoed, with a snort. 'Things are OK, thank you. Mum's resting – she's been sleeping a lot lately but she says it's a good sign, that it helps her body fight. A nurse came by earlier and spent some time with her but I think she's doing all right, considering.'

'That's good, ki— Andy. I've got my gig on Sunday and the song seems to be doing well. You're a famous songwriter. Shame you can't be there – I'd get you a backstage pass but Pam said Debbie's not quite well enough and you wouldn't want to come without her.'

'No, Gran said your concert's on the radio, so we'll tune in … she still calls it the "wireless".' Andy sniggered and

McKenzie could hear Pam shout something in the background about being cheeky. McKenzie chuckled too.

'Don't go upsetting Pam, Andy – you need her sausage and mash,' McKenzie said with a smile. 'Yes, it's on the radio. Atkinson can't do anything by halves. He went and struck a deal with Signal Radio to broadcast it live across their network. Talk about adding pressure. We've even got a big screen above the stage for the first time, so people at the back can see my face – if they really want to.' He laughed. 'Technology's coming on fast. My microphone doesn't even have a wire now; they call it a "radio mic". It'll feel strange moving around the stage without hauling a wire behind me. Atkinson keeps telling me to "move with the times", like I'm some old fart.'

'It sounds amazing,' said Andy. 'I've never been to a concert.'

'We'll make sure that happens soon – you and your mum will be my VIP guests. Tomorrow morning, I'm on *Going Live!* with Philip Schofield and Sarah Greene, answering kids' questions on the phone-in. It's terrifying. I'm amazed any of them even know who I am – maybe they won't and their first question will be, "Who are you?" Anyway, I'll be back up next week after the gig. I might not be in a fit state on Monday but definitely mid-week. I'll try to bring Charley too – I know she'd like that.'

'OK, thanks, McKenzie … McKenzie?'

'Yeah?'

'I hope the gig goes well. It must be scary going out in front of all those people.'

'Thanks, Andy. You and your mum … you'll be on my mind. I'll be thinking of you both and I'll be there soon – I promise.'

McKenzie navigated the Saturday morning kid's TV phone-in just about unscathed …

Did he have a pet? *Erm no … that's a bit boring … think of something … talk about Buddy, your dog who inspired the song, 'Heaven Sent'. Great, that seemed to go down well with a big 'ahhhh' from the studio.*

What was his most embarrassing moment? *Brilliant – bring out the TISWAS story. That got quite a laugh, you're on a roll!*

What was his favourite song he'd written? *Hmm, Atkinson would kill him if he missed this opportunity to namecheck his current song – it was 'Silent Struggle' because it held a lot of meaning for him. Nice moment, but atmosphere in studio dipped.*

Why wasn't he married? *Wow – bit of a curveball, that one. Mind your own business, you nosy little pipsqueak. No, don't say that, quick joke about no one being able to put up with him and besides, they'd have to listen to his songs all the time and who would want that? He even managed a bemused 'what a question!' look into the barrel of the camera to the audience at home. Studio loves it – back in business.*

Did he still get nervous performing? *Great chance to praise his fans who he said made him feel comfortable when out on the stage and if he did get nervous it was only because he wanted to give them the best show. What a creep. Mention the screen above the stage and the new radio mic, kids love a bit of state-of-the-art technology … and it's a strong finish!*

Walking off the studio set, McKenzie breathed a sigh of relief. He knew it had gone well when Atkinson slapped him on the back as they made their way out of the TV studio.

'Good stuff, Mack, good stuff. At least you've avoided doing something embarrassing and ending up on *It'll Be Alright on the Night* with Dennis Norden next Christmas. I wasn't sure you'd pull off a kids' phone-in, but you did it … just.'

'Thanks for the backhanded compliment, as always, Atkinson. Pub? I need a stiff drink.'

Atkinson lit his cigar and puffed a few times to get it going.

'Good grief, Mack. I've been working non-stop, booking you the greatest gig of your life and you want to head to the Dog and Duck? Absolutely not. You're rehearsing this afternoon. Then, my friend, you'll be getting yourself all tucked into bed with some lemon and honey, resting that angelic voice of yours and getting some shut-eye.'

'Yes, Atkinson. Erm, Atkinson, I don't think you're supposed to smoke in a studio, especially not a kids' TV one.'

***

More people loitered around the rehearsal that afternoon, their attention once again drawn to McKenzie. The men in suits were back, music execs, swarming around him like they had in the early days – eager and ingratiating, all with one thing on their minds: *money*. They milled about the theatre, watching the rehearsal's progress. With so many Roamers and Filofaxes on display, Atkinson was in heaven – it was like a competition to see who had the biggest bulge … in their pockets. The execs could hardly disguise their glee at signing a fading star, only for him to suddenly become hot property again. McKenzie had invited Charley to the rehearsal and she sat on the front row of the theatre, her smile warm and encouraging. They exchanged regular eye contact, giving McKenzie the boost he needed. He didn't want to let Charley down – he wanted her to see him at his best. As the rehearsal ended, the new suits leapt to their feet, offering handshakes and backslaps, showering praise on how great the band sounded. McKenzie measured the state of his career by the condition of his back – a backslap-free back meant his career was in the doldrums; today, his back felt raw from the onslaught of forced praise. McKenzie and the band stood around the makeshift stage, sipping bottles of beer, Charley joined them for the customary debrief that followed every rehearsal. Behind them, one of the new suits shared a cigar and a glass of champagne with Atkinson, who was in his element: 'McKenzie's going to go stratospheric again, Atkinson – congratulations, you must be thrilled. The public love a returning underdog and nothing's going to stop you guys for the rest of the decade. Once the gig's done, we need to meet again, Atkinson. Let's talk numbers on that advance for the next album you mentioned.'

21

The phone on the bedside table rang shrilly, jolting McKenzie from a deep sleep. Disoriented, he struggled to gather his scattered thoughts. *Sunday?* It must be Sunday. The day of the gig – *exciting*, but why was someone calling so early? He squinted at the clock beside the phone: 7:19 a.m.

If it was Atkinson, he had some nerve – especially after insisting McKenzie get a good night's sleep. Atkinson knew McKenzie liked to sleep in on gig days; the longer he slept, the less time there was to wallow in nerves.

So what was he playing at? Maybe it was Charley. Please, let it be Charley. Or Andy. Or Debbie …

'Mack? Atkinson!'

Damn.

'Mack, I want you to go downstairs and pick up the stack of Sunday newspapers from your letterbox. Take them into your sitting room and I will call back in five minutes. Do that now, Mack.'

The line went dead. McKenzie stared at the phone, now fully awake, a knot of dread tightening in his stomach. McKenzie knew Atkinson well enough to sense he was using every last ounce of self-control to hold it together. When Atkinson tried to rein in his tone, his voice hit a strained pitch – a smidge higher than usual. McKenzie recognised that sound all too well, a familiar warning from years of Atkinson's volatile mood swings.

Mack's Midnight Meetings with AIDS Victim!

Perched on the edge of the sofa, newspaper in hand, McKenzie wasn't shocked by the headline. He'd known this would get out eventually. All it took was one person spotting him at the hospital, tipping off *News of the World* and a reporter eager to turn whispers into a headline. A couple of hundred quid for exclusivity, a handful of flimsy details and they'd spin it into a sensational story. McKenzie knew how it worked. Scanning the article, he noted the glaring factual errors about his visits to the so-called 'secret ward'. The phone rang beside him and he continued reading as he reached to answer.

'Mack? Atkinson!' Atkinson barked, as if he hadn't just told McKenzie he was phoning back. There was a pause. 'Well, Mack? Have you *nothing* to say? You are on the front page of the bloody *News of the World* because you've been travelling to Manchester to see some woman with AIDS. Mack, I just … I don't … I mean what the *hell*? It's like you're trying to destroy everything we've worked for. How can I represent you when I don't even know what on earth is going on with you? I knew you'd been sneaking around – *flowers* indeed. I should've kept you closer. This is going to ruin you – what are you thinking, Mack?'

McKenzie flicked to page two, where the story continued.

'Calm down, Atkinson, you're going to make yourself ill again,' McKenzie replied. 'It's not true.'

'Oh, thank God. I knew you wouldn't get involved in something ridiculous like this. We'll get a rebuttal out there, a short statement and bury the story dead. Let's threaten a libel too – they might print a retraction then. At the concert tonight, maybe between songs, you've got the perfect chance to make a bit of a joke of it – something about the journalists needing a torch so they can shed light on the actual facts. Befriending an AIDS patient, I mean, I know you've gone off the rails recently but I knew that was stretching it even for you! We'll sort it, Mack.'

'Well, that part's true. It's the "midnight" nonsense they fabricated – why would I sneak into a hospital ward at midnight? I went during visiting hours, like everyone else – I had to fight a Mini Metro for a parking space. I doubt they'd even let me stroll in at midnight, even on Ward 14A, where they seem to make up their own rules. And it's not some "secret ward"; it's just ignored because it treats AIDS patients. Oh, and I'm thirty-seven, not thirty-eight – the cheeky sods.'

McKenzie clenched his teeth, fully aware that Atkinson's jaw was likely hanging open, speechless, and steeled himself for the fireworks. He counted to five, bracing himself for Atkinson's inevitable explosion.

'What are you talking about, Mack – you *have* been going to the hospital? My God, you're talking like this ward actually matters to you. Who is this person with AIDS and why are you getting yourself involved? We've just rebuilt everything and now you're risking it all over this? Have you even thought about the risks? Your insurance won't cover this. The article mentions a woman and a boy. Who *are* these people?' Atkinson thundered.

McKenzie had never heard him this furious – and he'd heard Atkinson furious *a lot*.

'They are Debbie Townley and her son, Andy. Debbie is suffering from AIDS and I've offered them' – McKenzie hesitated, he wasn't really sure what he'd offered them – 'my support.'

'Debbie and Andy *Townley*,' Atkinson repeated. 'Where have I heard that name before … Oh please God no, Mack. *Townley* – they helped you write the bloody song! The name of someone with AIDS is written on the back of your record? We're finished.'

'It was actually her twelve-year-old son, for what it's worth,' McKenzie said meekly.

Atkinson ranted for a full eleven minutes, scarcely pausing for breath, before he eventually began to transition into the 'action plan' phase of his fury. There'd be no official rebuttal but at tonight's show, McKenzie would play it cool – a few nudge-nudge, wink-wink comments about his lawyers and *News of the World*. Enough to cast some doubt on the story, but with a light, casual tone.

Atkinson's main concern was that, with McKenzie now linked to the AIDS crisis, some fans might be deterred from attending. McKenzie let him ramble, nodding and murmuring in the right places. In the background, *Breakfast with Frost* played on the television, featuring a brief news item about McKenzie's song as a contender for that night's number one spot and touting his gig as 'the most in-demand ticket of the year'. Frustration simmered in McKenzie. Was he not even allowed to show compassion without it being exploited to sell papers? The saddest part was how it made him cautious. How could he possibly keep supporting Andy and Debbie when every visit risked someone tipping off the press – or worse, paparazzi following him? It wouldn't be fair to Andy and Debbie.

McKenzie's morning unfolded with the same restless energy that always gripped him before a gig – an unshakeable tension that made settling into anything impossible. He tried watching a few videos on his VHS machine, popping in different tapes, but couldn't focus on any of them. He wandered down to his basement and strummed a guitar for a while. It felt surreal, knowing that while he paced around at home, the venue would already be a hive of activity: roadies darting across the stage, building, screwing, drilling and hauling equipment into place – all for him. Just last night, Whitney Houston had performed at Wembley Arena and by dawn, her crew had dismantled everything, loaded it into massive haulage trucks and cleared the stage for McKenzie's set-up. In the early days, McKenzie loved arriving early to soak up the atmosphere of a venue in full swing – the banter, the laughter, the quick problem-solving when the stage didn't fit or the electrics acted up. These days, though, he arrived in the late afternoon. The band would run a forty-five-minute sound check, fine-tuning levels and getting a feel for the space. After that, there'd be just a few hours to kill before showtime.

McKenzie called Andy later in the morning and was delighted to hear that Debbie was up and sitting on the sofa. She'd managed to make it over to the phone – her voice was weak and her speech slow and strained, but it was wonderful just to hear her.

'We've seen the paper, McKenzie. I promise you it wasn't us who told them. Reggie brought it round. He couldn't even tell his mum he was here. Andy was really upset when he saw it,' she said.

'I know it wasn't you – I didn't think that for a moment. Someone's made a quick few quid tipping off the paper, they won't be the first and they won't be the last. Don't worry.'

'I hope it doesn't cause you any trouble, McKenzie. But honestly, how many mistakes can one article make?' Debbie croaked.

'That's what they do – take one bit of truth and invent a story around it,' replied McKenzie.

'Look on the bright side, they said you were only thirty-eight. I thought you were at least ten years older,' rasped Debbie breathlessly.

'I see your illness hasn't dulled your cutting humour, Debbie.' McKenzie laughed.

'They got one thing right, though, Mack,' she said. 'They called you a friend of the family – and you are. I hope everything goes well tonight. We'll be listening. Let me put Andy on.'

McKenzie heard Andy take the phone.

'You OK, Andy?'

'Yeah, I guess.'

'You sure?'

A long pause followed.

'Reggie said everyone's parents have told them to stay away from me. They say that our house is dirty. He said someone at school on Friday told him that if he's friends with me, he'll catch AIDS too. He said Mr Harris heard it and did nothing – just turned away.'

'Oh, good heavens, what did Reggie say?'

'He smacked them one and got sent home for the rest of the day …'

McKenzie fought to keep from smiling. 'I don't condone Reggie's reaction, Andy, but I can't say I blame him.'

'I just don't understand how everyone can be so horrible. They were my friends, my form group. Mr Harris was so nice.' Andy's voice held genuine confusion.

'I think fear has made everyone go a bit mad, Andy. They're scared of something they don't understand. No one's really against you – it's AIDS they're afraid of, because not enough has been done to give people the right information … I know that doesn't make it any easier.'

'Maybe you're right, but it's still horrible. You're getting better, you know …' Andy said quietly.

'Getting *better*?' McKenzie replied, bemused.

'At talking. You're getting better.'

'Thanks, Andy. That … means a lot.'

Atkinson called multiple times throughout the day, reassuring McKenzie, and channelling his own unusually nervous energy into repeated assertions that, if handled sensibly, the *News of the World* story would soon blow over. McKenzie's driver arrived to collect him at 3:45 p.m. A small crowd of fans had gathered outside his house, clapping and calling McKenzie's name as the driver ushered him into the car. Atkinson was already in the back, dressed in a typical ensemble: a black suit paired with a grey cashmere turtleneck sweater and a pair of Ray-Ban Aviators perched on his nose, despite the overcast sky.

'Don't start going all Princess Di again, Mack, for Christ's sake. You've done your stint of saintly behaviour –

got it out of your system – so let's focus on selling records and planning your next tour. I get that you're having some kind of mid-life crisis, but you're not Mother bleeding Theresa. You've nearly finished me off today. My poor ticker can't take much more of managing you. I'm wiped out already. I think my age is catching up with me – but you're not helping.' Atkinson took a sip of champagne and a cigar smouldered in his left hand.

'I'm not sure either of *those* are helping, to be fair, Atkinson. How many cigars do you smoke each day? How many glasses of that stuff do you drink?'

Atkinson glared at him over the sunglasses, affronted, as McKenzie waved the cigar smoke away and lowered the window an inch or two with the press of a button, to emphasise his point.

'You really are turning into Florence Nightingale, aren't you, Mack? Look, let's just enjoy today – we're back at the pinnacle. London is yours tonight. Tomorrow morning, we'll discuss a strategy for our next move. For now, go out there and make sure you're at the top of your game.'

'No problem, Tom,' McKenzie said, staring straight ahead.

'*Tom*?' Atkinson asked, raising an eyebrow.

'Tom Cruise. The *Top Gun* wardrobe department will be sending out a search party for Tom's sunglasses,' McKenzie quipped, as he began to hum 'Take My Breath Away' from the same film.

Atkinson glared once more, this time with a clear let's-take-today-a-bit-more-seriously look on his face.

The drive across London to Wembley Arena took thirty minutes. When they arrived, the buzz was palpable. Despite the blacked-out windows of the sleek Rolls Royce Silver Spirit they were travelling in, fans were already waiting, hammering on the glass and shouting McKenzie's name. The scene crackled with anticipation, reminiscent of the 1970s when he first tasted the thrill of success in enthusiastic countries like Australia and Japan – before the United Kingdom caught on.

The first thing McKenzie did upon arriving at Wembley was wander onto the stage – it was a vital part of his pre-show ritual. He liked to stand at the very edge, right on the brink and take in the vast, empty arena. This was the moment when a familiar wave of imposter syndrome always hit him. Could there really be enough people eager to watch *him* to fill this space? He scanned the stage and the bustling activity around it: the stage manager, sound engineers, lighting technicians, rigging crew, security personnel and now a video technician – all of them here, ostensibly, because of him. It didn't feel real. He was certain that someone would tap him on the shoulder at any moment and reveal it had all been a terrible mix-up. It was actually someone else people had intended to buy tickets to see.

The sound check was already underway, the crew line-checking instruments and microphones, *one-two, one-two*, ensuring everything was linked to the sound system. Behind him, a roadie struck a few chords on the piano and the sound echoed through the arena, sending a shiver down McKenzie's spine. Atkinson joined him at the stage edge, hands in his pockets and a cigar between his lips, and they stood there in quiet companionship, gazing out at the sprawling arena.

'It's quite something, isn't it?' Atkinson said, his voice unusually quiet. 'We did it, Mack. You're back where you belong, filling venues like this.'

McKenzie nodded slowly, a modest smile tugging at his lips.

'I still remember the first time I saw you at The Black Lion,' Atkinson went on. 'You were a miserable git even back then, but you had something – aloofness, but real talent. I saw it. I knew you were going somewhere and I had to be part of it. It's been one hell of a journey, Mack – how many countries have we played in? Thirty-five? Forty?'

'Thirty-six,' McKenzie replied instantly. He had a map upstairs, pinned with every place he'd performed – his little geeky secret. 'I am grateful, Atkinson. For what you've done, I mean – behind the anger issues and toxic attitude, you've had my back all these years. Maybe part of what drives me is the need to stick two fingers up at you and say, "I've still got it. I can still write a song and people still want to see me." I still need your bloody approval.'

'We're a team, Mack – a great team. And we've only just begun,' Atkinson said, flicking his cigar butt into the vast auditorium. He glanced around, then lowered his voice. 'Listen, Mack, this AIDS thing – don't turn it into a crusade. You barely know these people. It could seriously come back to bite you on the arse. We've got a VIP chill-out lounge backstage tonight. Rock and roll royalty's coming down. Bowie and Jagger might be there, Lionel Richie's definitely in town and half the *EastEnders* cast, too. You can't get hotter than that. It's Wembley tonight – after that, I'm thinking we push to crack America again. Maybe Madison Square Garden's within our grasp. We never quite made it last time. Don't blow it, Mack … Mack, are you listening?'

McKenzie turned to Atkinson, smiled and put his arm around him as they walked back up the stage.

'I'm listening, Atkinson. I always listen. Come on, you know me – I like a few hours to be grumpy before showtime.'

'That's music to my eyes, Mackie boy,' Atkinson replied, exhaling a thick cloud of cigar smoke.

After a smooth sound check, McKenzie grabbed a quick bite to eat in his dressing room, nibbling on cold meats, cheese and bread. He never overdid it before a show – just enough to keep him going. He'd learned the hard way that a heavy meal could lead to indigestion or, worse, an uncomfortable bout of gas. A massive belch blasting out to 12,000 people at 115 decibels wasn't exactly the kind of memorable moment he was going for. McKenzie entered the VIP chill-out area with Atkinson, which, despite its boxy, makeshift feel – with a hastily set-up bar and a few temporary drapes under neon lights – was bustling. Atkinson had been right: this wasn't just any gathering; it was the heartbeat of the music world. As McKenzie stepped in, a cheer rose up and for a fleeting moment, all eyes were on him. David Bowie clapped McKenzie on the back, his mesmerising eyes sparkling with generous approval. Mick Jagger gave him a cool nod, adding that the stage and video screens looked 'pretty neat'. But it was Brian May, one of McKenzie's guitar heroes, who made his heart skip a beat. The Queen legend told him how much he loved 'Silent Struggle' and he took a genuine interest in the song's meaning. McKenzie couldn't help but ask after Freddie, hoping he might be coming. Brian replied that Freddie didn't go out much any more and preferred a calmer life these days. McKenzie knew that none of these icons were there purely out of goodwill. They were, no doubt, checking out the competition, scouting for fresh ideas, making sure no one was surpassing them. Some might even secretly wish for his failure. But in that moment, none of that mattered. What mattered was the respect – this was the very recognition he had been chasing back in the '70s and it was here, from the very people he'd looked up to for years.

Just before 7 p.m., Snakes adjusted the hi-fi, which had been playing a rough cut of McKenzie's new album and tuned it into Radio 1's Top 40. The room quieted, a collective suspense hanging in the air, as Bruno Brookes's voice filled the space, announcing the latest chart rundown.

'Straight in at number one … and no one was expecting *this* – McKenzie McCall is back with a bang … and he's back at number one! This is "Silent Struggle".'

The room exploded with cheers and applause. Bowie let out a whoop, pulling McKenzie into a bear hug and lifting his arm for him in triumph. To McKenzie, it felt almost dreamlike – surrounded by a sea of familiar faces, some of them his musical heroes, all applauding and celebrating him. In the corner, Atkinson was holding court with a group of women who were giddy with excitement at being in the presence of so many celebrities. He gave McKenzie a nod and raised his glass. McKenzie nodded back and smiled. That simple exchange was enough – fifteen years of highs and lows didn't require anything more.

As if things could get any better, Charley appeared in the doorway, her shy smile lighting up the room as she scanned the crowd until her eyes found McKenzie. She gave a bashful wave and made her way over. She wore high-waisted jeans paired with white leather stilettos, an electric blue blazer and a white belt cinched tight around her waist. McKenzie could feel the room's gaze following her every move. When she reached him, she slipped her hand into the crook of his arm, leaned up and whispered in his ear – someone wolf-whistled, followed by a few excited 'wooos'.

'McKenzie,' she said into his ear, 'I'm sorry, but there's a phone call for you in your dressing room. You need to come.'

And just like that, the buzz of the concert, the energy of the room and the exhilaration of a number one record all evaporated. McKenzie was snapped back to reality.

***

'Mum's back in Ward 14A, McKenzie,' Andy said, his voice full of fear. 'She was struggling to breathe, panicking, saying she couldn't see. She told me to phone an ambulance, just to be safe, but they took her straight away. She told me if anything like this happened, I was to call Gran first – and then call you.'

'I … I'm so sorry, Andy.' McKenzie's stomach churned. Andy's anxiety was palpable but he was holding it together, as always. It made McKenzie's heart ache. He glanced at Charley, who stood nearby, her wide eyes full of worry.

'I'm coming,' McKenzie said firmly. 'I'm going to come to you right now.'

Charley's face shifted to an expression of alarm.

'You can't come now, McKenzie,' Andy said, carrying a maturity beyond his years. 'You've got a show to do. You know Mum would be furious if you let all those people down. She probably just needs more antibiotics or something. Please, don't come now.'

'Is your gran coming for you, Andy? Are you going to the hospital?'

'Mrs Silva is here. Gran's on her way and we're going straight there.'

In the background, McKenzie heard Mrs Silva's voice. 'I *told* Debbie …' He didn't catch what she said but the tone was unmistakably Mrs Silva-like.

'OK, I'll be there tomorrow, Andy. I hope she's comfortable tonight and feeling a bit better in the morning. Listen, if there's anything … just call again, OK? I'll walk off that stage to answer, if needs be.'

'Thanks, McKenzie … McKenzie?'

'Yeah?'

'We'll be listening, in the car and at the hospital. Maybe Mum will be able to listen too. I hope it's the best gig ever.'

McKenzie glanced at his watch. *Christ!* He was due on stage in twenty-five minutes.

22

'**D**rone's started, Mack. Audience is electric tonight.'

Snake's head appeared at the door, just as it had hundreds of times before, giving him the final nod: *showtime*. The low, resonant hum of the drone pulsed through the sound system – a subtle cue that never failed to spark the crowd's frenzy. As the lights dimmed, a ripple of shrieks swept through the audience. The drone, both haunting and thrilling, played on a loop, its monotony stretching the tension to its breaking point. Sometimes it would loop far beyond its usual five minutes – if someone needed to dash back to the dressing room for McKenzie's lucky plectrum, or when nerves struck and McKenzie needed a moment to pull himself together. Tonight, though, he moved slowly through the labyrinth of corridors towards the stage, the energy from the arena vibrating through the walls. He absorbed it, letting it surge through him.

McKenzie stood behind the curtain at stage left, the crowd's anticipation thrumming in the air. His drummer waited out of sight behind the centre-stage curtain, poised to slip behind the kit at the back. The bassist, guitarist and keyboard player lingered at the side of the stage, their slight jitters barely contained. From where he stood, McKenzie could hear the audience – a restless mix of chatter, cheers and the occasional chant of his name. He looked down at his feet, taking a slow, steadying breath before closing his eyes. This was why he'd always wanted to be a musician. Moments like this – charged, electric – something only a few artists ever got to experience. Yet here he was, top of the charts and about to play to a packed arena. Lifting his head, McKenzie nodded to a waiting stage technician, who promptly relayed a message into a walkie-talkie to the control desk at the back of the arena. In response, the lighting rig behind the stage began to rise, accompanied by flashes of light, a crackle of thunder and clouds of dry ice – an effect that sent the audience wild. There was no turning back now. Once the lights began to lift, it meant McKenzie was ready.

The synthesizer intro to 'It's Tonight' began, its slow build-up the perfect way to open the show. Though it had only been a minor hit, the track always came alive on stage. As the chords reached a crescendo and hung in the air, McKenzie heard the guitar, bass and drums kick in, signalling the rest of the band's entrance. The crowd erupted, jumping and clapping to the infectious riff. The band sounded incredible and McKenzie's chest trembled with the music. He coughed softly, one last effort to clear his throat, then fixed his gaze on the curtain before him as it was pulled open. With his arm raised, fist clenched, McKenzie strode across the stage, his face set with purpose. Wearing slim black jeans, a white T-shirt and a black jacket, his stage outfit was complemented by his trademark cowboy boots. He'd done this hundreds of times and the audience loved it. Reaching the front of the stage, arm still raised, he cast his eyes over the crowd and nodded to them. The roar that followed nearly sent him stumbling backwards. McKenzie gulped. The auditorium illuminated in a flash of lights. He forced himself to steady his breathing, aware that his nerves couldn't show. An audience had to believe in his power. His guitarist played a repeating chord, a steady pulse. McKenzie held the crowd's gaze for a moment longer – almost glaring at them, daring them not to enjoy the show. Then, in one fluid movement, he turned to the band and dropped his arm. On cue, the bass and drums crashed back into life.

McKenzie always performed the first song without his guitar. With no barrier between them, he believed it helped him connect with the audience, but he couldn't deny the slight discomfort of being without his usual prop to hide behind. McKenzie was always anxious until he'd sung his first line or two. That opening verse told him everything he needed to know about the condition of his voice for the rest of the concert. On long tours, the strain began to show and he had to pace himself through the middle of the show, avoiding the higher notes to ensure he could finish strong. His band were excellent vocalists, knowing exactly when to step in and carry him. They could sense when his voice was faltering and would seamlessly pick up the slack with powerful backing vocals, helping to create their signature sound. This allowed McKenzie to tackle the rousing choruses in a lower key, without pushing his vocal chords to breaking point.

The show flew by in its usual whirlwind, a blur of energy that barely paused for breath. Atkinson and Charley stood at the side of the stage, Atkinson nodding along to the beat with a cigar in hand. His mind would be racing with post-concert tasks – keeping the press satisfied, ensuring McKenzie was happy and juggling a thousand other responsibilities. Charley, on the other hand, was more animated – beaming and clapping along. It was the first time she'd seen McKenzie perform before an audience. Having Charley there, her presence always just at the edge of his vision, brought a new dynamic to his performance.

McKenzie's show followed a familiar formula – start with the rocky, fast-paced tracks to ignite the crowd, before slowing it down with ballads and lesser-known songs. Then give the band members their solo spots, allowing them well-deserved attention while McKenzie took a brief respite for an outfit change and a drink. Then they'd ramp up the energy again, raising the volume and pace to rock out for the rest of the show. The set always closed with his standard crowd favourite, 'Here as One' – the song that had the audience swaying and singing along. But today, there was an addition to the usual routine. After the final song, McKenzie and the band would leave the stage, confident the audience would call them back for more. When they returned, they'd perform 'Silent Struggle', their new signature encore. That was the plan.

During the band's instrumental break, McKenzie slipped through the curtain at the back left of the stage. Just beyond it lay a small, private retreat – a den-like oasis set up for him to catch a breather mid-show. A selection of drinks stood neatly arranged on a table – both soft and alcoholic, depending on his mood and how the show was going – alongside a bowl of bananas for a quick energy boost. Despite the industry's temptations, McKenzie had never relied on drugs – perhaps a rarity among his peers. He didn't trust himself with anything addictive and hated the idea of losing control. A stage technician greeted him with a towel, which McKenzie used to wipe his face and neck. He poured himself some Perrier into a large plastic cup and took a couple of gulps, the cool water feeling great on his parched throat. Then, with some help, he shrugged off his jacket – a tricky task when hot and damp from performing. McKenzie changed into a lighter outfit – grey jeans paired with a denim shirt left open to the navel, revealing an assortment of dog tags and necklaces he had collected over the years. Feeling refreshed and more comfortable, he knocked back a shot of Jack Daniels, before the technician carefully lifted McKenzie's *Old Special* over his neck, readying him for the final section of the show. Standing just behind the curtain, McKenzie listened, always impressed by the band's skilful improvisation. They were seasoned pros, effortlessly reading the mood of the audience. If they sensed even a flicker of restlessness, they would begin to wrap it up. A subtle signal – three quick consecutive chords – would cue McKenzie that they were nearly done.

Tonight, the audience was with them every step of the way. The band stretched the improv, relishing the freedom and joy of the moment. McKenzie stood just behind the curtain, breathing deeply as he regained control of his breath. Suddenly, a heavy arm draped over his shoulders and the unmistakable mix of breathy alcohol, smoke and expensive aftershave filled the air. Atkinson was beside him, like a trainer coaching his boxer through the middle rounds of a bruising fight.

'You're killing it, McKenzie. What a night!' Atkinson exclaimed, his voice a mix of excitement and urgency. 'Just keep it tight now. Another half an hour and we've nailed it. This'll get column inches tomorrow. We'll cut a live album from the recording for the Christmas market – maybe a video too.'

McKenzie nodded and took another swig from his cup. He turned towards a mirror hanging on the rail, shaking his head to loosen the hair that had fallen over his face. The unmistakable sound of three sharp chords cut through the air. McKenzie straightened his jacket, offered a fist bump to Atkinson, who returned it with a grin, then prepared to step back on stage, raising his fist in salute. Just as the curtain was about to open, Atkinson's voice rang out from behind.

'Oh, and Mack – Charley said this is the best gig she's ever been to. She's amazed by how good you are.' Atkinson flashed one of his best car salesman smiles, followed by a wink. 'Don't mess that up either, with Charley, I mean. You and her, you're—'

But McKenzie didn't catch the rest. The curtain swung open and a barrage of lights hit him as the drums, bass, and guitar slammed back into the groove. McKenzie strode onto the stage, greeted by a thunderous roar from the crowd. He felt invincible.

The show raced towards its climax. McKenzie, now completely at ease behind his trusty *Old Special*, strutted across the stage with a confidence he hadn't felt in a decade. Singing 'Give Me the Freedom', followed by 'Here as One', he could barely believe the show was nearing its end.

The stage lights lowered on the hydraulics, now horizontal and aimed outward, lighting up the sea of faces in the audience. Swaying in unison, they sang along, their voices soaring above McKenzie's. It was always an emotional moment as the show drew to a close. When a gig had been this great, the euphoria was almost overwhelming, but

McKenzie had to focus on the song, pushing through the lump in his throat to maintain the strength of his voice.

But then, out of nowhere, an image of Debbie and Andy flashed in his mind and for a moment it caught him completely off guard. He saw Andy sitting on Debbie's hospital bed, vulnerable yet radiating quiet loyalty, listening intently to the gig on the radio. McKenzie was unable to stop tears from welling in his eyes. Atkinson would consider this pure gold – the veteran rock star breaking down, overcome by the love from his fans. McKenzie knew that once the show ended, he'd have to face some serious responsibilities – responsibilities for people he hadn't known a few months ago, when he'd stumbled upon a random news item on TV during a particularly hungover lunchtime. As the song ended, the audience erupted, raising the roof. In a perfectly timed move, the lights cut out, and the band left the stage to wipe themselves down, grab a quick drink and hope the crowd picked up on the hint that the concert wasn't quite over. Sure enough, they did, stomping their feet and clapping, calling for *more*. A chant started in the back row, slowly spreading through the auditorium – 'Mc-Ken-zie, Mc-Ken-zie, Mc-Ken-zie.' Leaving it until the last possible moment, McKenzie and the band strolled back onto the stage to a deafening roar. McKenzie slung his guitar back over his head, wiping his forearm across his face. The drummer kicked the bass drum to check the kit was still miked, while McKenzie and the lead guitarist each strummed a chord, making sure everything was in order. McKenzie stood close to the mic stand, played another chord and the audience quietened.

He hated talking during a show – it always ran the risk of sounding corny and interrupting the flow. He preferred allowing the music to do the talking, but as a solo act, avoiding it completely was impossible.

'You know,' McKenzie began, his voice echoing around the arena. He could appreciate the intricacies of his singing voice in the studio, but he hated hearing his speaking voice. 'I want to thank you all for coming down and making this a special evening. It's been the best gig of my life – I love you all.' The crowd erupted in cheers and applause.

'We've got to thank the band – how amazing are these guys? Gus on guitar, Dillon on bass, Jack on drums and Stevie on keyboards.'

The audience went wild once more and the band raised their hands in acknowledgement.

'This isn't going to turn into an Oscars speech, but I've got to thank the crew too. They pulled this show together on short notice. You don't see them but they've been working non-stop ever since Atkinson, with his usual lack of consideration for anyone, decided we were playing Wembley. We all know Atkinson's an absolute pain in the arse but … we're all here because of him, I guess, so we should probably thank him too.'

The crowd laughed and cheered, and McKenzie turned, smiling in Atkinson's direction. Atkinson, never one to miss a chance to be the centre of attention, stepped out of the shadows, shoved his cigar in his mouth and gave a double wave to the crowd before returning to his spot next to Charley, who playfully elbowed him in the ribs.

'I can't forget to mention Charley Okorie,' McKenzie said, his voice steady but tinged with something deeper. 'She's the genius behind the production of our new album and I think – I *hope* – you're going to love it. Not only is she insanely talented at what she does, but … she also believed in me when I wasn't sure I could believe in myself.'

There were more cheers from the audience and out of the corner of his eye, McKenzie caught the way Charley's face lit up. Yet, McKenzie's thoughts began to spiral again. He looked down, strumming another chord, before glancing sideways. His eyes met Charley's for a fleeting moment and she responded with a quizzical, expectant look.

McKenzie turned to face the audience. A hush fell over the crowd. They knew 'Silent Struggle' was coming. Those at the front, leaning against the crash barriers, watched him intently. McKenzie's jaw tightened as he played another chord, this one louder, harder. He knew the band were waiting for a cue. McKenzie thought about Andy and Debbie, about Ward 14A, the talented young men in the music industry who had disappeared and anyone affected by this crisis. He felt an overwhelming wave of anger on behalf of every one of them. *Another chord.* A whistle cut through the air and the atmosphere shifted, becoming uncertain. Someone shouted, 'Come on!' from the back of the arena. The band glanced at Atkinson, who hissed McKenzie's name across the stage. McKenzie took a deep breath. He knew Atkinson would be panicking about how this was playing out on the radio. Radio stations hated dead air.

'The next song is "Silent Struggle",' he said. The crowd cheered but McKenzie raised his hand.

'But first … I … I need to talk about the real silent struggle that far too many people are facing – people living with AIDS. This struggle is happening right now and it should be shaking the world to its core. You've seen it on TV, you've read about it in the papers, but unless it affects you or your family, you can't truly understand what it's like. We need this silent struggle to stop being silent. We need to make some noise about it.'

The auditorium was now unnervingly quiet. Every eye was on McKenzie.

'Oh. My. God,' Atkinson said through the side of his mouth to Charley, his cigar dangling from his lips. 'I knew this was a bad mistake, he wasn't in a good place and now, now it's game over. Stop him, Charley. Do something, he'll listen to you.'

'Shush, Atkinson. He's doing something … *important*,' Charley said, staring out at the centre of the stage. The figure of McKenzie with his guitar was silhouetted by the huge spotlights and she felt something momentous happening.

'Some of you may have read a certain newspaper today and it's true – I have visited a friend who happens to have AIDS.'

'*Oh, sweet Jesus*,' Atkinson said, his voice rising with disbelief. '*Someone* has to stop him. This is it. He's on self-destruct. I should have checked him into The Priory months ago.'

There was a sharp intake of breath across the auditorium, followed by a few whistles – protest? McKenzie wasn't sure. But he had to keep going. The truth was, he didn't really know what he wanted to say, which, in front of 12,000 people was a terrifying prospect.

'The fact is … erm, the fact is, right now, all over the country, all over the world, there are people lying in hospitals, in their homes, in their childhood beds – shadows of the people they once were – dying from this relentless disease with no cure. Gay people, straight people, people of every ethnicity. But it's not just about the disease; they're also victims of fear, ignorance and prejudice. While their bodies slowly stop fighting, they're made to feel as though they've done something wrong.'

The whistles grew louder. McKenzie's eyes darted to the aisles, where a few people were climbing the stairs towards the exits. Were they heading to the restroom – or were they actually leaving? His wafer-thin confidence was crumbling. Then it started: first one or two voices, then more joined in, until *booing* rang out across the auditorium. Not lots, but enough to throw him off his stride. McKenzie wanted to get offstage – he knew he'd blown it. There was no turning back. All he wanted now was to play the bloody song and leave, but from the side of the stage, he heard clapping – Charley. He turned to find her, her eyes pleading with him – not to stop, not to give up. A few people in the front row joined in and a small ripple of claps spread through the crowd – pushing back against the whistles and boos. McKenzie had nothing to lose now, so he went for it.

'There's been so much misinformation from people who should know better. You cannot catch AIDS from toilet seats, utensils, or petrol pumps. AIDS spreads primarily through sexual contact, so ensure your sexual contact is safe – whether you're gay, straight, or otherwise. This disease is not a judgement or a curse; it's a tragedy. Those suffering need our compassion and care. The antidote to fear is empathy, not to demonise people. Thanks to the press and the government, AIDS has been stigmatised and weaponised against the gay community. But knowledge is our greatest tool. There are no silly questions when it comes to AIDS – we need to spread understanding and educate ourselves.

Tonight, "Silent Struggle" is dedicated to those battling this disease and to everyone who raises awareness, challenges the prejudice and pushes for a cure. As a special friend once said to me, we need to rock the world. Let's lift our hearts and voices together – this is "Silent Struggle".'

A muted, relieved cheer echoed across the auditorium. All McKenzie wanted now was to get to Andy and Debbie. His career was over and he wanted to get off the stage. The drummer counted to three and the band started in unison. McKenzie's hands shook and his voice wavered through the first few lines as he fought to keep the adrenaline from taking over. As the first verse transitioned seamlessly into the heartfelt chorus, the band's voices harmonised beautifully, lifting the song to another level.

> *Silent Struggle – with dreams that fade away.*
> *Silent Struggle – when the night turns into day.*
> *Silent Struggle – they're carrying the light,*
> *Silent Struggle – fighting the fight.*

When they reached the second verse, McKenzie closed his eyes. *In the quiet whispers, hearts are torn apart.* Lost in the music, he felt every word resonate deeply, drawing a raw, unshakeable power from within. As the second chorus began, the band's harmonies soared again and McKenzie slowly opened his eyes. Before him stretched a sea of swaying lighters, held aloft in the darkness – a breathtaking constellation of flickering lights, like stars scattered across the night. The audience's voices rose together, singing as one. McKenzie's voice cracked and he dropped his head, momentarily falling silent. The band pressed on, undeterred and the crowd rose to the occasion, their singing filling the gap. Drawing a deep breath, McKenzie reclaimed the lead, his voice surging back with a newfound power, the band locking in behind him for the final bridge – the dramatic resolution. As the song reached its crescendo, the final chord reverberated through the arena. A wave of goodwill rippled through the crowd, erupting into a thunderous roar. The lights rose, revealing a sea of overhead clapping, a cacophony of cheers, whistles and applause. As the band set down their instruments, they moved to the front of the stage to embrace McKenzie. Together, the five of them stood, arms around each other – drained but triumphant.

'Good night. We love you. We'll see you again soon. Stay safe. Thank you,' McKenzie called out, his words heartfelt but brief. He was never one for long goodbyes. After a few more waves to the adoring crowd, they walked slowly offstage, the euphoria still ringing in their ears. McKenzie had a habit of stealing one last glance at the crowd. He never knew which concert might be his last – there would be a final show someday. So he made sure to take it all in, savouring the moment before the lights dimmed.

In the wings, they were met with towels and robes. Charley was waiting for McKenzie, greeting him with a kiss on the cheek.

'Well *that* was bloody brilliant,' she said, her eyes sparkling with pride.

Nearby, Atkinson was pacing in tight, agitated circles, the Roamer pressed to his ear. He ended the call abruptly when he spotted McKenzie, his expression volcanic.

'What on earth are you playing at, Mack?' Atkinson roared, his voice echoing in the narrow corridor. 'We had it in the bag – in the bag! And you just couldn't make it to the end without doing everything possible to throw it down the plughole. They were in the palm of your hand! Why the self-righteous sermon? *Why*, Mack?'

Atkinson paused, his tone shifting from fury to a desperate pragmatism. 'We might have *just* got away with it. All those lighters – that's an image the press will struggle to ignore. We'll spin it somehow. I've already been on to *The Sun*. I promised them an exclusive backstage pic for a positive write-up. Let's get you to the dressing room, the photographer's on his way. We'll sort it, Mack.'

McKenzie let out a quiet sigh, rubbing the towel through his damp hair. Without a word, he nodded towards Charley, signalling her to follow him.

'Dressing room's this way, Mack. Mack? Dressing room!' Atkinson barked, his tone sharp as he hurried after McKenzie and Charley. The two strode purposefully down the long corridor towards the back of Wembley Arena. Roadies darted in every direction, shouting congratulations as they passed. Reaching for Charley's hand, McKenzie quickened his pace, heading towards a fire exit.

'Come on, Mack, back to the dressing room!' Atkinson called, his voice rising with panic. 'We've got press to do. Mack, stop walking down this corridor *right now*! McKenzie, I am asking you – no, I'm telling you – turn around *this instant*!'

Atkinson puffed along behind them, unused to following anyone. People usually followed *him*. His voice cracked with a mixture of anger and desperation. 'Mack, this is *your* night! We've got an after-show party booked at Kensington Roof Gardens.' He switched tactics, his tone veering towards pleading. '*Spandau Ballet* will be there!' he squeaked. 'Mack, *step away* from the door … Mack, *do not* put your hands on that fire door … Mack, *do not* open that door!'

With a decisive push on the fire exit bar, McKenzie swung the door open. A rush of cool air hit him, filling his lungs and clearing his head. It felt incredible. Without a word, McKenzie reached for Charley's hand again, his grip firm and reassuring and together they stepped through the door and into the night. Behind them, Atkinson stumbled to the doorway, his blotchy face a deep puce. He clutched the frame for support, panting for breath – struggling desperately to shout after them.

McKenzie and Charley stepped onto a concrete concourse behind the arena, the night air cool and fresh. A handful of fans milled about and they watched open-mouthed as McKenzie led Charley towards a row of metal barriers, where two security guards stood near a line of limousines.

'Uh, excuse me?' McKenzie said, flashing a sheepish smile. 'Hi, McKenzie McCall here. I've just, erm, done a concert in there.' He pointed over his shoulder towards the arena. 'Would it be alright if we slipped through to one of those cars? Thanks ever so much.'

The nearest security guard blinked in surprise, his eyes darting between McKenzie and Charley. Stepping forward, he shifted the barrier aside without a word, recognising the star of the show before him.

'Thank you!' McKenzie said brightly as he and Charley walked to the first limo in line. Sliding into the backseat, McKenzie leaned back, exhaling deeply. The driver turned around, his professional composure just barely masking his excitement at having the headliner in *his* car.

'To the after-show party, sir?' he asked, gripping the steering wheel with practised calm.

'No,' McKenzie said firmly, looking at Charley.

'*Manchester*, please,' they said in perfect unison.

23

After booking into a hotel in Manchester, McKenzie
and Charley had been on call for Andy for several days
following the drama of their departure from Wembley
Arena. At first, Debbie had seemed quite lucid, though
extremely fragile, and there was hope that she might defy
the odds again and improve once placed on a drip.

In the dim light of the small, sterile room, Debbie
seemed almost ethereal, a delicate shell of the vibrant, slightly
indignant person she once was – her skin drawn tightly over
her cheekbones, leaving her gaunt and skeletal. Her hollow
eyes, once sparkling, grew distant, the light within them
gradually dimming. Despite Debbie's physical decline, there
were still moments of humour and bursts of chattiness,
though she was becoming increasingly confused and spent
more time drifting in and out of consciousness. Andy, with
his characteristic devotion, was fiercely determined to keep
fighting for her. Yet his eyes betrayed a heartbreaking mix
of pain, shock, denial and sadness as he clung to Debbie's
hand. Charley and McKenzie remained close by, sometimes
sitting with Andy in the room, other times waiting in the

visitors' lounge to give him space. They made sure he ate, stayed available for him to talk to and coordinated with Pam. Charley offered comforting hugs, while McKenzie gave reassuring hair ruffles, yet both felt painfully helpless. They understood this was now a long-haul commitment and didn't even discuss returning to London.

***

That night, Andy dozed off in the armchair beside Debbie's bed, curled up with a blanket, as comfortably as he could manage. His sleep was restless, his senses honed over time to detect even the faintest sound. He had developed an unspoken connection with Debbie, a sixth sense for when she stirred in the night in case she needed him. As he shifted in the quiet hours of the night, he instinctively turned towards her. In that hazy moment of wakefulness, he saw her lying still, her eyes open, gazing into the darkness. In the last few months, the nights had been long for Debbie – her discomfort robbed her of rest, leaving her to face the endless hours alone with her thoughts, quietly grappling with the enormity of her fate.

'Mum?' Andy whispered.

Debbie turned her head slowly and attempted a smile as she reached out her hand.

'Hi, love,' she said, her voice barely audible. 'You shouldn't be here, Andy. You need a proper bed – and some sleep.'

Andy shrugged off the blanket and moved closer to the bed, taking Debbie's hand in his once again, for what felt like the thousandth time. The dim light from the hallway filtered through the glass in the door, casting a soft glow over the room.

'I was thinking earlier, Mum,' Andy began eagerly, 'when the royalty money comes, maybe we can do up the house – decorate each room, get new carpets?'

Debbie swallowed painfully, her breathing shallow as she blinked slowly. She attempted to turn a little towards him. 'Andy,' she said softly, her voice strained but tender, 'you know you're going to be OK, don't you? Gran and Grandad will take care of you – they'll make sure you're looked after. You've always loved their house, haven't you? Remember how much you enjoyed going there when you were little?'

They looked into each other's eyes, Andy and Debbie – the team. In that fleeting connection a silent understanding passed between them – clarity about what this conversation was. A conversation they'd stumbled into but somehow Andy knew Debbie couldn't rest, she couldn't let go, until it had happened – it was goodbye. He saw the deep, unspoken sorrow in his mum's eyes, mixed with her love and concern for him. Her lips curved into a slight smile and it almost shattered him. Months of being brave, months of fighting and bottling up his feelings and it was all too much. A desperate feeling of sorrow at not being able to fix this and the inevitable outcome he had so far managed not to face up to all crashed over him. He put his head gently on top of Debbie and cried into the bedsheets.

'We're not ready,' he sobbed. 'You can fight for longer, I know you can. One more time, you can come home one more time.'

***

Debbie gently stroked his head with a hand connected to an IV drip. She longed to protect her child from pain, to give him the stable upbringing she had always wanted for him but that dream had been stolen. She ached to tear the drip out, scoop Andy up and take him home – to have just one more night, one more day of normality – but the strength to do so had slipped away from her. Her head pulsed with a distant ringing, her body throbbed from within and even the simple act of swallowing felt like a monumental effort.

'I'm just sorry that you're going to have a tough time ahead. I'm sad too, but I'll be with you every step of the way, big guy. Just try to feel me around you and I'll be there, I promise. I don't plan to miss a single moment, even if you can't see me.'

Maybe, in some way, Debbie was comforting herself too.

'You know I won't let you down, don't you? I'll work hard and do my best. You'll be proud, Mum.' Andy's voice shook, and she knew he was desperate to say the right things while he still could.

'I'm already so proud of you, Andy. I know you'll be brave – you've been so strong for me. I wouldn't have made it this far without you.'

'But I *need* you, Mum,' Andy choked out, switching between courage and sorrow with the blink of an eye.

Debbie's hand gently cupped the back of his head, her fingers stroking his hair. 'You're going to be just fine, Andy. Hold on to the memories but don't let them hold you back. You're a very special person. Go out and show the world what you're made of.'

Tears streamed down Andy's face as he nodded. 'I don't want to say goodbye.'

She lowered her head and kissed him softly. 'I'll be in your heart, in your thoughts and I know you'll carry me with you everywhere you go. So it's not goodbye, not really.'

'I love you, Mum.'

'Love you, Andy.'

***

The sterile hum of the hospital room faded into the background, muffled by the weight of the moment. In that space, it felt as if they could have been back home, curled up on Debbie's bed, hugging as they had countless times before. The air was thick with the scent of antiseptic but Andy could still catch the faint fragrance of Debbie's perfume. He held her tighter, needing to feel her close, to imprint that feeling into his memory. The tighter he clung, the longer she stayed with him and in that tender moment, he wished time could stand still forever.

***

The next day, McKenzie and Charley retreated to the visitors' room for an afternoon cup of tea while a doctor was with Debbie. Angie entered quietly, gathering a few mugs from the low table in front of them.

'How is Matthew doing …?' McKenzie's question faltered. He knew the answer.

Angie placed the mugs down in the sink. 'He passed away, McKenzie. I went to his funeral on Friday.' She hesitated, her voice catching slightly. 'It was my eighteenth funeral in the last three months.'

'It's so sad,' Charley said softly, breaking a moment of silence. 'How do you cope?'

'I don't,' Angie admitted. Her gaze dropped for a moment before meeting Charley's. 'The team here, we try to remind ourselves that we're bringing as much comfort, support and dignity to the patients as we can. I focus on the small victories – making someone smile, giving them a moment of peace, helping someone feel less alone when their family decides not to come. Thank you, by the way. For what you said at your concert, McKenzie. I was listening. It makes a difference.'

McKenzie nodded, his expression resolute. 'I … we all … know more needs to be done. I hope Mark – Matthew's partner – is going to be OK. We'll try to keep in touch with him.'

Angie left the room, and for a while, McKenzie and Charley sipped their tea without speaking.

'Thank you for being here, Charley,' McKenzie said at last. 'You've put your life on hold for this – for Andy and Debbie. I couldn't have done any of it without you.'

'You're right, you couldn't have,' Charley joked with a smile.

McKenzie returned the smile but then he frowned.

'There's something else I need your support with,' he said after a moment. 'Debbie has asked me to do something …'

***

It was definitely the right address. Although it was an early summer's evening, the clouds were grey and the wind swept around them as they contemplated the weathered door. The paint was peeling on the timber frame and the glass was cracked. To their left, they could see the skyline of Manchester in the gloom and there were other concrete blocks of flats towering around them. The outdoor corridor they stood in was dimly lit, crisp packets swirled on the ground and discarded items cluttered the corners, remnants of lives lived on the margins. A history of neglect clung to the building – places like this had been low on the government's priority list. McKenzie slipped the piece of paper from his pocket and double-checked Debbie's scrawled writing. Shivering, he wished he'd worn a proper coat, not just his denim jacket. In her khaki green parka jacket, Charley had been more sensible. Between them was Andy and they acted as a protective sandwich. Just an hour earlier, Charley and McKenzie had stepped quietly into Debbie's room, where she lay asleep, her breath heavy and rasping. Andy looked up at them with wide, searching eyes, immediately sensing the gravity they were trying to mask on their faces. Charley perched beside him and placed her arm around his small shoulders, a silent gesture of comfort. McKenzie knelt to meet Andy's gaze, his voice low and steady as he explained they were going to find Andy's dad. For a moment, McKenzie's heart twisted, wondering how much more this child could bear. But Andy, with a resolute nod, readily agreed without hesitation.

As they stood at the door, McKenzie and Charley both shifted in a little closer to Andy. Andy met McKenzie's eyes briefly before looking to Charley. McKenzie knocked on the glass hesitantly and it made a fragile tapping sound due to the broken panel. There was no answer. As they waited, the distant hum of motorway traffic, the wail of a police siren rushing down a nearby road and the faint strains of a ghetto blaster playing 'White Lines' seemed to swell in volume around them. McKenzie felt tense and instinctively put his arm over Charley's which was tucked around Andy's back. McKenzie knocked again, a little harder this time, though still gingerly. Still nothing. The net curtain twitched in the window of the flat next door.

'Come on, you two,' McKenzie said, looking back up the corridor towards the exit. 'We can try again first thing in the morning. We could maybe ask around if we get no answer tomorrow.'

'Sorry, Andy,' said Charley, hugging his shoulders. Andy thumped the wood of the door with his fist a couple of times then turned away.

'Let's go back to Mum. I don't want her waking up and wondering where we are,' he said, turning. McKenzie and Charley filed in behind him without question as they headed for the stairwell. But then, slicing through the stillness from behind them, came a man's voice – a shaky, disbelieving, raw whisper. '*Andy?* My God … Andy!'

The three of them froze and turned.

'Dad?' Andy said, his surprised voice carrying the faint tremor of a question.

Tony wore faded blue joggers with white stripes down the sides and an oversized, heavy brown jumper. The clothes hung loosely on his frail frame. McKenzie recognised his face from the photos – but only just. It wasn't the youthful, carefree face framed with short, spiky hair he thought he remembered; this face had aged twenty years – gaunt, with hollow cheeks and sunken, haunted eyes. His bony hands trembled as they gripped the doorframe and a deep, rasping cough racked his chest after he spoke. In that instant – no more than a millisecond – McKenzie, Andy and Charley understood. The realisation hit them all at once, leaving each to silently grapple with the shock. The skin stretched tightly over Tony's left cheekbone was marked by two dark, angry purple lesions, stark against his ashen complexion – Kaposi's sarcoma.

'You better come in,' he whispered, his voice hoarse and brittle.

The flat was thick with the musty odour of stale air. The hallway was carpeted in a swirling brown and orange floral pattern. To the right was a gloomy bedroom and bathroom; to the left, a small galley kitchen with dishes piled high in the sink and orange cupboards set against a lino floor. Straight ahead, the rectangular sitting room was dominated by a worn red carpet. A small, battered brown leather settee sat opposite a mismatched blue fabric armchair. On the wall beside the armchair was a wooden gas fire. By the window stood a small TV perched precariously on a cardboard box. The TV's portable aerial struggled for reception, rendering the picture fuzzy, with the unmistakable end credits of *Coronation Street* crackling through. A wonky coffee table in the centre of the room held a Liverpool FC mug and a scattering of medicine bottles. Next to the mug sat a matching Liverpool FC ashtray, overflowing with ash and stubbed-out cigarette butts. A packet of Benson & Hedges lay nearby, a lighter balanced on top. Through his shock, Andy noted, with well-practised practicality, how the cigarettes must be taking their toll on his dad's AIDS weakened chest. On the windowsill was a framed photo. It was Andy, younger and jubilant, holding a Man of the

Match trophy aloft from his days with the local under-11s football team. It felt like a different lifetime.

McKenzie, Charley, and Andy sat down on the settee at Tony's invitation. Tony slumped forward in the armchair, elbows resting on his knees, his hands cupping his face. He let out a deep, heavy breath, shook his head and coughed again before finally looking up at the three of them, squashed together on the settee in front of him. Charley offered him a warm smile. McKenzie's gaze wandered around the room. Andy's stare bored into him.

The man before Andy, with a pain-etched face, was a shadow of the figure he had expected to answer the door. As Andy looked into his father's eyes, he felt sorrow and pity replacing some of the anger that had consumed him moments before. It drained from him, as though someone had pulled a plug.

It wasn't just the physical change that stunned him; it was the realisation that his dad had been battling something so devastating, alone. Questions flooded Andy's mind. In that moment, a desperate need for his dad to speak overwhelmed him, to say something – anything – that might provide some answers.

'I'd offer to make you a brew, but … I think I'm out of milk,' Tony said eventually, his voice hesitant.

He fumbled for his cigarette packet, lit one with trembling hands and took a long, shaky drag. The smoke curled in the air as he exhaled. He began coughing again. 'I know it's bad for me, but, well … I haven't got much to lose right now.'

Tony nodded towards the TV, its screen flickering between fuzzy static and an episode of *The Bill*. 'Stupid thing – barely works half the time. I can't get a bloody signal.

Sometimes you have to stand there holding the aerial like a human antenna.'

The hit of nicotine seemed to ease Tony's nerves as he narrowed his eyes, studying his son and his two companions. His brow furrowed in confusion. 'You look an awful lot like McKenzie McCall and you …' He turned to Charley. 'You look familiar too.'

Andy watched as McKenzie took a deep breath, no doubt trying to control his emotions – much as Andy was trying to control his. But when McKenzie spoke, there was still a slight tremor in his voice, despite his attempt to adopt an authoritative tone.

'Tony, I am McKenzie McCall. Over the past couple of months, I've become a friend of the family. This is Charley – you might recognise her as a well-known music producer. The truth is, Tony, we're here because, well, Debbie asked us to come when she became … ill. She hoped that you would …'

There was a heartbreaking flaw in Debbie's plan, Andy realised. His dad was supposed to reappear from wherever he'd vanished to and step in as a parent when she was gone. But now, the weight of that unspoken reality hung heavily in the room as everyone silently filled in the gaps. Tony's face crumpled. Pressing his hands to his eyes, he broke into sobs.

'I hoped … For over two years, I've been *praying* Debbie was OK and getting on with life,' Tony said through his tears.

'You left us, Dad,' Andy snapped, his anger surging once more, tangled with tormenting emotions. 'You left us to deal with it – me, Mum … you deserted us. We were on our own. How dare you sit there … and … and *smoke*. Mum needed you.'

Tears streamed down Tony's face as he dragged his forearm across his face and sniffed.

'It was … it was for the best. *Look* at me, Andy,' Tony croaked back.

'You *left* us,' Andy repeated. 'Mum's been poorly … *she* didn't leave. I've looked after her but you weren't there and you should have been.' Andy gulped, fighting to control his fury. 'How could you treat Mum like that? Did you give it to her? You're … you're a disgusting man.'

Andy leaned forward, tears stinging his eyes, and jabbed a finger at Tony. 'You ruined everything. You've ruined all our lives, haven't you? *Haven't you?*'

'Andy, come on,' Charley said softly, leaning forward and resting a hand on his knee.

'Maybe we call it a day and meet again another time,' McKenzie suggested gently. 'We've all got a lot to process.'

Andy sank back on the sofa, his voice quieter now. 'I would've looked after *you* too … if you'd stuck around.'

Tony sat in silence, his head bowed, nodding in resignation. 'I have ruined everything, Andy. Sorry isn't enough, is it? But please, before you go, hear me out. Please just listen.'

He took another drag from his cigarette, caught Andy's disapproving glare and stubbed it out.

'I loved Debbie,' Tony began. 'We were great together, me and Deb. We carved out a little life for ourselves and we laughed – we laughed so much. Sometimes we laughed so hard it turned into that silent kind of laughing and we'd just point at each other, trying not to burst and ended up laughing even more. I think about that a lot.'

Tony smiled briefly at the memory, looking around at his visitors. Charley nodded warmly. Andy scowled but stayed silent, and Tony clearly took this as permission to continue.

'Then you came along, Andy,' Tony said, his tone soft. 'Having a baby – it's tough. It's like an explosion in your life. No one warns you about that. But you were so loved. It was … perfect. The three of us – we were strong, we were close. You must remember that?'

Andy crossed his arms, but his anger was subsiding.

'I loved our family,' Tony said quietly. 'I'd spend all day at work, just so excited to come back to our little home.'

He stared out of the window for a moment, as if his memories were hidden there.

'But there was a problem, Andy … and I'm going to find this very difficult to talk about.' His voice dropped to a hoarse whisper, like he was unaccustomed to talking this much. He reached up, feeling around his throat and glands.

'Are you OK to carry on, Tony?' Charley asked.

Tony took a couple of deep breaths and grimaced slightly, holding his chest.

'Please carry on,' Andy's quiet voice said, '… if you can.'

Tony locked eyes with him and a grim determination registered on his face. He clenched his jaw, leaning forward.

'Well this is the tricky part and I'm sorry for it all – I'm so ashamed.' He paused and took another deep breath. 'As a teenager, well, I suppose I was one of the boys – after the girls. Like my mates, there was always someone we were chasing. But there was something else there, I ignored it – it wasn't something I was going to do anything about, but I suppose… I suppose it wasn't *just* the girls who caught my eye. I hoped it would go away. You have to understand what it was like, Andy. You could be fired from your job if they thought you were … gay. It had only just been made legal. Before that you could end up in prison – a *criminal*. You could be beaten up, an embarrassment to your family – so you hid those feelings, you buried them and cracked on with life. Then I met Debbie and none of it mattered anyway because she was … *is* … perfect and I loved her – still do. But time went by and it gnawed at me and I reasoned if I just explored that little side of me, I could get it out of my system and then focus on Debbie and you for the rest of my life. The world was changing and gay people were becoming more accepted and more visible. I was aware nightclubs were opening just for gay people and that's where I started going, on my own at first, but I quickly made friends and became part of a little group. I started going out more and more. To my shame, I told Debbie I was meeting work mates and I could tell it was getting to her. Then I met someone who I became close with – Paul. He was kind and patient and I felt comfortable around him – we were … close.'

Tony lifted his eyes from the floor, dragged a hand through his hair and met the faces in front of him, waiting for him to continue. 'I kind of started taking stock, realising I was hurting Debbie by being out so much, while also knowing I maybe wasn't being true to myself. I was at a crossroads – completely torn apart by it. But then the stories started to appear in the newspapers and there were whispers in the clubs about this new illness. It soon had a name – AIDS. There was disbelief, fear, confusion but an awful lot of denial. People started disappearing from the scene. One minute they were there full of life, the next minute they didn't socialise any more. My whole group of friends became ill or died, one by one.'

He reached for his chest again, taking another deep breath. Andy's eyes didn't leave him, fully aware of where Tony's story was headed, yet still needing him to continue.

'Then I realised I hadn't seen Paul for a while,' Tony continued, 'and I started to worry because I was feeling run down, my glands were up all over my body and I was sweating at night. I had a bit of a rash and I looked rough. Man flu, Debbie joked, but it felt different – I'd always been healthy and I couldn't shake it off. So I went to the doctor and sat there listening to how I had a virus and I just needed a bit of rest and it'd blow over, but to take some antibiotics just in case. As I got up to leave, I just blurted it out. *I think I need an AIDS test* and the doctor looked shocked and disgusted. I thought you said you had a young child, she said. The test was booked and it took five days to hear – positive. They gave me a leaflet and suggested I tell my wife about my *lifestyle*. Thanks for that, I thought. I mulled it over for a few days, in shock more than anything and decided I had to leave – I was panicking. I thought I was doing the right thing, taking myself off … to die without bringing any shame to Debbie and most of all, without putting her, or you, at risk. You've got to understand that at that time, even those with it thought we might be able to pass it on just by hugging – there wasn't much information out there and very little support.'

Tony went to pick up his cigarette packet but decided against it. His voice became more desperate.

'I didn't know I was carrying a virus, no one did – not at first. Debbie and I still occasionally did things married couples do. But as soon as I thought there might even be the slightest chance I was at risk, I was careful – very careful.

The newspapers were saying people with AIDS were facing God's wrath as punishment for being homosexual. The gay community was … *is* … being vilified. I didn't want Debbie being associated with that, so I packed a bag and left – the coward's way out. I prayed she'd get over me and live a healthy life. She doesn't deserve any of this. I kept working for a while, but then I had a couple of fits. I think someone who'd spotted me out once put two and two together and they terminated my contract. They said my safety was at risk working with the machinery – just to spare us all from the real reason. I signed on and came here. I only ever leave the flat to go to the shop every few days. There's an old guy who lives a few floors up, alone. I've bumped into him a few times in the lift, he took one look at me and I could see in his face he knew. He leaves me little bags of shopping at the door and we've never even said a word to each other. All this time, I've thought of you and Debbie, Andy. Most of all, I hoped you were OK and getting on with life. Stupidly, I actually hoped that because she was a woman, she might have been safe.'

Tony's eyes lingered on the cigarettes again and this time he grabbed the packet and removed one. His hand was shaking so much he struggled to find the end of the cigarette with the lighter. The whole thing was just so awful and helpless that no one really knew what to say.

'I can't speak for Andy,' Charley said after a pause, 'but no matter your feelings – whether for women or men – you shouldn't feel ashamed. No one could have predicted that a virus would come along and devastate an entire community so quickly. It's tragic. All of this is so tragic.'

Andy stood and for a brief moment, Tony flinched,

thinking Andy was going to hit him across the face. But instead, Andy sat on the arm of Tony's chair and gently draped an arm around his shoulders.

Tony leaned in, his face full of anguish. 'I'm so sorry, Andy,' Tony whispered. 'I want to get to know you again. For as long as I'm here, I'll be a dad to you the best I possibly can – if you'll have me. Am I … am I allowed to visit Debbie?'

24

For the next two days, Debbie slipped in and out of consciousness. Her room on Ward 14A became heavy with a poignancy that was almost too much to bear – a fading life and profound reflection. On the bedside table was the photo of Debbie, Tony and Andy in front of the Christmas tree, framed and standing as a bittersweet reminder of brighter days, lovingly placed there by Andy. The room held a serene stillness, sadness touching every person differently. Andy refused to leave, steadfast in his vigil, still sleeping in the armchair by Debbie's side. McKenzie, Charley, and Pam took turns staying with him and Debbie, their quiet presence a fragile comfort.

In Andy's dreams, Debbie was her old self – vibrant, bubbly and alive. The visions were so vivid that waking was a cruel jolt, leaving him momentarily expecting to see Debbie sitting up, smiling at him. Debbie lay mostly still, propped up on pillows. She seemed impossibly small in the bed, her ailing frame barely denting the mattress. Her translucent skin, marked with lesions, bore the cruel evidence of the disease that had ravaged her body. Occasionally, Debbie would stir, her faint whispers for water barely audible through the oxygen mask. Andy would gently help her, each time trying to coax her to take a bite of fruit, a morsel of anything, clinging desperately to the hope that food might kindle some spark of strength. But she slipped back into sleep before he could even put the cup down.

In a fleeting moment of clarity, Debbie's eyes locked with Andy's as he told her he had visited Tony. There was a glimmer of recognition and he was certain she gave a faint accepting nod. Did she know why Tony had disappeared? Was that why she had let him go so quietly, without anger or protest? Andy was never to know. Tony arrived by bus, venturing further than he had in months to join Andy at Debbie's bedside. His visit was heartbreakingly brief. Tears coursed down his face as he grasped Debbie's frail hand, the faintest squeeze meeting his touch. He held on tightly, desperate to believe it was a silent acknowledgement of his regret, his love and his sorrow. No one could truly decipher what this reunion meant, a reminder that everything was now beyond anyone's control. Seeing Tony's exhaustion, McKenzie and Charley drove him back to his flat, leaving him with his memories.

On Debbie's second-to-last night, as she continued to slip further away from them, Pam stood at the payphone in the corridor, desperately pleading with Brian to come. When she returned to the room, she shook her head sadly at Charley. But as the light outside faded, Brian arrived. Stepping into the room with hesitant, unsteady steps, he took one look at Debbie and collapsed to his knees at her bedside.

'My little girl,' was all he could keep repeating.

Late into the night, as Andy slept under a hospital blanket, Debbie's eyes flickered. Brian leaned forward and took her hand. A faint smile touched her lips and in a voice barely above a whisper, Debbie murmured that she hadn't thought he would come. She thanked him – for being there, for the stubborn streak she'd inherited from him and for simply being her father.

Brian's voice wavered as he whispered, 'I'm so proud of you, Debbie – always have been, always will be.'

The sun rose and a golden light filtered through the curtains. Debbie's breath became more laboured and fear grew in her eyes as she struggled. Brian stroked his daughter's hand and calmed her, reassuring her that she shouldn't hang on for them. Debbie relaxed again – her dad's presence easing her towards peace. During the day, Andy took up his usual spot, perched on the bed. Brian's and Pam's memories flowed freely and McKenzie, Charley and Andy listened and laughed at the anecdotes of happier times with smiles and teary eyes. McKenzie and Charley found themselves alone when Pam, Brian, and Andy stepped out for a quiet break, seeking some lunch and fresh air in the hospital garden. Debbie stirred and murmured something McKenzie couldn't quite hear, prompting him to lean closer. Her shaky hand removed the oxygen mask and her voice – faint yet carrying the ghost of the feisty woman he had first met – whispered weakly in his ear. McKenzie listened intently, nodding as he gently reassured her.

With her final message delivered, those were Debbie's last words.

As night fell, a sense of peace settled over the room. Angie arrived on her shift and she came with a doctor who administered medication to ensure Debbie's comfort – free from pain. Debbie's chest had developed a loud rattling noise with each breath but Angie assured Andy that Debbie was comfortable and that she could likely still hear him. Angie encouraged him to speak to her whenever he needed to. There was no way out of this, no way to shield him from reality.

By midnight, Andy had crawled up the bed to lie next to Debbie, nuzzling into her as he dozed fitfully. Debbie lay on her back, her face turned away from him, towards the window and the night sky. This comforted Andy – was she facing heaven? He woke often, craning his neck to kiss her cheek, whispering, 'Love you!' each time. Pam and Brian sat on either side of the bed, both with glistening eyes filled with pain. McKenzie and Charley sat at a distance, forming an outer ring. Andy willed Debbie to move, to roll over and snuggle him as she had done countless times when he'd scrambled into her room each morning. Her breathing had grown shallow and he watched her chest rise and fall with almost imperceptible movement. Suddenly, Debbie's head turned, resting her cheek gently against Andy's hair. His heart soared, but in the same moment, he knew – the soft exhale, the last of her breath – and she was gone.

'Gran …' Andy looked up at the exhausted faces around him. Pam lifted her head, her eyes drawn and heavy. 'Mum's gone now.'

Pam stood up and wobbled slightly, her eyes locked on her daughter in disbelief, the plastic chair sliding backwards in the haste of the movement. There was no surprise in what had happened but the shock and pain etched in Pam's face told a different story – like a blow she had been bracing herself for but wasn't ready to endure – grief crashing down on her.

'It's OK, Gran. She looks happy.' It was true. For the first time in weeks, Debbie's face looked almost serene, a euphoric expression lighting up her features. The pain had gone. Charley instinctively rose and put an arm around Pam's shoulders. McKenzie stood by Brian, who was crying silently in his chair and placed a hand on his shoulder. Andy remained with Debbie.

'I'll get Angie,' said Charley, ever practical.

'Don't,' said Andy. 'I want us to have longer, just us. Not yet.'

And that's how he stayed. Andy and Debbie – their last moment of teamwork together, guiding her on her final journey. Angie did come in but she understood – she'd seen it so many times and discreetly left. No one was going to suggest Andy move, understanding that this moment was going to stay with him for the rest of his life. As the sun rose on the first day without his mum, Andy lay exactly where he was, holding on until he was ready.

25

True to his word, McKenzie honoured Debbie's final whispered wishes with unwavering dedication. He and Charley rented a house in Manchester, close to Pam and Brian, where they temporarily made their home, focusing entirely on supporting Andy as Debbie had asked. While Andy primarily stayed with Pam and Brian, he spent much of his time at McKenzie and Charley's house. Together, they helped him with work from his textbooks, reminisced over photos and even found moments to laugh amidst the heartbreak. At times, Andy would withdraw into himself, retreating into silence. McKenzie and Charley waited patiently until he was ready to talk, offering quiet reassurance through their presence.

Andy had returned to his old street in Massleforth only once, but he couldn't bring himself to step inside the house. It remained frozen in time, just as it had been since the day Debbie left for the last time. The mere thought of crossing the threshold felt too raw, too overwhelming. Mrs Silva, ever thoughtful, had tidied up and emptied their fridge and freezer. One evening, she invited them all over for tea. 'Andy, you're so thin! Mack, you need to feed this boy!' she exclaimed, her hands on her hips. Pam, Brian, Charley, Mack and Andy squeezed around makeshift tables stretching through the Silvas' sitting room, while Mrs Silva carried in pot after steaming pot of mouthwatering dishes.

Whether it was an oversight due to the odd number of guests or a quiet, unconscious gesture by Mrs Silva, one place at the table was left empty. Andy noticed it. Later that night, after shedding muffled tears into his pillow, he shared the ache in his heart with McKenzie.

At the church funeral in Massleforth, Andy sat in the front pew, flanked by Pam and Brian on one side and Charley and McKenzie on the other. Tony was further back, his thin frame swallowed by an ill-fitting black suit. Mr and Mrs Silva were there as well, embodying their steadfast and resolute dignity, just as they had throughout Debbie's illness. Reggie arrived with his mum, wearing his scruffy school uniform but making an earnest effort to neaten his hair into a side-parting with a comb. Yet the church wasn't full – not by a long stretch; a sobering reminder that some people from Debbie's life had chosen to stay away. From the pulpit, Andy spoke to those who *had* gathered, his voice steady but full of emotion. He shared how proud he was of his mum and the way she had held her head high through everything she had faced. Andy then read lyrics from a song he and McKenzie had been working on – 'The Empty Chair at the Table'. McKenzie then took up his guitar, performing an acoustic version of 'Silent Struggle'. His voice cracked, emotion echoing through the church. Brian stepped forward to read the poem *You Can Shed Tears*, a heartfelt choice suggested by Charley.

***

The newspapers inevitably latched on to the story, splashing it across the front page: *Mack's Silent Struggle at AIDS Victim's Funeral.* In truth, the media had been relentless with McKenzie since his no-show at his own after-show party. Sensing a bigger story, they were determined to paint him as unhinged, running daily headlines like *Mack in a Muddle Over Manchester Move!* McKenzie, however, remained unfazed. His loyal fans would stick by him, and as for the rest? That was their issue. If need be, he'd go back to playing pubs – or just retire altogether. *For Those Who Come Next* had been released and earned McKenzie his first chart-topping album in a number of years, garnering widespread critical acclaim. Yet now, his name was invariably accompanied by labels: *the eccentric singer* or *the reclusive singer* or *the AIDS activist singer.* McKenzie turned his attention to fulfilling his second promise to Debbie – not only ensuring Andy was supported in his grief but also helping to take care of Tony. Tony gradually spent more and more time with them and he and Andy began to bond, their connection rekindling over games of cards, *Monopoly* and *Subbuteo.* Together, they tentatively worked to rebuild their relationship.

Andy often brought out Debbie's cherished photo albums and he and Tony would flip through the pages together, memories spilling out with each turn. It gave them focus and a chance to reflect on the past.

'I just want to turn back time,' Tony would murmur.

McKenzie knew it wouldn't be long before Andy's royalties came through. In his grandparents' name, Andy could finally buy a house for his family – if that was what he chose to do. McKenzie would ensure care workers were provided for Tony. One thing wasn't in doubt: Tony would eventually need Ward 14A, just as Debbie had. McKenzie had already decided where his share of the proceeds from 'Silent Struggle' would go – Ward 14A needed funding to provide incredible professionals like Angie with the resources to support people living with AIDS, including Tony, Mark, and countless others.

They scoured the news, clinging to any hope of a breakthrough treatment for AIDS. It was clear that Tony was weak and after their experience with Debbie, they all recognised the familiar signs and progression of the disease. McKenzie arranged for Andy to receive tutoring while decisions about his education were being made. Reggie visited regularly, joining Andy for games on his Spectrum. It was heartening to hear their laughter as they pummelled the joystick on *Daley Thompson's Decathlon*. Reggie couldn't quite hide his indignation that Liverpool had finished the season in second place, nine points behind a plucky Everton.

And Atkinson? There were a few phone calls – discussions about newspaper headlines, a potential autumn tour and perhaps a follow-up album – but Atkinson seemed unusually subdued. Charley and McKenzie speculated about this, wondering if he was sulking. Had he finally decided McKenzie was too much trouble? Maybe he was already scouting for a new act – someone more malleable, more receptive to his manipulative, malevolent ways. Atkinson thrived on control and now that he had lost it, it was a possibility that need had been diverted elsewhere. The second, less-discussed theory was that – just maybe – Atkinson had decided to give McKenzie the room to focus on those around him and take his time before his next career move. McKenzie and Charley quickly dismissed that idea. Atkinson, willingly offering anyone room to breathe? That was *never* going to happen.

One evening, Andy and Tony sat at the coffee table, laughing and tossing playful accusations of cheating over a game of *Cluedo*. Charley and McKenzie lounged on the sofa – Charley at one end, propped up with a cushion, her feet resting on McKenzie's lap, giggling at *The Two Ronnies* on TV.

McKenzie felt something unfamiliar: contentment. The absence of Debbie was a huge hole in their lives and there was no doubt that dark clouds loomed on the horizon for Tony. But for now, his T-cells were stable – low, but stable. Being back around Andy seemed to have given Tony a boost. When the telephone rang and McKenzie reached for the receiver from the side table, he felt a sudden appreciation of normality. A warmth of domesticity he realised he'd been craving and a sense of family, in its own way.

'Mack? Atkinson.'

'Hi, Atkinson.'

'Mack, we … *I* have a problem …'

***

At the other end of the phone, Atkinson held his Roamer to his ear with his right hand. He stood before the fireplace in his sitting room, where a grand marble mantel adorned with intricate gold detailing was framed by an ornate brass surround, gleaming against bold floral tiles in the hearth. A large, gilded mirror above the fireplace reflected the opulence of the room, with plush velvet curtains and lavish accessories. But it also reflected something else – a man Atkinson barely recognised. He knew it was him, yet this version seemed smaller, his face carrying an expression almost foreign to him – fear. The illusion he had painstakingly created, maintained and protected was on the verge of shattering.

His left hand rose, shifting the heavy gold chain that hung around his neck to one side – a symbol of the status he had always cherished, the gleaming marker of his wealth and success and an accessory to his swaggering bravado. He wasn't sure why he felt the need to check again; it was unmistakable.

A dark, purplish lesion, irregular in shape and slightly raised, lay concealed beneath the chain – much like Atkinson's carefully guarded private life had remained out of sight for so long. He could no longer push it to the back of his mind or pretend it wasn't there. He knew what it was. He knew what it meant. He knew the outcome.

Atkinson heard McKenzie take a sip of something at the other end of the line.

'Whatever it is, Atkinson,' McKenzie said, 'we'll sort it.'

26

Dear Parent/Guardian of Andrew Townley,

First and foremost, we are writing to express our deepest sympathy for the passing of Mrs Townley. We cannot imagine the shock and grief you are experiencing and the thoughts of everyone at Massleforth High School are with you during this difficult time.

Our Senior Management Team and Governing Body recently met to discuss and reflect on our ongoing risk assessment with respect to Andrew's return to school. After careful consideration, we have concluded that, when Andrew feels ready, he will be most welcome to reattend school.

On his first day back, we kindly ask that Andrew present himself discreetly to the school office with a negative AIDS test result, in order to ensure peace of mind for all involved.

We would be most grateful if you could provide the school office with at least one week's notice prior to Andrew's return. This will allow us to make necessary preparations and help ease Andrew's transition back into his new form group. It is our priority to ensure Andrew feels safe, supported and accepted every step of the way.

Yours sincerely,

Senior Management Team:
Mr Dean
Mrs Dawes
Mr Harris

Massleforth High School

Rock the World

The air is electric, but the stage feels cold,
Dreams on the edge, like a story untold.
Shadows are creeping, doubts take their aim,
But deep in our hearts, we still feel the flame.

The spotlight is fading,
Darkness is closing in.
The weight of the silence,
Like a battle we can't win.
But we hear the thunder,
A whisper turns to a roar,
It's time to …
Rock the World.

The walls are closing, they're trying to keep us out,
But we've got the fire and we're breaking out.
Lightning inside us, breaking through the storm,
Rising from ashes, we're ready to transform.

The spotlight is fading,
Darkness is closing in.
The weight of the silence,
Like a battle we can't win.
But we hear the thunder,
A whisper turns to a roar,
It's time to …
Rock the World.

Every fall, every fight,
Built the fire burning bright.
Through the void, we'll ignite,
A revolution in the night.

The spotlight is fading,
But we're still shining within.
Darkness is breaking,
Our battle is where we begin.
We are the thunder,
We are louder than before,
It's time to …
Rock the World.

(McCall)

Acknowledgements

The book was loosely inspired by the remarkable life of Ryan White, a courageous young haemophiliac from Indiana, whose battle with AIDS brought global attention to the stigma surrounding the disease in the 1980s. Ryan contracted AIDS through contaminated blood and was banned from attending his local school, facing prejudice from his community. Determined to challenge misconceptions about AIDS, he fought for his right to an education and worked to raise awareness. His story garnered the support of incredible musicians like Elton John, who stood by him in both his personal and public fight against the disease.

Further inspiration was drawn from several powerful documentaries about AIDS that I have watched over the years. While I may not recall the titles or the exact moments I first encountered them, certain poignant scenes and emotions have stayed with me and may have subtly woven their way into the fabric of this story.

Lastly, my lifelong love of Freddie Mercury and Queen has inevitably influenced aspects of the narrative, with a few unapologetic nods to this extraordinary band.

Nevertheless, this book is a work of fiction and a tribute to all those affected by AIDS – a celebration of compassion, courage and the enduring legacy of those who challenged ignorance, fought for justice and offered hope in the face of fear and adversity.

About the Author

Keith Campion, a primary school teacher from Cheshire, is the proud father of his two amazing young sons. His debut book, *The Last Post*, has been used widely in schools for English and History lessons and was adapted into a touring theatre production. His novels *The Flower Boy* and its sequel, *Flower Power!*, delve into the challenges faced by a socially anxious child transitioning from primary to high school. Keith's fourth book, *The Chemist*, is a vivid portrayal of life in post-war 1950s Britain.

Rock the World is Keith's fifth book and his first foray into fiction for adults.

ALSO BY THE AUTHOR

*"We were all just desperate men who wanted to
be home for Christmas with the ones we loved; our
hearts torn between the duty to our country and
the warmth and shelter of our families."*

The wartime correspondence between a son and his father
during the Great War. As 1914 draws to a close, William's
letters are full of hope. Well, they said the war would be over by
Christmas, didn't they?

Helpful questions for
discussion and First World War
research ideas included.

In a gentle way, you can shake the world.

James frequently needs to escape, to walk the streets of his local village and lose himself in his thoughts. James isn't finding his final year at primary school easy, and he wishes he had a brain that allowed him to chat and laugh like his classmates. Having spent his life avoiding trouble, it now seems to follow him wherever he goes.

When he stumbles into Mrs Samuel in the churchyard one autumn day, nothing is the same again. For Mrs Samuel, the present is a blur but the past shines clearly in her mind. Her tales about the village's history bring the past to life and ignite something deep within James. Without realising it, Mrs Samuel helps turn James's world from black and white to colour and inspires him to become... *The Flower Boy*.

But as Mrs Samuel loses her smile, will James find his?

Without fear, there cannot be courage.

James's first year at high school has an inevitability even he couldn't have predicted. Having a mind that stops him talking freely and a strong desire to be invisible, were always going to provide a challenge in the rush to make new friends. James's spark has gone – even the churchyard and growing roses have lost their appeal. When his relationship with his dad starts to break down, neither of them are really sure why. Not knowing what has happened to Mrs Samuel doesn't help his mood either.

When James finds out what they have planned for the churchyard, it's the final straw. But when things are going wrong, and life is far from a bed of roses, James will be reminded of the true value of kindness. Will James bloom again and find his... Flower Power?

Hopes, Dreams, And Nightmares In Post-War Britain

THE CHEMIST

KEITH CAMPION

It's 1955, and Richie is living a rather solitary life in post-war London, but it's all he's ever known. He can see signs that a colourful and exciting new world is emerging from those dark days of wartime.

Until one day tragedy strikes and Richie's life changes beyond anything he could ever have imagined.

London is soon a distant memory, as Richie and his mum reluctantly move north to the Chemist Shop where they are expected to toil under Aunt Beatrice's menacing eye. Richie, overwhelmed by the work he is expected to do, longs for his previous life and is unnerved by the mysterious presence of a boy called Peter.

Is Peter just a figment of Gran's imagination, and will Richie forever remain under Aunt Beatrice's domineering control or will he and his mum escape from the misery of life at… The Chemist?